A lost book holds the secre

Archaeologists excava York City cemetery make a gruesome discovery: stacked like cordwood are skeletal remains going back decades, but all have one thing in common. Each skull bears a hole in the exact same location. When their friend is murdered investigating this bizarre discovery, Jake Crowley and Rose Black set off in search of the killer. Their path will take them to abandoned hospitals, hidden chambers, and into the depths of the strange world that lies beneath New York City in search of Edgar Allan Poe's secret journal.

An occult murder mystery wrapped in an action-packed thriller!

Praise for David Wood and Alan Baxter

"A genuine up all night got to see what happens next thriller that grabs you from the first page and doesn't let go until the last." Steven Savile, author of *Silver*

"Mixing history and lore with science and action, David Wood and Alan Baxter have penned a thriller that is hard to put down." Jeremy Robinson, author of *Island 731*

"Bone-cracking terror from the stygian depths. Explodes off the page!." Lee Murray, author, *Into the Mist*

"One of the best, the most thoroughly delightful and satisfying, books that I've read in quite some time. A serious out-of-the-park type of home run hit." Christine Morgan, *The Horror Fiction Review*

"A sinister tale of black magic and horror – not for the faint hearted." Greig Beck, bestselling author of *Beneath the Dark Ice*

"With mysterious rituals, macabre rites and superb supernatural action scenes, Wood and Baxter deliver a fast-paced horror thriller." J.F.Penn, author of the bestselling *ARKANE* thriller series

REVENANT

A Jake Crowley Adventure

David Wood
Alan Baxter

Adrenaline Press

REVENANT- A Jake Crowley Adventure
Copyright 2019 by David Wood

Published by Adrenaline Press
www.adrenaline.press

Adrenaline Press is an imprint of Gryphonwood Press
www.gryphonwoodpress.com

ISBN-13: 978-1-950920-02-0

BOOKS BY DAVID WOOD AND ALAN BAXTER

The Jake Crowley Adventures
Blood Codex
Anubis Key
Revenant

The Sam Aston Investigations
Primordial
Overlord

Dark Rite

BOOKS BY DAVID WOOD

The Dane Maddock Adventures
Dourado
Cibola
Quest
Icefall
Buccaneer
Atlantis
Ark
Xibalba
Loch
Solomon Key
Contest

Dane and Bones Origins
Freedom
Hell Ship
Splashdown
Dead Ice
Liberty
Electra
Amber
Justice
Treasure of the Dead
Bloodstorm

BOOKS BY ALAN BAXTER

PROLOGUE

Charles Winthrop shivered and pulled his coat tighter about his shoulders. The cold and damp soaked through is inadequate coat, making his skin clammy. He wished to be anywhere but in such cold, damp woods in the middle of the late autumn night. Surely there were easier ways to do this. His breath puffed and clouded in the light from a bright half-moon that speared between leafless trees. Somehow, the silver illumination made him feel even colder.

He hurried to catch up with the Witchfinder. "Sir? Are we nearly there?" He loathed the weak whine in his voice, but no longer felt his feet for numbness and wanted to be sure he would survive the night. The lot of the apprentice witchfinder bore many discomforts, and it seemed he learned a new one almost daily. Charles wished for a flask of warming alcohol. Aqua vitae! The water of life! The thought brought a fleeting smile to his face, his first on this miserable night.

The Witchfinder slowed his pace and glanced down. Physically, the man was almost the opposite of Winthrop's short, stocky rotundity. Tall and thin, almost insectile in the precision of his movements, he nonetheless traveled with an easy grace. He turned his sharp-featured face to Winthrop, looking down his long nose. His dark green eyes were lost in shadow, pools of night under the ledge of his brow, crowned with gently curling dark brown hair. In the moonlight, his teeth glistened brightly as he smiled, but there was no warmth to be had there either. The Witchfinder's smile was as cold as the night, and entirely predatory. It reminded Winthrop of the scar the Witchfinder bore across his chest, from left shoulder to just beside his heart. Wide and puckered, perpetually pale, it looked like something close to a mortal injury had been enacted upon the man there. Winthrop had asked him once how he had come by such a wound, for it must have been quite a blow to heal with such a broad scar.

The Witchfinder had fingered the scar almost reverently and then pulled his shirt down over it as he continued dressing. He had said, "There are more dangerous things in this world than witches, sometimes." The enigmatic reply was all Winthrop had ever been able to learn. And now, looking through the night at that smile, he wondered if perhaps the Witchfinder himself wasn't one of the more dangerous things anyone might have the misfortune to encounter.

Now, the tall man smiled, charismatic as ever. "You suffer, Charles?"

"Honestly, sir? Yes!" Winthrop was thankful for the conversation not least to remove his thoughts from the forefront of his mind.

"We all suffer, Charles. Some of us more than seems fair, more than seems reasonable for our burden as agents of God, wouldn't you say?"

Winthrop looked at his feet, ashamed. The Witchfinder's wife lay deathly sick at their home, and would surely soon fall victim to consumption. Winthrop knew his master watched impotently as her lungs threw out more and more blood, her body weakened and failed, knowing she would eventually die in pain and fear. A terrible fate for her, an awful burden for the Witchfinder, both of them a sufferance far greater than any degree of cold feet.

But that didn't lessen the immediate suffering Winthrop endured now, though perhaps he should have kept it to himself. The cracks were beginning to show in his mentor's demeanor. The Witchfinder had become temperamental, erratic, quick to anger. And Winthrop realized that for all his smiling here, the man's eyes no doubt sparkled on the edge of fury.

"I'm just very cold, is all, Sir. And hoped we were nearly there. No distance is too far, of course."

"Of course." The Witchfinder strode off into the woods and Winthrop hurried to catch up.

Thankfully it wasn't long before a cottage came into sight, a couple of warm orange squares in the cold night marking the windows, a heavy shingle roof above reflected the moonlight. The building was of stone, heavy gray chunks, roughly hewn. The Witchfinder raised a hand and the two of them crouched, creeping forward as silently as the damp leaf litter would allow. Soon they crossed a small garden, more a simple clearing in the woods than anything deliberate, but a vegetable patch and herb garden were clearly well-attended to one side of the dwelling. As the men drew near, voices came to them, jovial and relaxed. The mixed strains of several women.

The Witchfinder raised one long, bony finger to his lips and moved in a low crouch to one of the brightly lit windows. Winthrop followed, the warmth emanating from the thick glass almost mocking as his feet pressed numbly into soft grass at the base of the cottage wall. Together they edged their eyes up over the sill and looked inside.

A group eight of women, six of them on the most recent list of the accused, stood in a rough circle before a crackling fire. The logs in the hearth glowed a deep red and dozens of candles on tables and sills around the room made everything bright as day inside. The room was homely, busy with old, but well cared for, furniture that had been pushed aside to clear the space directly before the flames. The friendly chatter waned slightly and then one woman brought them all to order with a quiet word. They smoothed their circle and joined hands, began a soft chant, almost like a child's playground rhyme, but slow and ominous.

Another woman entered, helping along a young boy no older than eight or nine. He was stripped to the waist, his trousers threadbare and stained with dirt, his bare feet grubby. Against his chest he held one withered arm, his left, supported protectively by his right. The woman helping him had one hand lightly on his shoulder. With a friendly smile and a nod she guided him into the circle. He ducked under the joined hands of one pair and stood in their midst, turned a slow circle with an expectant though slightly fearful expression on his face.

"Lie down," the woman who had helped him said. "Relax, Thomas, you'll be fine. I promise."

The boy nodded, his trust in her apparent, and laid on his back on the floor. His thin chest heaved as he took a deep breath, then he closed his eyes. The woman who had brought him in gently touched the hands of one pair of women and they parted to let her join the circle.

"Just in time," the Witchfinder breathed. "Now we shall see." His hand rested on the hilt of the dagger he kept always on his belt.

"Sir, shouldn't we stop this?" Winthrop whispered, his heart hammering. Were they really going to stand by and simply watch witchcraft performed upon this innocent boy child? Were these witches about to offer him to Satan? To sacrifice him?

"We need proof these women are the darkest of witches.

We must wait."

Winthrop swallowed a lump in his throat, tried to keep his voice strong, though quiet. "Proof?" he asked. "But that little boy..."

The Witchfinder glanced at him, eyes flashing with anger. Here was more of that erratic behavior Winthrop had noticed, more irrational and confusing anger. "I regret whatever may befall the boy, but we have to think of all the lives that will be saved if we can root out all the witches in the colony. In order to do that, we must first find the real witches, the leaders, the coordinators. Or are you perhaps ill-suited for this particular apprenticeship, Charles?"

Winthrop swallowed hard. Though he feared the tall thin man, his confusion won out. "Are you suggesting the witches we've already hanged were not real witches, if we didn't witness their devilcraft firsthand?"

"Be quiet, Charles. Get down! It's starting. I will take the risk of observation while you protect your sensibilities."

With one surprisingly strong gesture, the Witchfinder put a hand onto Winthrop's shoulder and pressed him to the grass. Winthrop fell back onto his rump, instantly damp and cold from the night dew. Stunned, he sat there, staring up at the Witchfinder's face, glowing like fire in the light of the window. Unable to see any inside longer, Winthrop watched his mentor instead, tried to ascertain the activity by his master's expression. The Witchfinder was clearly enthralled.

Winthrop heard the chanting increase in pace and volume and soon began to feel something, a palpable energy surging forth in waves. It made his heart race, his hair stand on end, his skin prickle with gooseflesh. He tried to stand, but his legs were weak, his breath suddenly shallow. He looked up at the Witchfinder and saw an expression of wonder on the tall man's face. The light from inside flickered, as every candle suddenly guttered in a gust of wind, then stilled, and then brightened further. The sounds of the women's voices and the brightness of the candlelight both grew, faster and brighter, ever more intense. A pressure built inside Winthrop's head like the onset of a sudden and debilitating headache. He squeezed the bridge of his nose, squeezing his eyes tightly shut, and bit his lower lip to keep from crying out, terrified of what might be happening inside. Surely he had never been closer to Satan in his life. He pushed up again, trying to call out, tell the Witchfinder to put an end to it, but the tall man pushed him down again. What was occurring inside, and why would the Witchfinder not allow him to see? He felt he needed to bear witness also, even though a significant part of him had no desire to watch. The pressure built further, the chanting louder and faster, the light seemed to burst brighter than ever and then everything stilled.

Silence. For a moment, Winthrop thought it had fallen dark, but realized the candles and firelight were back to their normal luminescence and his eyes quickly adjusted. He looked up again to see pure wonder on the Witchfinder's face, his expression almost beatific.

"Sir? What happened in there? The boy, sir? Is he well?"

His question remained unanswered as the man stared.

"Sir?" he pressed. "What now? Let us end this blasphemy!"

Smiling again, that predatory showing of teeth, the Witchfinder reached down and took Winthrop's hand, hauled him to his feet. Winthrop began a smile of his own, about to turn and look into the cottage to see for himself what had held his master so enraptured, when he felt a sharp, heavy punch into his chest. He looked down to see the Witchfinder's pale, bony hand gripping tightly the hilt of his dagger. The blade was buried between Winthrop's ribs. His heart still, pain exploded and darkness flooded into the edges of his vision.

"I am sorry," the Witchfinder said quietly, almost kindly. "But I cannot have you telling anyone."

CHAPTER 1

"Not the most impressive sight." Jake Crowley and Rose Black stood outside The Edgar Allan Poe House on West Third Street, in New York City. Already the place was proving to be something of an anti-climax. The three-story home had been completely engulfed by a much larger building, the façade itself a recreation of the original structure. The whole thing had the impression of a pretty flower swallowed by wild grasses, homogenous and desperate.

"Don't start with me, you grumpy old badger," Rose Black said. "We're going to relax and enjoy ourselves."

"I'm not grumpy, only tired. You kept me up late last night."

Rose grinned. "I think it was the other way around. I was the one tired from our road trip, but you had other plans."

Crowley smiled, slipped his arm around her waist, and gave her a squeeze. The pair had been through a hell of a lot in the past few weeks. Their search for Rose's missing sister, Lily, had led them across the pond to the United States on the trail of a lost Egyptian artifact. They had also learned some unwelcome news about Lily and where her true loyalties lay. In the ensuing chase, Lily's small plane had crashed. No bodies had been recovered from the wreckage as far as they knew. Surely no one could have survived a crash like that.

"I just hope agent Paul doesn't learn we're still in the country," Crowley said. The FBI agent had instructed them to return to England and had provided airline tickets to help them along the way. They'd decided to extend their stay by rescheduling the flight from New York to London by two weeks, then taking their time leisurely road-tripping across the United States. Little had he known that middle America, especially Kansas, made for endless, mind-numbingly boring scenery.

"Technically, he didn't order us to leave the country on any specific date," Rose said. "We're just stopping off for some sightseeing and to visit your Aunt Gertie."

Crowley laughed. "Remember I'm the only one allowed to call her that." Gertrude Fawcett, known as Trudy to everyone but Crowley, was his favorite aunt, and he was like a son to her. Hence the special dispensation for the juvenile nickname.

Rose's attention had already returned to the Poe House. She scrolled on her phone, looking up details. "This is a reinterpretation of the original house where Poe once resided," she said disdainfully. "He lived here only a little while anyway, from 1844 to 1845. Apparently, New York University demolished the historic structure when they built Furman Hall here. What a letdown! But we can have a look inside, and it's the ghost that intrigues me anyway."

"The ghost?" Crowley asked.

"Yeah, legends have it that Poe's ghost is seen here often and no one really knows why, given it was such a short-lived residence, such a tiny part of his life really. It did coincide with some of the man's first significant successes as a writer, so it has its relevance, but not really for haunting. There are several theories as to why he's here so often, but none of them really make much sense."

"It's all a bit..." Crowley paused, searching for the right word.

"Lame?" Rose offered. She grinned. "It really is, huh? But this whole area has some cool ghost stories." She turned and pointed across the street at a building of orange and yellow brick, four stories standing a little taller than the more modern structures either side. The second, third, and fourth floors each had three tall windows, but the first floor featured a large black, arch-topped door. Above it, gold letters on black proclaimed FIRE PATROL, a bold number 2 on each corner level with the sign. "That's former Fire Patrol Station #2," Rose said. "Now a private residence, some news anchor or other lives there, but it has a long history. Built by Ernest Flagg in 1906. It's said to be haunted by the ghost of a firefighter by the name of Schwartz."

"Why would he haunt there? Did he die fighting a fire? Surely he'd haunt that place, not his station."

Rose shook her head. "It's better than that. In 1930 he hanged himself from the rafters in there after he discovered his wife was cheating on him. Other firefighters, for a long time afterward, claimed to hear strange noises when no one was there. And some said they saw the shape of Schwartz suspended in mid-air."

Crowley let out a small, uncomfortable laugh. "You really dig all the macabre stuff, huh?"

"I still need to educate you on the good horror movies! There are so many cool and creepy things you need to see. But right now, we can concentrate on what's right in front of us." Rose grabbed his hand and hauled him up the steps of the Poe house. "Come on, let's see Edgar's ghost!"

They went inside and now Crowley did laugh, a lot more mirthful this time. "Lamer and lamer," he said in a low voice. No need to offend anyone who might work here.

"Holy crap," Rose said, not as quietly. "What a bust!" She laughed too, the whole thing too absurd for words.

Before them lay a single room, closed off entirely from the rest of the building. Around three of the walls were a selection of glass-fronted cabinets containing a variety of items. Some black and white photos, a few early contracts signed by Poe, a couple of fountain pens he had allegedly used. One side of the small space held the largest cabinet and in that stood a writing desk, scratched and worn, with a few items haphazardly scattered across it.

Crowley slowly walked the perimeter of the space and shrugged. "Oh well. I've seen bigger bathrooms!" He squinted into one of the cabinets. "Mind you, it's not entirely without interest. I mean, look at this here. It's pretty cool to think that Poe actually held these pens, signed his name there with them. I can imagine every writer aims to have the kind of recognition someone like Poe enjoys. I imagine most writers would want that recognition while they were still alive to enjoy it."

"I suppose so," Rose said. "Of course most would like to live to see their success. Poe had a decent career, but so many scrape and scratch through life only to succeed after they're dead. Take Lovecraft, for example. Can you imagine if he could see how much his work is still current and the amount of other work that has sprung from it."

Crowley nodded. "Well, maybe he's somewhere we can't fathom, kicking back with the Elder Gods, laughing at his posthumous popularity."

Rose laughed. "You're not entirely uneducated then, Jake Crowley."

"Not entirely, no. Hey, this is interesting." Crowley pointed into another glass cabinet. "It's new."

"What do you mean by new?" Rose joined him, and together they looked down at a small, tatty leather-bound journal sitting on a clear plastic display stand.

"Fine, recent then. It was only put on display here last month," Crowley said. He read from the small placard sitting in front of the old book. "Found during repairs to an older part of the foundations below this very room, bricked into a basement wall. New York University uncovered a metal lockbox containing several items, including this journal of Poe's containing a variety of mostly indecipherable writings."

Rose turned to him, frowning. "Indecipherable in what way?"

"Too messy to read, or too complicated to understand maybe? It doesn't elaborate."

"How weird. I wish they displayed it open, at least we'd see one page."

Crowley shrugged. "Oh well. If an ineligible old notebook is the most interesting thing here, I think we're done."

"Yep," Rose agreed. "Sometimes people really draw a long bow trying to make a place interesting."

"It's just as bad in England," Crowley said. "King Henry the Eighth once spent a night in this Inn on his way somewhere else far more exciting!"

Rose laughed. "Queen Elizabeth the First once farted in this cottage!"

Both laughing now, they left the small room behind and walked back out onto Third Street.

"Come on," Crowley said. "Let's go and see the Statue of Liberty."

CHAPTER 2

The Dakota was an iconic part of New York City history and spoke volumes about Aunt Gertie's immense wealth. Crowley was embarrassed to reveal this side of his personal life to Rose, a little self-conscious of the always open line of credit Gertie made available to him should he ever need it. But Rose had known him as a working man and knew he paid his own way as much as he could. Aunt Gertie's dollars had helped them here and there during their recent adventures, and he felt he should, at the very least spend some time with her as a thank-you. This visit was as good a way as any to do that.

As they walked along 72nd Street heading for the building and Gertie's apartment inside, Crowley said, "Brace yourself, okay? It's all quite opulent. But Gertie herself is down to earth and lovely. She wasn't born into wealth, so she's, you know, mostly normal." He grinned.

Rose laughed. "Normal like you? Sure, Jake. You don't need to make excuses for her, I judge everyone by their actions and personality, nothing else. But ever since you said she lived there, I've been aching to see it. I mean, so much has happened in that building, so many famous people lived there."

"So many still do! Although it's amazing to think of people from history living there. Larger than life folk like John Lennon, for example."

Rose laughed again, seemingly somewhat giddy with excitement. "More than that, he died there!"

"You are so damned sinister."

"No, it's not that. It's such a historical moment, don't you think? That famous archway, the crowds."

Crowley smiled and gestured. Rose turned and gasped, looking directly at the very arched entrance she had been describing. The building stood before them, surrounded on two sides by taller, more modern structures, it nonetheless commanded the eye with its splendor. It occupied the northwest corner of 72nd Street and Central Park West, in the Upper West Side, its pale tan brick stark against the whites and grays and silvers around it. High gables and steep roofs held a profusion of dormers, terracotta spandrels and panels, niches, balconies, and balustrades, giving it a German Renaissance character.

"It's a square," Crowley said, as Rose stared. "Built around a central courtyard. The arched main entrance is large enough for a horse-drawn carriage because back in the day they would drive right in to allow passengers to disembark safely from the rain, or prying eyes."

"*Porte-cochère*," Rose said quietly.

Crowley frowned. "Bless you?"

"No, idiot. *Porte-cochère*. It's French. It's what that kind of entrance is called."

"Ah, now I'm with you. Smartypants."

Rose smiled at him. "You know I like to know things. But I don't know about this place, so go on!"

Crowley shrugged. "I don't know much more to be honest. Gertie once told me that while the outside is German-influenced, the layout of the apartments is in the French style. All the major rooms are connected to each other." He looked at Rose pointedly and said, "In enfilade."

"What?"

"Ha! You're not the only smarty pants with some French. It's from the French enfiler, 'to put on a string.' I know it because it's a military term. A formation or position is 'in enfilade' if weapons fire can be directed along its longest axis. A trench if the opponent can fire down its length. Or a column of troops is enfiladed if they can be fired on from the front or rear."

Rose grinned at him, one eyebrow raised. "Really, Jake?"

"If a line of advancing troops is fired on from the flank it's defiladed," he said with an exaggerated nod.

"Okay, well done. That's one point each on obscure French vocabulary."

"Two points to one, actually, my favor. I gave you two words."

"Technically, *porte-cochère* is two words too." Rose held up one hand. "But let's just agree we're both smart, shall we?"

"Okay, fair call."

"So you could fire a weapon the length of a Dakota apartment, is that what you're trying to tell me?"

Crowley grinned. "Yeah, I guess so. But there's also access from the corridor or a hall, so it's not like every apartment is a straight line, just the main rooms. It's high society nonsense again, to be honest. The idea being that you could move guests from one room to another easily, but staff could discreetly service them without being seen coming and going."

"Look at us," Rose said. "A museum researcher and a high school teacher, trying to out-nerd each other."

"Made for each other, you mean?" Crowley said with a smile.

Rose kissed him, then turned her attention back to the building, staring up at it. "It's weird to imagine, isn't it? No thought like that really goes into the design anymore."

"Well, that's not such a bad thing. When you design a home so the servants can work and not be seen, it says a lot about society."

"Yeah, we certainly need to move on from that kind of thinking. It's just that buildings are so boring now. Look at this place! It's amazing. Such character and style."

Crowley turned to gaze up at it with her. "It really is. Aunt Gertie told me all about the layout and said the other cool thing is that the apartments are open to the outdoors on two sides, the street and the courtyard, which was pretty rare at the time. The idea of that much space in New York City is bewildering."

"Rare at the time and even rarer now. Not to mention the overall size of the apartments, I'm guessing."

"You're not wrong. Aunt Gertie's main room is about fifty feet long, the ceiling is fourteen feet high. And the floors are all parquetry, in different shades of wood. There are ghost stories here, too, by the way."

"John Lennon haunts the gate?"

"Yes, actually! If you believe the stories. And construction workers in the 60s apparently saw the ghost of a young boy, though no one knows who he is. And more recently, the ghost of a girl in turn-of-the-century clothing was reported by painters working here."

"How do you know all that?"

Crowley half-smiled, sheepish. "I looked up ghost stories while we walked here after your firefighter one."

"Ten out of ten for effort, Jake. You know, there's another creepy angle to this place for horror fans."

"Is there?"

"It's the building they used for filming *Rosemary's Baby*." When he didn't acknowledge the relevance, she said, "Roman Polanski, 1968? Jake, that's iconic cinema even if you're not a horror fan!"

"Sorry."

She shook her head. "We need to start planning regular movie nights."

"If you say so!" In all honesty, he relished the idea. He may not be much of a horror movie fan like Rose was, but the fact she was planning their future made him warm inside. And maybe with a good education from her, he'd come to appreciate horror movies the way she did. "Come on," he said. "We'll be late."

They crossed the street with the traffic light, and Crowley went up to the door, pressed the button for his aunt's apartment. A few seconds passed, then her robust and vibrant voice came through.

"Jake, darling! Come in, come in!"

Crowley threw a smile at the camera and pushed the door open when it buzzed.

As they walked for the elevator, Rose said, "So where does Aunt Gertie fit in your family tree again?"

"Call her Trudy," he reminded her. "But she's actually my great aunt. You know I never knew my dad. He was killed in the Falklands while my mum was still pregnant, but I knew Gertie well."

"She helped raise you?"

"Sort of. My mum and paternal grandmother, my dad's mother, raised me. Gertie is my Grandma's sister. So she was always around, always kind. Grandma was a bit of a hard case, it really hit her hard when my dad died. Must be a hell of a thing to lose your son. But she loved me and cared for me, even if she was tough. But Gertie was always soft and kind, she saw how tough it was for all of us, I guess. Then, when I was about twelve or thirteen, Aunt Gertie met and married Charles Forsythe, an incredibly wealthy stockbroker, and moved here to New York." Crowley pressed for the elevator, uncomfortable talking about his connection to so much privilege. "Only a year or two after that, my Grandma died from a very aggressive cancer. Aunt Gertie said she always felt guilty to have moved away and would fly back to England regularly to visit us, and she always insisted on passing over some money to keep us looked after. In her sister's memory, she always insisted. Plus, Gertie and Charles never had kids, though they tried for ages before giving up. I think that only made her more keen to keep an eye on me. And she has ever since. The Army looked after Mum and me as well, of course. So losing my dad was terrible, but we were fortunate in other ways."

The elevator pinged and the ostentatiously decorated doors slid silently open. "So why is she a Fawcett and not a Forsythe?" Rose asked as they stepped on.

"Well, sadly Charles dropped dead from a massive heart attack at 67. It was big New York news for a while, and after that, she went back to her maiden name. It was difficult being so closely associated with such a prominent New York name, she said. She wanted to have a more quiet life and has largely slipped out of high society since. At least, as much as she can with her money, living somewhere like this."

"Life has a way of messing up any plans we make, huh?"

"You're not wrong. She's also proud of her heritage, she's a Fawcett, distantly related to the explorer, Percy Fawcett."

"Really? Oh, that's interesting. He was, like, the real Indiana Jones, wasn't he?"

"I think he was one source of inspiration," Crowley said.

Rose nodded. "How long have you been waiting to drop that bombshell?"

Crowley quirked an eyebrow. "Bombshell? Most of the people I meet have never heard of him."

"Lucky for you I'm not most people."

The elevator pinged again and stopped, the doors slid open.

From an open door just along the hallway, a well-dressed lady waved. She was slim and stood tall, with neat iron-gray hair in a modern style, her smile warm and welcoming. "Jake! So good to see you!"

"Not bad for a woman in her seventies, huh?" Crowley said sidelong to Rose, then strode up to hug his great aunt. "It's been too long, Aunt Gertie!"

She scowled good-naturedly and pinched his cheek like he was a schoolboy. Then she kissed his forehead and stepped aside to shake Rose's hand. "And you must be the delightful Rose. Please, call me Trudy."

Rose shook. "It's lovely to meet you, Trudy. I've heard so much."

"All wicked, I hope? Come along, inside we go. Can't stand in the hallway like vagrants."

They walked in, heels clicking on the beautiful parquetry floor Crowley had mentioned before. He enjoyed watching Rose take in the enormous rooms, high ceilings, all the artistic touches of architecture never seen in the modern age. Gertie kept the place neat and tidy, enough furniture that it didn't feel minimalist, but nothing too grandiose. Artworks hung on the walls, Crowley remembered Charles had been an avid collector. Those alone were probably worth more money than he or Rose had ever seen. His great aunt led them through into the smaller lounge room and gestured to the floral couch under the window.

"Please, have a seat. Gabriela is making tea so we can chat before dinner."

That was a name Crowley hadn't heard before. "Gabriela?"

Gertie made a rueful face. "Honestly, Jake, it feels terrible to have a staff. So bloody colonial, you know? But I'm not getting any younger. It's not that I feel old or infirm yet, but at my age, you can't be too careful. And I do tire more easily than I ever did before. Anyway, long story short, I have Gabriela now. She lives with me, takes care of small things, and keeps the place clean, vacuuming, dusting, that sort of thing. And it makes me feel much safer to know that someone is always here should I have a fall or something like that."

"Well, that makes perfect sense," Crowley said. "Actually, it makes me feel better to know someone's here for you too."

"I did have a fall a few months ago. Nothing serious," she said quickly at Crowley's look of dismay. "Just some bruises, mostly to my pride. But for a little while I couldn't get up, and that frightened me. If it had been more serious, I might have been in rather a lot of trouble."

"So you employed Gabriela after that?"

"Exactly. She's a lovely young thing. Only twenty, recently come to New York. Mexican, you know."

Crowley nodded. "Cool."

"And what about you, dear?" Gertie said, turning her attention to Rose. "You have a look of the Orient about you. What's your story."

Crowley cringed, caught off-guard by the casual racism of the older generation. "Aunt Gertie, please–"

Rose lifted a hand, smiling. "No, it's fine, really. My mum is Chinese, from Guangzhou. Dad is a Londoner from generations back."

"That part is the same as our line, then," Gertie said. "Jake's is age-old English stock on both sides."

Crowley opened his mouth to change the subject when the other door to the room swung in, and young Latina with long black hair in a loose ponytail came in carrying a tray. It bore a ceramic teapot, cups and saucers, and a jug of milk. A small silver bowl held sugar cubes and tiny serving tongs. You can take the woman out of England, Crowley thought, but you'd never take the England from the woman.

"Ah, thank you, Gabriela," Gertie said. She gestured to Crowley and Rose. "This is my grand-nephew I was telling you about, Jake, and his lovely partner, Rose."

They made polite greetings all around, and as Gabriela was about to leave, the door intercom buzzed again.

"That will be Matthew," Gertie said. "Could you let him in, please, Gabriela? Then you can head off, we'll be okay."

"Yes, Mrs. Fawcett, of course. I'll be in my room if you need me."

As the young woman headed for the door, Crowley said, "Matthew?"

His aunt gave him a smile that had a cheeky edge to it, her eyes sparkling. "You're not the only one introducing a new partner tonight."

"Is that so?"

A few moments later, a man appeared at the door to the lounge. They all stood, Gertie moving to squeeze his hand and plant a kiss on his cheek. A tall man, and thin, he bent to receive the kiss and favored Gertie with a warm smile. He had a head of gently curling gray hair, neatly combed, and wore a sharp three-piece suit of dark pinstripes, and a burgundy cravat. The word "dapper" came immediately to Crowley's mind. His shoes were so shiny they could have been used as mirrors.

Crowley stepped up and offered his hand to shake. "Jake Crowley, Trudy's grand-nephew." He chose not to play with the Gertie business, in case it confused this gentleman.

"Matthew Price," the man said, his shake warm and firm, but not aggressive in that alpha way, so many insecure men seemed to use. "I've heard a lot about you."

"Is that so? I've heard nothing at all about you." Crowley grinned to show there were no hard feelings, but he turned a raised eyebrow to his aunt all the same. She gave him a mischievous look. "And this is Rose," Crowley said.

As Rose shook hands, Aunt Gertie said, "There are still lots of things I do for myself, and cooking for family is one of them. You three get acquainted while I see to dinner. It'll be ready any time now."

When his aunt went off to the kitchen, Crowley and Rose

sat once more. Price joined them.

"Tea?" Crowley asked.

"Thank you."

"Have you and my aunt known each other long?" Crowley asked, not sure how polite it was to ask, but desperate to know the story.

Price smiled good-naturedly. "We've known each other a little while now, yes. We met at a charity lunch where we were both donors, and we hit it off right away."

"That's great," Crowley said, and he meant it. He was pleased his aunt had found company that seemed to make her happy. "And what do you do? Or are you retired?" It was hard, Crowley realized, to guess the man's age. Gertie barely looked seventy, and he thought perhaps Price had that same well-preserved demeanor, probably associated with wealth as much as genetics. He certainly seemed to be younger than Gertie's early-seventies, but Crowley had no real inkling by how much.

"Mostly retired now," Price said. "But I worked in pharmaceuticals and still keep my hand in. I run a company called SaleMed."

"New York company?" Rose asked.

"All over, really, but I'm from the east coast, yes. I've lived in dozens of places, never really had a home town. Even as a child, I moved around. But I live in New York City now, just moved back in the last year or so after traveling for most of my career."

The man was personable and open, and Crowley found himself relaxing. He had been nervous at first, wondering what this new companion of his great aunt's might be like. Perhaps he need not worry after all. But he saw Rose's expression was guarded as she watched Price, and he thought she was less at ease. He wondered why. Only time would tell.

His great aunt called them through to the dining room with its silk-covered chairs and highly polished rosewood table that could seat more than a dozen people comfortably if necessary. The four of them sat amiably around one end of it, and Gertie served up a delicious roast dinner in the old English style. Lamb with mint sauce, roast potatoes, carrots, parsnips, and Brussel sprouts.

The meal progressed well, the four of them chatting about all manner of things, though most of it superficial. Crowley and Rose talked about their road trip and Rose's first impressions of

New York City. They avoided anything to do with why they happened to be in the US in the first place, both wordlessly agreeing to avoid any talk of the Anubis Key or Rose's sister. But they didn't get away with that for long.

"I had a work thing over here," Rose said quickly when Price enquired about the reason for their trip. Then she had gone on to talk about her role as a historian, researcher, and guide for the Natural History Museum in London. She diverted the question nicely. But then Crowley wondered about it if her job was still secure after their recent absences. He knew his own job teaching high school history was probably tenuous by now. They would both have a lot of reparations to make to their employers when they finally returned to London in another week.

Throughout the meal, Crowley noted Rose's discomfort with Price. He didn't think his aunt or Price himself would notice, but he knew Rose well enough to recognize her distrust of the man. Her slightly narrowed eyes, her lips pressed a little flatter than usual. It was subtle body language, but there. He didn't see the problem himself, he thought Matthew Price seemed to be a decent, stand-up guy. He'd ask Rose about it once they were alone again.

Fully sated by the delicious meal they retired back to the lounge and its comfortable couches for nightcaps. Aunt Gertie produced the best Cognac Crowley had ever tasted, and Rose seemed equally impressed. A little tipsy, they eventually hugged and promised Crowley's aunt they would visit plenty of times during their week in New York City. They would all catch a show one evening and spend some days sightseeing together.

"And any time you get the urge to make another meal like that, you let us know!" Crowley said, kissing his aunt goodbye.

As they left the Dakota, stepping out into the still busy street, Crowley asked, "You don't trust him, do you?"

Rose grimaced. "Was it that obvious?"

"Only to me, I think. Why not?"

"I don't know. Nothing I can put my finger on, that's what was bugging me. There's just something about him that puts me on edge." Rose looked back to the building, the large darkened archway of the entrance, and started. She turned quickly, all attention on the shadows.

"What is it?" Crowley looked too but saw nothing.

"There was someone there." Rose walked back the few

steps they had taken, looking carefully around the entrance.

"Someone there?"

"I glanced back, and a man was standing right here, in a three-piece suit and shiny shoes."

"Was it Price?"

"No, definitely not. Wrong size and shape. But he seemed only half there or something, I couldn't see too clearly. As I turned for a better look, he was gone."

"What do you mean, gone?"

"Exactly that! He was there, then he wasn't. He looked... I don't know. Sort of old-fashioned." Rose looked at Crowley, eyebrows raised.

Crowley smiled, put an arm around her shoulders. "All this talk of ghosts and a couple of strong brandies, maybe got your mind spinning overtime?"

"No, Jake. He was there." She frowned, shook her head, and let out a short laugh. "I think I just saw a ghost!"

CHAPTER 3

Matthew Price left the Dakota Apartments not long after Jake Crowley, and Rose Black had said their goodbyes. It's wasn't especially late, but Trudy always started to wane after ten p.m., and it was almost a full half hour past that already. Taking a deep breath of not especially fresh New York City air, he decided to forego a cab and walk home. He needed the exercise to help him think. Besides, the walk was one of the best in the city. The Dakota Apartments let out onto Central Park West Avenue, directly across the street from Central Park itself, and Price's current home was in the Upper East Side on East 73rd Street, a casual stroll directly across Central Park, then only three blocks to the other side of Park Avenue. Long enough a stroll to be contemplative, not so long as to be taxing.

As he waited for the lights to change and let him across Central Park West, he let his mind wander, considering the night's varied conversations. He had things settling into a good routine with Gertrude and loathed any interruption to their lives. But of course, he couldn't begrudge visits from what little family was still left to her. The crosswalk sounded, and he went across the road and into Central Park. It cast its magic immediately, the sheer size and bustle of the city instantly cut off. Though the traffic was still audible and the buildings even on the other side visible here and there, towering above the treetops, the calm stillness enveloped him. Price took a deep breath and let it out with a sigh.

He set a leisurely pace, enjoying the deep shadows cast by the trees and before long came to the Bethesda Terrace, midway across the park between west and east. Rather than carry on directly, he went to the stone railings and looked down at the fountain and Central Park Lake beyond. The pale, sandstone steps had intricate stone balustrades and large square posts at the end. The red herringbone tiles below stood out even in the darkness, pools of lamplight turning some parts orange.

Where the central steps led down into the brightly lit gallery, and from there on to the fountain, Price stopped and looked at the large pillars either side, each almost twice the height of a grown adult. One each of the four square faces, intricate indentations had been carved. Each indent, the shape of a three-leafed clover, held a bas relief design; an owl on a branch, an open book with a crescent moon above. Price ran one index finger over the sour-faced witch flying on her broomstick over a church and a carved pumpkin and chuckled to himself. So many memories, so much history.

He turned away again. History had its place, but the here and now was more important, and his evening had left him mildly troubled. Gertrude's nephew, Jake Crowley, seemed all right, but Price had his doubts about the man's story of being a teacher. Or at least, that couldn't be all Crowley had been. No man got that demeanor from life indoors with students. And Price knew beyond a doubt that Crowley's girlfriend, Rose Black, didn't seem to like Price himself much at all. She was clearly a strong woman, and strong-willed, no meek partner or quiet wife material there. She had a formidable nature about her that Price found alluring in its own way, but more troublesome than anything. Perhaps the pair of them might cause trouble, and that was something Price dearly wanted to avoid.

Gertrude doted on her nephew, she'd admitted as much. She said how she kept a healthy trust fund running for him to ensure he'd only ever need teaching for the fulfillment, not financial stability. He'd had a tough early life, Gertrude had said, and she intended to see his adult life ran more smoothly. Price smiled. He had a feeling Crowley himself avoided any semblance of an easy life, whether money was an issue or not.

As Price turned to continue on towards home, his phone beeped. Good timing, he thought, as he pulled it out. The message, as he had expected, came from an employee Price had tasked with a little digging. He opened the message and scanned the quite extensive contents.

It seemed Rose Black was indeed the museum historian and guide she had claimed to be. Not that long ago she had ended a long relationship with a woman named Alison Stokes, but was clearly very much in love with Crowley now. Singularly uninteresting in the greater scheme of things, and nothing to give Price too much pause.

Ah, but Jake Crowley's history was a lot more complicated. A broken home, father died at war before Crowley was born, Crowley himself in the Army for years, quit after his second stint in Afghanistan. Price's eyebrows rose, and he read the last paragraph again, a small smile tugging at one side of his mouth.

Crowley's exit from the Army was possibly the most interesting thing about the man, and he wondered and how many other people knew. Did Rose Black know about this particular episode in the life of the mild-mannered schoolteacher?

"Well, well, well," Price said quietly to himself. "Aren't you quite the bad man, Jake Henry Crowley!"

CHAPTER 4

When they had arrived back at the Algonquin Hotel the night before, Rose stood outside looking up at the pale stone building with its distinctive green awnings, lit up with bright spots.

"Penny for your thoughts?" Crowley had asked.

To head off the question, she'd answered, "You ever hear about the Round Table here?"

"Arthur and his knights? That's Camelot, not New York."

Rose gave him a long-suffering look. "You're not as funny as you think you are, Jake."

"I'm bloody hilarious."

"You're full of brandy. No, this place, the Algonquin, it's designated as a New York City Historic Landmark these days, probably because if its architectural significance. But I like to think it's also because of its journalistic history. For the better part of a decade, back in the 1920s, a whole bunch of journalists, publicists, authors, actors, all gathered here and shared gossip and cutting-edge reports on the New York scene. They became known as the Algonquin Round Table. Privately, they referred to themselves as the Vicious Circle."

Crowley smiled. "That's pretty cool. Can you imagine the kind of stuff they talked about?"

"That's exactly what I was thinking about when you asked me. The history of places like this is fascinating. And because I think I saw a ghost earlier, it reminded me. Quite often, guests at the Algonquin claim to spot members of The Round Table in the halls or rooms. Famous people were in the group, like Dorothy Parker, Robert Benchley, Harpo Marx, Edna Ferber. Loads more I can't remember."

"Ghosts, huh?" Crowley asked.

She glanced at him. "I'm telling you what I saw back there was weird!"

"It sure was." Crowley gestured at the hotel. "So how do you know about that Round Table stuff?"

Rose smiled. "I was here once before, with a journalist friend. She told me all about it."

Crowley narrowed his eyes. "Did she now?"

"It was a long time ago."

With that, they'd gone inside and were soon tucked into bed, where they didn't bother talking for quite a while, and not long after that, they were both asleep.

It had been a long time since Rose was last here. Back then she had been in a relationship with Alison Stokes, and her journalist friend, Jasmine Richards, had tried everything she could to corrupt it. Rose couldn't help a smile at the memory. There was something undeniable between her and Jazz, that was certain. If it hadn't been for Alison, who knew what might have happened, but Rose was a loyal lover. And now she was back in New York and back in a relationship, this time with Jake. So she felt a little bad about what she was considering, calling up Jazz, but the reporter was the only local contact she had. Of course, there was Cameron Cray, Crowley's old Army intel buddy, but that was Jake's business, even though she considered Cam her friend too now. But Rose didn't feel comfortable calling him about this. Though she also didn't feel comfortable ignoring her nagging suspicions about the strange and enigmatic Matthew Price.

Catching up with an old friend in New York was nothing to worry about, after all. It was an entirely reasonable thing to want to do. Just because Jazz was also a damn fine investigative journalist for the New York Sentinel was a bonus. And she didn't need to feel guilty. If she hadn't given in to Jazz's charms when she'd been with Alison, there was no reason to think she would now that she was with Jake. Besides, Jazz would surely have moved on, probably had a partner too, so the whole concern was academic.

Rose had met Jazz the only other time she'd been to New York City. On an exchange program with the American Museum of Natural History on the Upper West Side, she'd spent a week in the greatest city on Earth, mostly in the bowels of the old museum building poring through research papers and retired exhibits. But she'd gone out too, exploring by night, checking out restaurants and bars. She'd met Jazz, quite fittingly, in a small jazz bar. When Rose saw the slim woman sitting alone at the bar, thick black hair held in a loose fat ponytail, dark skin like warm wood under the lights above the bar, she had gravitated to her, sat beside her for security as much as anything. Jazz had smiled, nodded hello, and over the noise of the freeform band had introduced herself.

"Jazz. Like the music," she'd said, jabbing one thumb back

over her shoulder.

"Rose. Like… the flower."

They'd laughed at that, immediately hit it off, and spent some hours getting drunk and sharing stories of two lives that were quite different on the surface, but that shared similarities.. Rose had been fascinated by the life of an investigative journalist looking into modern news and crimes the way Rose herself looked into old manuscripts and archeological finds. And it was apparent Jazz was into her, so she was careful not to lead the other woman along. She kept Alison front and center of her mind, even told Jazz about her relationship early on in their conversation.

"That's cool," Jazz said, "Don't worry. I'm not out to score tonight. Well, you know I wouldn't it turn it down, but it's not top of my agenda." And then she had continued to flirt mercilessly the whole time. Which, if Rose were honest, she had enjoyed.

Sitting on the edge of the hotel bed in the morning sunlight, remembering that night, Rose whispered to herself, "Jasmine Richards. I wonder if you could help me out." It couldn't hurt to give her old pal a call.

"What was that?" Crowley asked, emerging from the bathroom.

Rose smiled. "Nothing. Just thinking out loud."

"Want to come to the gym with me?" Crowley flexed his arms, pumped his chest. "Got to keep this fine machine in shape."

Rose looked him up and down with a half-smile. He certainly did have a fine physique, fit and strong, and he kept it that way with the discipline he'd developed in the Army. And the truth was, they worked out well together. She stayed in shape too, mostly through kickboxing and amateur soccer. It seemed like years since she'd played and her life back then had been so much simpler. Life now was exciting, sometimes not in a good way. "I think I'll skip it this morning. But you go on."

"You'll be okay?"

"Of course. I can amuse myself for a couple of hours, Jake!"

He kissed her, then grabbed a towel and a bottle of water and headed out for the hotel gym. Rose pulled out her phone and stared at it for a minute. It would be good to see Jazz regardless of her concerns about Matthew Price. They had kept in touch, regularly making gags on each other's Facebook pages and stuff like that, but there was no substitute for genuine human interaction.

Rose tapped up the Facebook app, opened Messenger, and sent a quick note to Jazz.

Guess who's in town. Want to grab a coffee?

She put the phone down and went to take a shower and brush her teeth. When she came back, there was a reply.

Girl, you here now? Why didn't you tell me you were coming?

Rose smiled. *Last minute detour. You around?*

The response was immediate. *Hell, yeah. Where you wanna meet?*

Rose knew Planet Hollywood was not far away and suggested it. Jazz called her a *damned tourist!* for choosing such a kitschy place, but said she wasn't too far from there and they arranged to meet in half an hour. Rose pocketed the phone and headed out.

Inside Planet Hollywood, Rose was mesmerized by the movie memorabilia/ She found a photo of Doug Bradley in his makeup as Pinhead from Hellraiser, and the actual puzzle box used in the film. The Lament Configuration, it was called, and Rose smirked at the typo in the display box, calling it the Lamont Configuration. It was also known as a Lemarchand Box, after the fictional artisan who made them. Rose wondered if she should tell someone, to have the error corrected, but figured it would be pointless. She took a photo anyway and posted it on her Facebook page with a snarky comment that would amuse her horror aficionado friends.

She wandered around the other exhibits, ignoring the noise and bustle of early drinkers and people eating, and then found a seat right near a glass display box containing Freddie Krueger's red and green striped jumper and his glove of long razors. Her love of horror films made the thing feel like a holy grail of sorts, and she stood staring at it for several moments, mesmerized. Robert Englund had really worn those exact items as he terrorized Nancy in her dreams. Rolled gold film history. She took a selfie in front of it and messaged it to Jazz, knowing her friend was also a fan. She added the words, One, two, Freddie's coming for you!

There was no reply, and Rose sat and ordered a non-alcoholic cocktail of sweet juice and fruit pieces, enjoying the general vibe of the place. Before long, a heavy hand landed on her shoulder from behind.

"Three, four, better lock your door, bitch!"

Rose laughed and jumped up, pulled her friend into a hug. "It's so good to see you!"

"You too. It's been a long time."

"Too long."

"What the hell are you drinking?"

"Want one?"

Jazz laughed. "Sure, why not?"

Before long, they were chatting and laughing as if they'd never been apart. Rose quickly mentioned Jake, but Jazz didn't need the heads up.

"I've seen you two on Facebook. He looks like a hardass."

Rose nodded. Of course. As if she needed to worry about breaking the news of a relationship to Jazz. She internally scolded herself for being so ridiculous. Perhaps, she mused, it was because she harbored a strong desire for Jazz and felt some measure of guilt for that. She certainly wouldn't act on it, but maybe she needed to be a little more honest with herself about her feelings. And with that thought, she realized she hadn't noticed Jazz showing off any partners on her social media.

"He's tough," Rose replied. "But he's also gentle and kind. He's a great guy."

Jazz smiled, squeezed Rose's hand. "I'm happy for you, really." She left her hand there a moment longer, mischief playing her eyes.

"Cut it out!" Rose said.

Jazz lifted her hands in exaggerated surrender. "I'm not doing anything." But her grin was pure evil.

Rose laughed, tried to cover her flushed skin by hiding behind the umbrellas in her cocktail as she took a sip. "What about you? With anyone?" she asked, putting the large glass back down.

"Nah, no one special. Just fooling around, enjoying life. I got no complaints."

"That's good."

They fell to chatting, reminiscing about the last time Rose had been in town. Jazz talked about a story she was working on, hoping to bust something wide open, but she had to be cagey about the details.

"Talking of investigating," Rose said as the conversation lulled. "You ever hear of a big New York name, Matthew

Price?"

Jazz's nose wrinkled in thought, then she shook her head. "Don't think so. Why?"

Rose was a little deflated. She had maybe hoped the response would have been immediate and damning but knew that was unlikely. "No real reason. He's started seeing Jake's aunt, and he sort of gave me the creeps a little bit, that's all. He works for SaleMed, owns it in fact. Big pharmaceutical outfit."

"Well, if he's rich and into big pharma, I guess he's not a great guy," Jazz said.

"Not all pharma is bad, surely?"

"No, of course not. But it's enough to maybe put you on edge, no?"

Rose thought about that and wondered if perhaps Jazz was right. Maybe it was that simple. Maybe she just needed to do a little digging of her own, check out the company website. The director would surely have some profile on there, and she could put her mind at ease. She felt the need to turn the conversation elsewhere. "Remember you told me about the ghosts of the Round Table at the Algonquin?"

Jazz laughed. "Classic journalist story, that one. What, you saw one there? A ghost?"

"Not there, but I think I did see a ghost last night."

"Get outta here!"

"I'm serious. Jake's aunt lives at the Dakota."

Before she could carry on, Jazz sat back in her seat with a whistle, wide-eyed. "Damn, you need to marry that boy. You'll never need to work again if he has relatives that rich."

"Shut up, I like working. But yeah, it was a surprise to learn. I mean, I knew he had a decent bit of money, but I wasn't sure how. Now I know. Anyway, that's not the point. I saw a ghost outside the building when we left after dinner last night."

Jazz sat forward again, smiling, but her interest seemed genuine. "Looks like you got a spook from it too. You okay?"

"Well, we'd had a couple of drinks, and Jake was a little skeptical about it, so I didn't admit much to him at the time. I just told him it was an old-fashioned looking man. But it was more than that."

"In what way?"

"Well, earlier in the day we'd been to visit the Edgar Allan Poe house."

Jazz grinned. "You do love your horror stories."

Rose nodded, chewed her lower lip nervously. "I do, and maybe that's why this is creeping me out so much. But the ghost I saw last night at the Dakota, I'm sure it was him."

"Who?"

"Edgar Allan Poe!"

"Seriously?" Jazz said. "You don't think maybe he was just in your mind and you saw someone in the shadows..."

"No, I really don't think so. I hadn't thought about Poe for hours, then just saw him there in the darkness of the arched entrance. His hair was a little shorter than in the photos you always see, and he was wearing a suit and tie. It was old and worn, and he was carrying a hat in one hand, the kind men wore in the early 20th century, maybe. But I'm not kidding, it was definitely him. Or an absolute doppelganger."

Jazz leaned back again, shaking her head. "Well, I don't know anything about Poe ghosts, but I'll grant you that is pretty weird. You'll be going to see his aunt more while you're here?"

"Sure."

"Then keep an eye out. And maybe ask around, do some research, see if Poe has any connection to the Dakota."

Rose smiled, relieved Jazz wasn't ridiculing her. "I'm glad you're accepting my word for this."

"Well, I believe you when you say that's what you think you saw. Whether or not it really was what you saw, who knows? But I'll tell you what. I can't help with Poe ghosts, but I'll ask around about Matthew Price and SaleMed, see if there's anything obvious you should be aware of. Just in case, you know?" As she spoke, she was tapping a note into her phone.

"Thank you, Jazz. I really appreciate that."

"And don't leave town without us catching up again." She swallowed the last of her cocktail and stood. "I have to get back to work, but I want to meet this hardass new man of yours."

Jazz Richards headed back into the *New York Sentinel* offices, her mind on Rose Black. A damn shame she was seeing this Jake Crowley guy because Rose was as fine as Jazz remembered. Better even. Clearly hanging out with this guy agreed with her. Jazz was pleased for her friend. Rose was one of life's decent people, and there were few enough of them around, it seemed. Or perhaps she was getting more jaded, spending her life working on the kind of stories that sold. Which meant stories about the worst sorts of people. Although she got to do a feel-good piece every now and then, and she was doing a public service every time she exposed another predator or criminal. Jazz Richards was an ardent believer in the power of the press.

She headed towards her desk, thinking about Matthew Price. The fact the name had never crossed her path before made her think there would be little to find on the man, but she wasn't so lost in her own hubris that she thought she knew everything.

"Richards, over here!"

Jazz winced, Elena LaGuerta's summons could never be ignored. She turned to see her editor hanging off the doorframe of her office. The tall Puerto-Rican-American woman had an imposing presence, but kind eyes. She was a tough boss, but a fair one, and Jazz had developed a strong liking for her. Even if she was a pain in the ass sometimes.

She headed over. "What's up?"

LaGuerta went back inside her office and sat down. "Got a new assignment for you," she said, as Jazz closed the door.

"Oh yeah? Anything juicy?"

"I need you to head over to Washington Square Park."

"Another homeless person?" Jazz asked.

"Nope, much more interesting. You're probably going to enjoy this, it'll appeal to your sense of the macabre. Two previously undiscovered tombs beneath Washington Square were found this morning by water department workers."

Jazz had to admit that was a more interesting story than many she had to cover. Probably just an old dusty pit with a few bones from before history really mattered in the modern bustle of New York, but she had long since learned to never write anything off. An open mind and a keen eye were the most important aspects of her work. That, and strong analytical thinking. "Okay," she said. "I'll head over there now."

LaGuerta nodded and turned back to her computer.

As Jazz left her boss's office, an idea struck her. She pulled out her phone and called Rose.

"Miss me already?" Rose asked, a tease in her voice.

Jazz shook her head, gave a short laugh. "Always miss you. But something just came up that I think will interest you."

"Oh yeah? What's that?"

"Let's just say it's relevant to your professional interests. How about you join me at Washington Square Park to see a mass burial."

"Seriously?"

"Come on, Rose, I know you well enough. Trust me on this."

CHAPTER 5

Rose held Crowley's hand as they walked along the last bit of 5th Avenue to Washington Square Park. Across the busy street, the park looked inviting, open, and calm. Low, black iron fencing stood all around the perimeter, with gray paved walkways between green trees and neatly managed flowerbeds. People enjoyed the large grassy lawns, reading, napping, picnicking. The park entrance was marked by a towering white stone arch, an eagle with its wings spread at the apex, with intricately carved details all around. Two figures in statuary stood proudly on either side. George Washington on the right-hand side, Rose noted, not surprisingly given the name of the place. Was it also Washington on the left, in a long coat and tri-corn hat, or someone else of note? She realized her US history was incredibly limited when it came to ex-presidents and notable figures. She was about to ask Crowley when he spoke.

"Here we are then. So where's your mysterious friend?"

Rose frowned, sensing a bit of snark in Crowley's tone. Was he a tiny bit jealous? She had told him how she'd decide to pop out for a drink with her old pal while Crowley worked out and how it had been just like old times. Maybe that's what put him on edge. She sighed. Men could be so fragile if they felt anything but the most important person at any given moment. Rose refused to feel guilty about having friends, even if they were friends about whom she harbored carnal thoughts. Thought police were not in force yet, only actions counted.

Then again, if Crowley had said he was going for a drink with an old girlfriend, or an old nearly-girlfriend, Rose figured she might be a bit jealous, too. Maybe she should cut Crowley some slack. "Honestly, Jake, she's an old friend. That's all. You'll like her, I expect."

Jazz emerged from the other side of the large archway and waved. Rose snuck a glance at Crowley and smiled when she saw his reaction. Rose thought Jazz was a beautiful woman, and Crowley clearly shared that view.

"Hi again!" Jazz said. "You must be Jake?"

"That's right." He reached out, and they shook hands.

"Rose told me all about you."

Crowley looked from Jazz to Rose. "Did she now?"

"I did not!" Rose protested. "I just told her how great you were."

"In bed," Jazz said.

"Hey!" Rose looked at Crowley and laughed to see him blush. "I did not say that, Jasmine Richards, will you stop stirring."

"Oh, so he's no good in bed?"

Rose was thankful that Crowley laughed and joined in instead of being offended. "I'll have you know I'm bloody fantastic in bed, thank you very much. I've satisfied over three women in my lifetime."

"You didn't tell me he had a sense of humor," Jazz said to Rose, though her eyes never left Crowley.

"All right, enough," Rose said. "I think we need to change the subject. What's happening here that you think I'll be so interested in?"

Jazz handed Rose a new-looking Canon digital SLR camera and said, "Just play along, yeah? Follow my lead."

They went into the park and Jazz headed directly for an area between two lawns, marked off by orange cones and yellow tape. Two men stood beside the tape, talking.

"We got an early tip about this," Jazz said quickly as they walked. "It's the kind of thing that's often discovered in New York. You can imagine the layers of history, the city is constantly renewing itself, a modern layer put over the top of one that came before, time and again. There are all kinds of stories about underground places that are forgotten, bricked up, filled in even. Then every now and then, city workers will uncover some part of that lost history, a snapshot of what was here before.

"Now we know this park is historic in its own way, and city archaeologists knew there were supposed to be old tombs somewhere nearby, but were unsure exactly where. Then last night, city workers doing a dig for a water main discovered two burial vaults containing the remains of at least a dozen people, supposedly interred around two centuries ago."

"Two hundred years?" Crowley asked, aghast.

"Yep. And it's all only three and a half feet below the sidewalk. But that's all I know from the tip-off. It's probably all there is to know, a bit of old New York and that's that. But who knows, right? One day I'll luck into something special, worthy of a good story. This might be it."

They reached the two talking men and Rose realized she was smiling. Jazz did know her well, after all. This was a pretty cool thing to tag along for. Inside the barricade was an open manhole. One of the men standing beside it was clearly a construction worker, with calloused hands and a friendly face. His companion was altogether more academic, wearing a suit and tie. He was older, probably not far from retirement.

Jazz flicked a wink at Rose and stepped up. She flashed something in a leather wallet that Rose couldn't see, then said, "How are you guys today? Parks Department, here to have a quick look before the others descend."

"Others?" the academic asked, confused. He looked from Jazz to Rose to Crowley, then back again.

"That's right," Jazz said, "so we'd better be quick. Gotta make an inspection, a couple of quick preliminary photos, you know the drill, right?"

"Well, not really–" the man started.

Jazz bulldozed over him. "Hey, look, no matter. It'll take five minutes."

"We're waiting for the police," the construction worker said uncertainly. "I guess it's not a real priority though, not being an emergency."

Rose laughed. "No, it's hardly a crime scene, huh? You found the vaults?"

"Me and my team, yeah. We're contractors for the city department of design and construction. As we went to set up down there, an old wall fell in, and we saw the vaults behind it. I sent the team home, there's nothing we can do now until we get the all clear. You here to give us that?"

"Not my department," Jazz said quickly. "But I report to them." She turned to the academic. "And you are?"

"Professor Charles Putnam. I received a call, and I'm waiting on a couple of young researchers to join me in examining the site. I thought we were supposed to–"

"Of course you are, Professor, but red tape always comes first, am I right?" She stepped over the tape and gestured to Rose and Crowley. "Come on, you two. The quicker we get this done, the quicker these guys can get on with their job. I'm really sorry to inconvenience you like this."

Without waiting to see if anyone followed her or tried to stop her, Jazz strode over to the manhole and quickly descended the ladder. Suppressing a smile, noticing Crowley doing the same, Rose followed.

At the bottom of the ladder, Rose found herself in a low, rounded passage of brick. The walls and ceiling were coated in a white deposit that at first looked like peeling paint, but which she suspected was in fact a mineral deposit from centuries of damp. At the end of the rounded passage was a low doorway, and Jazz headed for it.

"You're right," Crowley said as they followed. "I do like your friend."

Rose laughed. "Told you!" She made sure to snap a lot of pictures as they went, though she wasn't sure how necessary any of them might be.

The door led to a short cross passage and only a few feet along that an old brick wall was half tumbled in. Jazz nudged a couple more bricks free to make enough room to step through, and then did just that, flicking on a flashlight as she went.

"Jazz!" Rose said, aghast. "You can't go blundering in there, surely?"

Jazz poked her head back out, grinning. "Oops. Looks like I just did. Come on!"

The room beyond was a rounded brick structure like the one they had descended into, this one coated with the same mineral deposit, but here a good half inch thick, no doubt undisturbed by even light for over two hundred years. Rose only had moments to marvel at that before she realized all the broken wood on the floor was actually the remains of about twenty coffins. Some dusty, gray bones lay scattered among them, but not many. Rose swallowed, the presence of death sudden and impossible to ignore. Everything seemed instantly much more serious. But, she had to admit, exciting too.

She snapped pictures as they went through the long space and eventually came to another doorway. "You think they even realized this was here?" she asked, gesturing at the next door.

"I doubt it," Jazz said. "Seems they spotted this space and immediately ceased work. Clearly not as curious as us. I guess they don't get paid enough for complications."

The door before them was wooden with diagonal supporting slats, hanging by iron hinges. Or maybe copper, Rose mused. Unable to help herself, she gave it a gentle push. It shifted slightly, so she pushed harder. Scraping against the grit on the floor, it slowly opened and Jazz shined her flashlight inside.

There were dozens of skeletons piled up against one wall, stacked like cordwood, with bits of clothing and hair still clinging to them. Rose gasped at the sight.

"Holy hell," Crowley breathed.

Rose quickly took more photographs, then turned to take pictures of another pile of bones, disarticulated skeletons making a confused pile of skulls, femurs, and other aged and broken bones, many crumbled to dust.

Crowley pushed the door all the way open to reveal the other side of the space and Jazz swore eloquently.

Another stack of bodies filled that side, but these weren't ancient skeletal remains. Rose saw right away that there were distinct layers. The bottom layer was clearly the oldest, evidenced by the clothing and jewelry, a pocket watch in the dust, but even they weren't that old. Decades more than centuries, certainly. As her eyes lifted to take in the scene, her gorge rose too. Rose let out a yelp of shock as Crowley joined Jazz in swearing. The bodies on top were obviously no more than a few weeks old, dressed in modern clothes.

"Get photos," Jazz said.

Swallowing hard, Rose lined up the camera and took several. The two recent corpses were a red-haired young man and a blonde young woman, well-dressed. The man at least had the brown stain of dried blood on the back of his head, though the angle at which he lay made it impossible to see the wound the blood had come from without getting closer. Rose was reluctant to do that. She took more photos, the flash like lightning bolts in the dim room. She hoped her trembling wouldn't make the images blurry.

Jazz put a hand on her arm as she lowered the camera. "We'd better get back up right away and tell Professor Putman to hurry those police along. Looks like this is a crime scene after all."

CHAPTER 6

Crowley stood back while Jazz told the professor and construction worker what they'd seen. She was doing a good job of skirting around her own credentials, and Crowley could tell she was anxious to be away from the crime scene. They could all get in a lot of trouble if they were caught here, especially having moved things down there and possible contaminated evidence. Something made his skin itch, put him on edge.

"You went past the fallen wall?" the professor asked in shock.

"We just stepped in," Jazz said. "We had to. We only had a quick look. But please, call the police. We could see further than you had before, and those bodies are fresh. This is serious."

"Holy crap," the construction worker said, pulling a phone from his pocket.

As they talked, Crowley scanned around. He saw a large man, broad-shouldered and thick-limbed, wearing a charcoal suit and dark sunglasses. His hair was a mop of dark brown curls, his skin pale. He held a cell phone awkwardly in his left hand, and Crowley realized it was because he was surreptitiously lining up for a creeper photograph of Rose and Jazz talking to the two men. The man checked whatever photo he'd taken, then tapped the screen to make a call.

Crowley was about to cross the square to confront the man when Rose pulled on his sleeve. "Come on, we need to go."

"Why the hurry?"

Distant sirens sounded, getting quickly closer. "That's why," Jazz said. "It'll be much easier for all of us if we make ourselves scarce. Otherwise, we'll have a lot of awkward questions to answer."

She was only voicing his own concerns of moments ago. "Okay." Crowley glanced back to where the man had stood, but he was gone. Scanning the crowds, Crowley saw his broad back heading away from them towards West 4th Street. Frustrated, he made a mental note of the man's appearance and then followed Rose and Jazz out of the arched gateway and back north along 5th Avenue.

Matthew Price was sat quietly reading, enjoying the sunshine through his apartment window when his phone shrilly interrupted the peace and quiet. He frowned at it, rude and intrusive device that it was, but then saw the name Carlo flashing on the screen.

He tapped to answer, immediately selecting speakerphone, so he didn't have sit holding it against his head. It always made him uncomfortable to use it that way. "What have you learned?"

"Constructions workers found the vault in Washington Square Park, just like you suspected. They have it all cordoned off, and the police have just arrived."

Price's eyebrows rose. "The police?"

"Yeah, seems they found something down there that caused a bit of a panic. There was some people around, then a few of them went down inside. When they came back up, they looked pretty freaked out. Had a conversation and then the police came. I moved along before the police got there, but watched from a distance. They've established a crime scene. But interestingly, the three who checked it this morning left again pretty quick, like they didn't want to be around for too long."

"Who were they all? Officials of some kind? Any idea?"

"Not all of them, no. The two who stayed behind are the city works guy and some academic. They were there all along. The three who turned up and went down into the vault were a strange bunch. They were acting all official, but it looked to me like a bamboozle. And I think I'm right about that because one of them I recognized, and she's no city official. She's a reporter with the *New York Sentinel*."

"How do you know her?"

"I read the *Sentinel*. They always put her picture by her stories, and I've always thought she was pretty hot. Her name is Jasmine Richards."

Price pursed his lips, thinking. If a reporter had gone down there and discovered something interesting, how long before it was public knowledge? "How did a reporter know to investigate already? The hot press grapevine is rather active, I suppose. What about the other two?" he asked. "Were they press as well, do you think?"

"They were with Richards, but I got no idea why. A man and woman. The woman was acting like she was the photographer, but I saw the reporter give her the camera when they got here, which seemed kind of weird. She was Asian-looking, maybe Chinese? But she had a foreign accent. Australian maybe. Or British or something. Who the hell can tell, you know? The guy had a similar accent, tall and burly-looking fella. Not huge, but sorta capable, you know what I mean?"

Instinct struck instantly, and Price's eyebrows rose further. "I do know what you mean. Did you get a photo, by any chance?"

"Not of the guy, he stayed a bit to one side when they came out. But the reporter and the other woman, yeah. Hang on."

There was scuffling as Carlo moved his phone around, then a beep and a grainy photo came up on the screen of Price's phone. He leaned forward to see Rose Black and an African-American woman talking to a construction worker and an academic. So the man was surely Gertrude's dear nephew, Jake Crowley. What an interesting development.

"I know which way they went," Carlo said. "I can catch them up easily enough, and have a friendly chat if you want to know more."

"No, thank you. Just keep an eye on the situation unfolding in the park for now, if you'd be so kind. Thank you, Carlo."

"No problem."

The call ended, and Price sat back, fingers tapping thoughtfully at his chin.

"What are we going to do about this?" he said quietly.

CHAPTER 7

"Well, I'd better get back to work." Jazz's face was alive with excitement, no doubt the adrenaline of their mischief and the subsequent macabre discovery.

Crowley shared that joy, but he also harbored darker thoughts, uncertain about Jazz and Rose spending time together. There was clearly a spark between them that he doubted would ever be extinguished. He also told himself not to be a jealous fool, Rose was with him, after all. But still, the nagging doubts persisted. It was one thing to recognize you were being a jealous fool, but entirely another to not feel it any longer.

"Thanks for that unusual sightseeing detour," Rose said. "A New York City experience most people would never get."

Jazz made a sarcastic curtsy. "You're welcome. I hope I get to follow this up, it could become quite the juicy exposé." She gestured with the camera she'd retrieved from Rose. "Especially as we got photographs of the bodies in situ. You want me to credit you as the photographer if I get a feature piece, get you an official *New York Sentinel* byline?"

"No, thanks! I'm happy to be photographer incognito," Rose said with a grin.

"I expect there'll be a lot of red tape before you're allowed your fun in the paper," Crowley said, and he heard the gruffness in his voice.

Rose glanced at him, frowning slightly.

"Sure, there always is." Jazz seemed unfazed by his attitude, and he was thankful for that. "But I have the best chance here to get something going. We'll see. LaGuerta, that's my editor, she can be a hardass, but I'll try to talk her around." She moved to Rose and hugged her. "See you more before you leave town, I hope?"

"Oh, most definitely."

They kissed each other's cheeks, then Jazz reached out a hand to shake. Crowley took it, wondering if the scowl he wore looked as obvious as it felt. He resented his feelings, didn't like to be jealous, but he resented the closeness of the women too. This wasn't how he had hoped their excursion to New York would play out.

"Really good to meet you, Jake," Jazz said. "You look after Rose, you hear?"

"I will. You can count on it."

"See you guys."

Jazz turned and strode away. Rose turned to Crowley.

"You okay?" Her brows were knitted, but more in concern than annoyance he thought.

"Sure, why?"

"You're a little grumpy, is all."

Crowley took her hand and squeezed it, kissed her lightly on the lips. "I'm sorry. A little out of sorts, I guess. But you're right, I'll try to shake it off. Let's get a coffee and go to Times Square. Be tourists again."

They continued north up 5th Avenue, and soon enough the road opened up into the large, long triangular precinct that for some reason was called a Square. Crowley loved this part of New York, so intense, so vibrant with colors, neon, noise, people. The digital billboards scrolled a riot of colors advertising all kinds of technology, movies, shows, cars, the full gamut of human achievement and excess.

Crowley pointed to a freestanding shop in the center of the pedestrianized precinct. It said *wafels & dinges* in bright yellow lettering. "I have no idea what either of those things are, but they sell coffee too, so let's go."

A few minutes later, oversized cups in hand, they moved to the red steps in the middle of Times Square designed as a kind of viewing platform for tourists. Glass sides surrounded the bright red plastic stairway, people swarming all over to get the best selfies at the top, the brilliance of Times Square framed just right behind them. Crowley and Rose sat on one side, only a few steps up.

Rose hefted the cup. "Everything in America is unnecessarily big."

Crowley grinned. "Yeah, that's their brand, I think. Excess in all things. Kind of exhausting, isn't it? A bit grotesque."

"It is, but invigorating too." She spoke without looking at him, her gaze roving the mad brightness all around them.

Crowley nodded. He had to admit, it was mesmerizing. He joined her in looking around, as fascinated by the huge array of people as well as the city itself. "I love to visit, but I could never live here."

"Too much for you?"

"I think so. It would be overwhelming. Then again, if I lived in New York, I wouldn't be in Times Square all the time, so perhaps the perspective is off. Other parts of the city, even parts of Manhattan, are entirely more relaxed. More so than here, at least."

"It's certainly not England," Rose said. "Not even London."

Crowley smiled. "Old Londinium has its own charms and bustles. But we're used to those."

"I guess. What do you think about what we saw with Jazz?" Rose asked.

"I don't know. Pretty bizarre to visit a vault supposedly undisturbed for two hundred years only to find fresh bodies in it."

"Yeah, exactly. So it obviously wasn't undiscovered. Someone knew about it and was making good use of it. That's just so creepy. You think we disturbed the lair of a serial killer?"

"Sounds like one of your horror movies." Crowley cast his mind back, picturing the gloomy crypt. "Did you notice how the bodies stacked up there were in layers? The two on top were fresh, but beneath they were kind of representing different time periods as they went down. Not by much, but the stack must have covered several decades, and that was only the one pile. Other piles seemed even older."

"I did. And you know, we were shocked by fresh ones, but the next couple of layers down weren't *that* old either. There was some relatively modern clothing rotting away down there."

"I saw that too," Crowley said. "But towards the bottom of the next pile over, the corpses were ancient. Little more than bone and rags."

"You think someone found that old vault and decided it was a good place to stash the more recently deceased."

Crowley laughed, but without much humor. "I guess so. Not a bad place in a city like this. I mean, you can lose a body in the wilderness easily enough, but a place like New York?" He gestured around, encompassing all of Times Square and the massive city beyond.

They sat quietly for a moment, sipping coffee. Then Crowley said, "You notice anything else about the bodies?"

"Like what?"

"Any… uniformities?"

Rose frowned. "I'm not following."

"Each one, at least all that I could see, had a hole in the skull. Same size and location every time."

Rose looked up, eyebrows raised. "Really? I saw blood on the back of that fresh guy's head but didn't see a hole. Even the older ones had it?"

"Yep, so far as I could see anyway. We only had a moment, but that's significant, don't you think?"

"It is. I wonder if Jazz noticed that? I should tell her."

Crowley sighed. Jazz again. "Already gone off the idea of ghost hunting?" There was a level of snark in his tone he hadn't intended, but he wasn't about to apologize for it.

"What's that supposed to mean?"

"Nothing, I just—" He was interrupted by his phone ringing. Feeling like a fool, he was thankful for the distraction. "Hang on." He thumbed to answer the unrecognized number. "Hello?"

"Jake, is that you?"

The voice was male, familiar, but Crowley couldn't place it for a moment. "Yes, this is Jake Crowley. Who's this?"

"Dear boy, it's Matthew Price. Your aunt was kind enough to give me your number."

"Matt Price! What can I do for you?" Crowley saw Rose's sour look from the corner of his eye and enjoyed a moment of juvenile pleasure from her disapproval. Give her something to worry about too. He wasn't sure why she was supposed critical of Price, the man seemed decent enough to him.

"Matthew Price, if you don't mind. I wondered if you'd like to have lunch tomorrow? I thought perhaps we ought to get to know each other a little better now we're both such a large part of Gertrude's life."

"Sure thing, sounds good. Where and when?"

"Let's say twelve noon at Riko on 8th Avenue? It's a wonderful little Peruvian place I've grown rather fond of."

"Sure thing, I'll see you then." Crowley hung up and grinned at Rose. "Aunt Gertie's loverboy wants to have lunch. Get to know me better."

One side of Rose's mouth twisted slightly. "I really don't care for Price."

"I know, but I like the guy. And hey, at least my friend doesn't want to shag me." He could tell by the sudden tightness in her face that he was pushing the teasing too far. "Only joking. I guess you can have lunch with Jazz then?"

CHAPTER 8

Price arrived at Riko early. The restaurant was small, a narrow frontage on 8th Avenue between a Jessie's Express Café and a place that served Thai and Japanese food. Riko was cozy on the inside, with dark wood tables and chairs and deep red painted walls. The whole place was as narrow as the street front, only eight or nine tables in two rows, four seats at each one, and a cramped bar and service counter at the far end. Beside the bar, a door led into the brightly lit kitchen. Immediately Price was assailed by the smells of grilling chicken and South American spices. The place was renowned for its wide selection of craft beers too, something Price had developed a taste for over recent years.

A large screen above the bar showed a sporting event, the nature of which Price didn't care about. He chose a table halfway down and sat with his back to the screen. It seemed like everywhere had to have a TV hanging up these days, and he hated it. Even a small family restaurant like this, with its wonderful food and careful service, sullied itself with the modern infection. It was the only thing about Riko he disliked.

A young girl came over, smiling broadly. She was full-figured, with thick brown hair and soft, friendly eyes. "Just yourself, sir?" she asked, her accent strong.

"I'm waiting for a friend," Price said.

"Okay." She laid two menus on the table and left. A moment later she returned with a bottle of water and two glasses, leaving again without a word. Price appreciated that.

He pulled his phone from his pocket – some modern inventions were useful rather than intrusive – and went over his notes again. Following the dirt Carlo had dug up before, Price had done his own extensive research on both Jake Crowley and Rose Black, but had found frustratingly little to work with. Despite the recent call and photo from Carlo, he knew Rose Black was neither a reporter nor a photographer for the *Sentinel*. He didn't need to research to know that, so he had no idea why she had been there with a camera. But he had found her on several social media sites, and Jasmine Richards was friends with her on most of them. So they had a connection that went back some years. And Rose most definitely was employed by the Natural History Museum in London, she was on their website listed as a historian and guide. An incredibly smart woman by the look of things.

Jake Crowley, however, was more of an enigma. He had next to no social media presence as far as Price could discover, and there was precious little information anywhere else online. He was listed as a teacher by his school's website, so that much was true. Price had even made a surreptitious call to the school asking for him to see what that might turn up, but all they had said was that he was currently on leave and they weren't sure when he would return. Strange activity for a teacher, Price thought. Rose had mentioned him a great dealt on her own social pages, so there was secondhand information about him there even if she didn't mention his name, or sometimes only referred to him as J. It was obvious who she meant. She had also posted a few photos, selfies as they were known, a phrase which bothered Price for reasons he couldn't quite explain. But even those photos were few and far between, and they did nothing to further his knowledge of Crowley.

But one thing had really piqued Price's interest. From before, Price knew Crowley was ex-Army, but Rose had recently posted a meme about snooping on your partner's phone, which conveyed its own questionable inferences, but she had added the comment, "When your man is ex-SAS" and included a laughing emoji.

The replies on that post seemed to confirm it wasn't a joke, and Crowley had indeed been in the SAS "a long time ago." Price had already discovered that little tidbit about Crowley's ignominious exit from the Armed Forces, but it hadn't revealed that he had been in the Special Forces. The SAS, which stood for Special Air Service, was a British Army special forces unit founded in 1941 as a regiment, and later reconstituted as a corps in 1950. Not unlike the American Green Berets, the SAS was responsible for things like covert reconnaissance, counter-terrorism, direct action, and hostage rescue. Despite a little digging on his part, Price had been frustrated to learn much more. Anything about the actions of the corps was highly classified due to the sensitivity of their operations. Regardless, it added new spice to the other things Price had learned about Crowley's final weeks in the Army.

Besides that, how long ago could it really have been, given

the man was only in his mid-thirties now. So very young. Price needed to chew over these details some more and decide how best to leverage that particular morsel of information. Perhaps he could dig a little during lunch, just scratch the surface in casual conversation and see what came up.

Beyond that, all the information he had about Crowley was rather dull. He enjoyed football, and was a West Ham fan, which was apparently an English soccer team, as the sport was known here. But Price needed to remember Crowley would refer to it as football. That might be another way to lower the man's defenses, but Price would be quickly out of his depth on that subject. And, again via Rose's comments, it seemed Crowley was a huge fan of William Golding's classic novel, *Lord of the Flies*. The whole exploration of savagery versus civilization explored in that book gave its own insight into Crowley's nature, if he really was as much of a fan as Rose implied. Precious little, the man was something of an enigma. Price smiled, deciding he would prefer to think of it as a challenge.

Movement in the doorway caught Price's eye, and he looked up to see Crowley enter. The man paused momentarily at the entrance and scanned the small restaurant, taking in the bar, the kitchen door. His eyes narrowed slightly as he glanced back at the entrance. It all happened in the space of a second or two, but Price recognized the trained eye of someone sizing up a place. Crowley had clearly logged everything about the eatery in that short time and had been perturbed that there was only a single way in and out. Of course, there would be a back door from the kitchen into some dark and fetid alley, and Price didn't doubt for a moment that Crowley would have considered that too. Such a fleeting moment that revealed so much about the man.

Then Crowley's eyes met Price's and he smiled, waved one hand. Price slipped his phone back into his jacket pocket and stood, extended one hand to shake. Crowley's hand was strong and rough, calloused in ways a schoolteacher's hands never would be.

"Glad you could make it," Price said.

"Good choice of place," Crowley said, sitting opposite. "I haven't been here before, but I love Peruvian food."

"Then I think you'll be coming here again. One of the best in the city, in my opinion. I recommend the seafood stew."

Crowley nodded, looking over the menu. "That just happens to be a favorite of mine."

Price smiled. "Maybe you're all right after all." It really was amazing the kind of minutiae a person could glean from someone else's social media. One photo on Rose's Facebook page of Crowley enjoying seafood, and Price had the man more at ease instantly. Honestly, people these days wore their lives like sandwich boards, no mystery or personal details kept close. And that was with Crowley hardly putting anything online himself. Price wondered if the man knew how much could be learned about him from Rose Black's almost continuous posting, and whether it might bother Crowley to realize that. Or did he not care? Price thought maybe he would try to find out obliquely, as it could always prove to be another lever at a later date.

The waitress returned, and the two men ordered. After considering the range of craft beers, Crowley picked a Kuka ginger and mango IPA. Price joined him, and they both agreed it was an unusual but quite pleasant variation.

The conversation moved easily and smoothly, though it was plain to Price that both men were sizing each other up. Crowley clearly had concerns for his aunt, and that was entirely understandable, but those concerns might well prove to be a considerable problem as things moved along. A shame, Price thought, as under different circumstances it was entirely likely he would have become good friends with the ex-SAS schoolteacher and his shady past. Perhaps they had more in common than Crowley would be comfortable admitting in polite company.

"So you're a schoolteacher," Price said. "That must be a fulfilling profession."

Crowley nodded as he chewed, swallowed. "For the most part it is. Funding makes the life difficult, those kids deserve more. But I do my best, and it's always gratifying to see young people grow and develop."

"Has that always been your desire, to teach?"

"No, it's something I came to a little later in life."

Price smiled, angling around to the subject of Crowley's previous career. "What were you before a teacher?"

A dark look passed over Crowley's face, then he smiled. "A soldier. I was in the Army. But I realized after a little while that it didn't suit me."

"Didn't suit? In what way?"

Crowley thought for a moment, lips pursed. "Probably best to say that I discovered I wasn't so good at blindly following orders. My father was a soldier, and I thought it was in my blood, but I wrong."

"So you quit?" Price wanted the dirt, but there was no way to ask for it directly. "was that easy?"

Crowley laughed. "Easier than you'd think, in fact, of the conditions are. But all that was a long time ago. I'm a teacher now."

Silence hung between them, and Crowley was clearly happy to let it end there, his last sentence like a full stop on the subject. Price tried not to let his disappointment or frustration show.

"You visit New York often?" Price asked, to fill the conversational lull.

Crowley swallowed a mouthful of stew and nodded. "As often as I can, but just lately not as often as I'd like. Gertie is getting older, and I feel like I need to stay closer. Partly to make the most of the time she has left, of course, but also to make sure she's okay."

There were veiled assertions to that seemingly innocuous statement. "It is a vibrant city," Price said, to head off more talk of Gertrude.

"Quite the jungle out there," Crowley agreed.

Price smiled, pleased with another opening he'd been working towards coming around so easily. "That strange juxtaposition between civilization and savagery, eh? It reminds me a lot of *Lord of the Flies* in many ways." Crowley looked up, one eyebrow raised. "I've often thought," Price continued, "that the big city and its millions of people is not so different to that small island and its group of British boys."

Crowley huffed a soft laugh. "You know, that's one of my all-time favorite books."

"Is it really? Mine too. I own a first edition in excellent condition, signed by Golding himself." Purchased earlier that day, though Crowley didn't need that particular detail. Price considered it $20,000 well spent if all went to plan.

"Seriously? A genuine first edition?"

"Absolutely. 1954, in excellent condition, signed on the title page. It's housed in a custom clamshell box, but I prefer to display it so I can enjoy its presence in my home. Perhaps you might be interested in seeing it?"

"I most certainly would!" Crowley's eyes were wide with wonder.

Price smiled, doing his best to remain relaxed and casual. "Well, you'll have to come to my house. I look forward very much to having you there." He looked down at his lunch so Crowley wouldn't spot the triumph in his eyes.

CHAPTER 9

Rose climbed the steps and entered the gray stone New York Public Library through the center arch of the three that fronted the impressive building. Doric columns and high eaves with intricate carvings of leaves and flowers towered high above her. Inside, the space was capacious, with polished marble floors and a high curved ceiling. Several archways led to various rooms on the first floor, with huge staircases to either side leading to a mezzanine style second floor. More arches, daylight streaming through them, marched around the second level. A carving front and center between the two levels announced that she stood in Astor Hall. On the giant square columns at the start of each staircase, the names of numerous benefactors were carved. Rockefellers and counts and even Astor herself among them.

Rose moved slowly through the huge building, marveling at the age and beauty. It wasn't old by British historical standards, but as an American institution, it held the weight of history. She tried not to resent Jake and his lunch with Matthew Price. She held her reservations about the man, and wouldn't change her mind easily about that. She had learned to trust her instincts. Most women she knew trusted their initial reactions to men, even if they might be proven wrong later. She also knew Jake was partly pushing back against her friendship with Jazz, and she could understand that too. An electricity existed between her and the reporter that only a fool would deny. But she had no intention to act on it and perhaps he would only believe that once he saw it to be true. Any promises on her part would fall on deaf ears in the meantime. Perhaps she simply needed to give that time and let Jake see the truth of it. Besides, she could busy herself here while he enjoyed lunch with his aunt's new beau. Maybe he'd return equally suspicious of Price and his motives after spending time alone with the man. She hoped so. That would achieve far more than Rose trying to convince him of her feelings, with no substance to back them with other than intuition.

She walked through a room with dozens of long desks, lamps with gold metal shades spaced evenly among them, three to a table. Lots of people sat at the desks, reading, researching, some simply enjoying the space, gazing around the huge room. A large wooden door with a convoluted frame stood at the far end. Above it, in gold letters, was the legend:

A good Booke is the pretious life-blood of a mafter ſpirit, imbalm'd and treaſur'd up on purpoſe to a life beyond life.

Rose smiled. Almost deliberately opaque in phrasing, but a fine sentiment nonetheless. She began searching for books to sate her need to know more about what she had seen with Jazz and Jake in Washington Square Park. While the news story would undoubtedly be the fresh bodies, there was a lot more to the place, a long history like so much of New York City. It was built in layers, after all, from its earliest settlement to the modern metropolis. Jazz's talk of layers had alluded to that, and it intrigued Rose to consider it.

Her research led her to discover a more morbid and macabre history than she ever imagined. In the late 18th and early 19th century, the area that became Washington Square Park was nothing more than a potter's field, a strangely euphemistic name for a mass grave site for the indigent, poor, criminals, and victims of epidemics. The term had biblical origins, referring to a clay-heavy area of land near Jerusalem that was bought with the thirty pieces of silver returned by a remorseful Judas to the chief priests. Worthless for farming, the land came to be used to bury strangers, and the name of a potter's field had been used to describe such places ever since.

What would become Washington Square Park was originally a farm, purchased in 1797 by the city for this purpose, and it remained a potter's field until around 1827 when Washington Square was legally declared a public space. But its history wasn't only sad, it was cruel. The site was also used as an execution ground, the last execution, that of a slave, took place in 1819, with the slave's burial taking place in the same field.

During celebrations of the 50th anniversary of the signing of the Declaration of Independence, the place was renamed the Washington Military Parade Ground, and transformed from a burial site to a bucolic green space. But the pleasant park retained its history, the bodies that had been buried there remaining undisturbed. Rose thought that was deliciously macabre. She found excerpts from a guide book called *Inside the Apple: A Streetwise History of New York City* by Michelle and James Nevius, who wrote that, "While estimates vary, it seems likely that over 20,000 people were buried in the land…. The bulk of the bodies were never disinterred, which means that they remain to this day under the grass and pavement of Washington Square."

Rose sat back from her research, equally fascinated and appalled. They had been walking over the remains of tens of thousands of people, unawares. Every day, thousands of living people did the same, and no doubt there were many such places in New York City. It really was an ideal place to hide fresher corpses if the perpetrator knew a way to secret them there. Of course, the waterworks in the park had interrupted that carefully laid plan. Those poor city workers must stumble across ancient corpses with some regularity. Of course, this time, the corpses, at least several of them, weren't ancient. That was something else entirely.

She read on, following the rabbit hole of research into potter's fields, which led her to learn about Hart Island, an uninhabited strip of land off the coast of the Bronx in Long Island Sound. If Washington Square Park had been macabre, this place was positively terrifying in its implications. The city had bought Hart Island in 1868 and used it as a burial ground and a prison for Confederate soldiers. For more than a century, the dead shared the island with living inmates of one kind or another, many of whom were likely to end up in its mass graves themselves. To this day, prison inmates, for 50c a day, bury the unclaimed dead there, stacked in plain coffins shoulder to shoulder like bricks in numbered trenches.

The corpses of the poor, the destitute, those executed by the state, or donated to medical science, and a thousand other sources, all filled trench after trench on Hart Island. New York, like many states, had added dissection to death sentences for murder, arson and even burglary by the early 19th century, circumventing an otherwise illegal practice. The demand for medical cadavers soon outstripped the legal supply of executed felons, and a black market in corpses bloomed. Slave owners "donated" or sold bodies of dead slaves to medical schools and schools in competition with each other smuggled in black bodies stashed in whiskey barrels. Potter's fields, almshouse cemeteries, and African-American burial grounds were regularly robbed as professors paid top dollar for corpses delivered without questions asked. These corpses would then end up later interred on Hart Island, stacked in the mass graves, forgotten, unrecorded, unlamented. Over more than one hundred and fifty years, in excess of one million people had been buried on Hart Island. That was a staggering number to imagine.

Rose found photos and drone footage of the island as it was now. Crumbling and derelict institutional buildings, including a lunatic asylum, a tuberculosis hospital, a boys' reformatory, slowly decaying around the open ground being reserved for ever more mass grave trenches, filled with forgotten bodies buried three deep, row after row after row.

Rose stood and moved away from her research, amazed at the stories, and deeply saddened by the seeming inhumanity that such dense populations triggered. And besides, the research was moving her away from finding more about Washington Square Park and the fresh bodies they had discovered there. While learning about Hart Island gave her a greater insight into what happened historically at Washington State Park, it didn't move her forward with new information.

She decided to change tack. Jake had said about the uniformity of holes in the skulls of all the bodies he had seen in that newly disturbed underground chamber. That had to be relevant, it had to mean something, but she couldn't decide what. When Rose closed her eyes and pictured the scene, she knew he was right. It took some time, a whole different approach to the angle of her search, but Rose was in her element, the historian in her reveling at the challenge. Why would someone put holes in skulls like that? What sort of practice might they be pursuing? Pre-death or post?

She had no idea how long she'd been at it, learning all kinds of things, when one particular article caught her attention. She paused, staring hard at the piece for several seconds before whispering to herself, "That is not possible."

CHAPTER 10

Jazz Richards rubbed her tired eyes and sat back to look over what she had gathered so far. It wasn't a lot, but like a shark that's able to sense a tiny drop of blood in a vast ocean, Jazz could sniff out a juicy story in a morass of mundanity. Fresh bodies in a crypt that had been undisturbed for decades, maybe even centuries, was the kind of hook an investigative journalist lived for, after all.

"Okay, Jazz," she whispered to herself. "Let's do this."

She collected up her work and headed to LaGuerta's office. She tapped on the door, and her editor's voice came through right away. "Yep?"

Jazz went in, shut the door behind herself. "Okay, I've been doing as much research as I can, and I need a bit more budget and time to do more, but I'm onto something here. Something big, I know it!"

LaGuerta held up one hand, frowning. "Wait, what are we talking about?"

Jazz gestured with the folders in her hand. "The follow-up to my story about the bodies in Washington Square Park? We ran the short piece about the discovery, but I've been looking into—"

LaGuerta interrupted again. "You didn't get my message? Have you even checked your messages?"

"What message?"

"I killed that story. It's done."

Jazz deflated, stunned. "What? Why?"

"Your sources wouldn't confirm. In fact, the archaeologist from the university flat out denies it even happened. Said he had no idea what you were talking about and they should probably sue for what we already printed. He denied you were even there, that you'd talked or anything. I challenged him on that, and he backed down, of course, but still. He refused to confirm anything else, said it was all a mistake, the gloomy crypt played tricks on your eyes or something. Regardless, we've got no source now and no further access. It's dead in the water."

"There were fresh corpses," Jazz said, aghast. "There were

dozens of skeletons with matching holes in their skulls, and a lot of them were a lot newer than the chamber next door. Dozens of bodies from recent decades, Elena! This is huge!"

LaGuerta shrugged. "So you said, but we have no access and no sources."

"But I've got photos!" Jazz protested.

LaGuerta smiled ruefully, shook her head. "But no permission to use them. And your photos have no context. Disturbing images inside a dark room. So what? It could be a haunted house. If the authorities involved deny the shots are real, we'll look like idiots."

"Elena, you know me better than that! This is something, why are you canning it so easily?"

"The story is dead, Jazz. Your photos don't matter. No sources willing to confirm, so no story. I imagine there's probably a mob angle or something, this city is corrupt as hell, we all know it. But there's nothing we can do about this and the *Sentinel* won't be dragged into legal hassles over it. It's not worth it."

Jazz stood dumbfounded for a moment, then said, "Who's pressuring you? It's not like you to let anyone gag you."

LaGuerta stood, slammed her palms down on the desk. "That's enough! Who do you think you are to talk to me like that? I've told you the story is dead, which you'd know if you checked your messages. And also in those messages you'll find your new assignment. Now get back to work!"

Jazz stared at her boss, a thousand retorts flying through her mind. Her clenched hands trembled in rage and impotence, one crushing the folder she held. Seeing the steely defiance in LaGuerta's eyes, Jazz swallowed any response and stormed out.

CHAPTER 11

Rose stood outside the Empire State Building entrance on West 34th Street enjoying the live action show of humanity cruising past. New York City was vibrant, unlike any other place in the world. She'd been to plenty of big cities, densely populated in so many different ways. Trips to Guangzhou and her mother's birthplace outdid NYC when it came to people crammed into urban spaces, after all. But nothing had the feel of this place. She had long ago decided that cities had personalities, whether the people made the city or the city made the people she had yet to determine. But nowhere else on Earth was like New York, just like nowhere else was like Guangzhou or London or Paris.

Jake came along the sidewalk, waving to catch her attention. They hugged and kissed, and she was pleased to feel genuine warmth there. The tension from earlier, his jealousy over Jazz and her concerns about Price, had maybe eased, at least a little.

"How was lunch?"

He smiled. "It was really good. Nice food, I'll take you there before we leave, I think you'll like it."

"You and Price best buds now?"

"Yeah, we're like brothers. We sliced our palms and made a blood pact."

She slapped his arm. "You're an idiot."

"That's why you love me."

She looked at him for a moment, eyebrows raised. For all their intimacy now, neither of them had yet said *I love you* to the other and they were swimming in that shallow water where it had to happen soon. Was Jake fishing? She decided to let it pass this time. "Seriously, though," she pressed. "He was okay? You still think he's a good guy?"

Jake smiled crookedly. "He's a weird one, I'll grant you that. But so far he seems decent enough. I'm not foolish enough to just instantly trust anyone, and my aunt's best interests are my first concern. So I'll proceed with caution. But so far, I think he's okay."

Rose was slightly annoyed by that, still inclined to trust her own assessment, but she needed to respect Crowley's feelings too. Despite her words moments ago, he wasn't an idiot. Not that kind of idiot anyway. "Fair enough," she said. "Wanna go up?"

"For sure."

They made their way in and lined up with all the other tourists to buy a ticket, then lined up again for the elevator.

"Holidays seem to be ninety percent standing in queues," Rose said, smiling.

Crowley looked around them. "Isn't it weird? The way we all want this experience, we all go to the same places and see the same sights, take the same photos. I mean, there's a million pictures online, from every possible angle, of all there is to see from the top of this building. And yet there's still a compelling urge to experience it ourselves directly, to feel it, smell it, know we've actually *done* it rather than simply see a picture."

"Your lunch was very philosophical, was it?"

Crowley laughed. "Not especially! But there is something about Price that brings out the... I don't know, the contemplative in me. He gives me pause for thought."

Rose considered that for a moment, recognizing a deep truth to it. "Perhaps that's why I don't trust him," she said. "He puts me on edge for some reason, and I can't define why."

"And I don't deny that." Crowley squeezed her hand and then relaxed his grip but didn't let go. She enjoyed the warmth of his touch. "I trust your instincts, and I am on my guard. But I like the guy. I don't get the same discomfort."

Rose shrugged. She appreciated his honesty. "I hope I don't have to tell you I told you so at some future point."

"I hope so too!"

The took their turn in the elevator, packed in like sardines, watching the information movie it played on the ceiling as the car shot swiftly up through the middle of New York's most iconic skyscraper. When they reached the top, they walked around the balcony in bright sunshine, the views across the city truly breathtaking. All the way across Central Park, the Hudson, the Statue of Liberty tiny in the distance just off the tip of Manhattan. Crowley pointed out Ground Zero.

"It is something else to be here, huh?" Rose said, looking down on the forest of buildings crammed shoulder to shoulder that from street level would have towered over them.

"Perspective is a trippy thing," Crowley agreed. Leaning on

their elbows side by side, mesmerized by the bird's eye vista south across the city, Crowley said, "So did you meet Jazz for lunch?"

He was casual enough, but Rose caught the hint of discomfort in the question. She sighed but couldn't resist a slight smile. Men could be so fragile sometimes. "No, she was busy, I guess. Didn't answer my call. But I did make myself useful. I went to the library, which is amazing enough in itself!"

Crowley nodded. "Yes, I've been there before. Incredible place."

"Well, I lost myself for a few hours falling into a research rabbit hole." She told him all about the myriad dead at Washington State Park, the whole concept of a potter's field, and how the park paled into almost insignificance next to Hart Island, still filling up with corpses every day. "But then I started looking into other details, trying to think laterally. I was thinking about the holes in the skulls, you know? All so uniform? You know what trepanning is?"

Crowley looked at her with a slight frown. "Drilling a hole in the skull to let the demons out?"

"Partly, yeah. It's a weird thing, it's been going on forever. They found a burial site dated about 6,500 BCE with evidence of trepanning. The medieval thinking is that it was done to let out bad spirits, but a slightly more evidence-based practice was to reduce pressure from a blood build-up in the skull, sometimes from blunt weapon trauma, that sort of thing. Sometimes people would subsequently wear the disc of removed skull as a ward against evil, which is a pretty bizarre concept."

"That would be a strange one to explain," Crowley said. "Kind of cool though, if you think about it. But where are you going with this? I can see that all those bodies were possibly trepanned, but as you've said, it could be for any number of reasons."

"Don't forget how recent some of them were though. Not just the two fresh ones, but others there from recent years, not hundreds of years ago, or even decades. Anyway, to answer your question, I learned that certain witch covens used to cut holes in skulls."

"Witches? Really?"

"It's as much a possibility as anything else you and I have encountered recently. But here's the thing, check this out." She took out her phone and pulled a picture she'd taken of a book in the New York library. "This is from a very old book on witchcraft, and how it pervades modern society. Obviously, this book is a bit sensationalist, and modern society, according to this book, was back in the nineteen fifties. But look at this." She handed over the phone and watched as Crowley zoomed in the image of the grainy photograph she'd snapped.

"It's not very clear," he said, frowning.

"The picture in the book is pretty grainy. But why have you zoomed in on that particular bit?"

He grinned crookedly and handed the phone back. "You know why."

"Well?" She really wanted him to agree with her, but the implications were too much to consider possible. "It looks just like Matthew Price, doesn't it?"

Crowley nodded, lips pursed. "It really does. But it looks like Price now, and that photo is more than sixty years old if it's from the fifties. I guess it could be a distant relative or something."

"Jake, it looks just like him!"

"Nah, Price isn't that blurry in real life."

She gave him a withering look and decided to let it drop. Give him time to ruminate on what she'd shown him and see if he came around at all. And besides, it was a grainy photo, and the likeness could easily be entirely coincidental. But it only added to her underlying concerns about the enigmatic old man. To change the subject, she said, "I learned other stuff too, and this might be worth following up. I copied the relevant sections you can read later, but in short, there was a scandalous experiment conducted at Bellevue Hospital back in the early 1900s. Bellevue is the oldest hospital in NYC. Anyway, a doctor was fired for conducting experiments on patients and covering up several deaths. There weren't a lot of details on the crimes, but the term "trepanning" came up quite a few times."

Crowley turned to look at her again, the constant breeze this high up riffling through his hair. "Really? Okay, now you've got my interest. But you're talking about more than a hundred years ago."

"Yes, but what if the hospital, or people associated with that doctor, might have secretly continued the experiments? And the mass grave at Washington State Park was a secret dumping ground for the corpses? They might have a means of ingress to that area that is otherwise unknown, so those water workers assumed they had uncovered a new, previously undisturbed crypt. But what if it has actually been in use fairly consistently since the early 1900s, or even before? It would explain the layer upon layer of increasingly recent bodies in there, all with signs of trepanation."

Crowley's expression was skeptical. "You're drawing a long bow here."

"Sure, but it would be fun to dig around a bit, wouldn't it?"

"Sounds to me like you've got the amateur sleuth bug after our recent adventures."

"Maybe. Haven't you?"

Crowley laughed. "I've always had it! But aren't we supposed to be on holiday?"

"Sure, but weren't you only just saying about how it's strange that everyone on holiday always lines up for the same things. This would make for a pretty unique New York City experience."

"And you can maybe help your mate Jazz out with her story along the way?"

Rose watched Crowley's eyes closely as he said that, but she saw no malice or real jealousy there. Maybe a touch of amusement was all. Perhaps he was finally getting over himself. "Sure," she said. "It would be kind of cool to be an investigative journalist for a while too."

Crowley rolled his eyes, but his smile was genuine. "All right then, Sherlette Holmes. Where to?"

CHAPTER 12

Jazz walked the night-time streets of Manhattan, doing her best to not let guilt or fear show. She had long since hardened to the sharp edges of living in New York City and refused to be cowed by it, but just like every woman, her life was one of constant threat assessment. It was also a life of risk mitigation, though she railed at anyone who questioned how a woman dressed or whether she'd been drinking whenever a case of assault came up. After all, a woman wearing what she liked or enjoying a drink was no crime and every woman's right, and perhaps guys should just stop raping people. But the world was a messed up place and walking the streets of the greatest city on Earth at night had its own incipient risks. Especially walking those streets at 3am. For safety, she carried a short tire, single bar iron, up the sleeve of her jacket, one flat end cradled in her cupped palm. She could straighten her arm and drop it into her grip in an instant should the need arise. Jazz Richards was no pushover.

Given that NYC hardly really slept, finding a quiet time to be out and about was difficult. But now, in the depths of the dead hours between midnight and dawn, it was as quiet as it ever got.

As Jazz entered Washington Square Park, she was briefly lit by the bright white lights shining up at the arch, then plunged back into gloom once inside. Her eyes quickly adjusted again. Nowhere was really dark in the city at night. Black metal lampposts, each topped with four round, white balls, made pools of brightness on the grass and paths. But there was no one else to be seen walking through. She stopped, suddenly startled by movement near low scrubby bushes on the grass to her left, then relaxed. A homeless person, rolled up in blankets with a collection of large bags beside them, had turned over in their sleep, nothing more. Jazz watched for a moment longer, but the person didn't move again, almost completely hidden in the shadows of the foliage. She shook her head, feeling a deep sympathy for anyone forced into a life of sleeping in parks, but alongside it was a complete impotence. What could she do to help, short of charity? The city itself, the country itself, needed to do better by its lost, its broken, and its poorest. Jazz crept on nervous feet across the grass and tucked a ten dollar note securely into a strap on the nearest bag. As she backed up, she made sure it wasn't visible from the path. Satisfied that it was the best she could do, she moved on.

Her alertness ratcheting up a notch, Jazz quickly headed towards the site of the crypt. She couldn't let the story drop, despite LaGuerta's insistence. Maybe even because of it. LaGuerta's resistance bore all the hallmarks of being actively shut down by someone higher up. Jazz had thought better of her editor, but then again, she had no idea of the kind of pressures that might be being applied. It made her think less of LaGuerta, and that annoyed her. She didn't need to think less of anyone. Everyone needed more people to look up to these days. Regardless, she had decided to return to the site of the burials, determined to get some proof of what she'd seen, some incontrovertible proof of the location and its secrets. Perhaps even a new angle to follow up. She didn't need to tell LaGuerta anything, at least until she had something more concrete.

She was fairly certain the freshest two corpses would have been taken to the coroner's office already. They had looked almost brand new, surely not dead more than a week or two. But the older ones, and the bones in various states of decay, would surely have been left in-situ until further study had been done. She had done some research and also learned that whenever old burial grounds like this were discovered in the city, which was surprisingly often, the dead were left in place rather than be disturbed. That seemed to Jazz and incredibly morbid secret of New York, but perhaps not surprising given the size of the city and the number of ancient interred citizens. If at all possible, the city simply continued to be built around them. Jazz wondered how often she'd leaned against the wall in a subway station unaware of a pile of corpses just on the other side of the tiles. Or how often she might have been below street level, with dozens of dead bodies lying just over her head. It was macabre, but also a kind of thrill to consider. Besides all that, these bodies, at least a large number of them, were not ancient dead. This was altogether more modern and current.

Jazz moved towards the area where they had discovered the entrance, expecting to see police tape, cones, maybe even solid temporary fencing. But there was nothing there. She stopped, staring. Everything looked entirely normal, even the works that had been started cleared up as though they had never been.

There was the maintenance cover on the ground, but nothing else. The only evidence at all were a few scuff marks on the ground, but even those showed evidence of having been brushed over, as though someone had tried to hide them.

Icy fingers crept up Jazz's spine, and she tensed. Taking her eyes from the ground, she turned slowly, looked all around. She had the distinct impression someone was watching her, she could almost feel their gaze pressing into her flesh. Ignoring the trembling that started in her hands, she turned slowly again, trying to look everywhere at once. Someone was there, she knew it. Like a soft breeze tickling her skin, she couldn't discern the source but knew beyond a doubt that someone watched her.

As she slowly turned a third time, a large man loomed up behind her. She shrieked, leapt back, bringing her hands up in front of her face in a defensive gesture, the short tire iron she carried raising too, now held in a tight grip. The man's odor reached her, rancid and sour. His pale skin bore a layer of black grime, his hair matted and thick. He wore several layers of ragged, filthy clothing and his eyes were wild.

"Calm down, lady, calm down!" His voice was gravel and tar. He raised his hands and edged crabwise around her, never taking his eyes off hers. "Just passing through, okay?"

Jazz gasped quick breaths, tried to calm her hammering heart as he moved by. She wasn't sure which of them had scared the other more. She watched him move away into the shadows between lampposts and took another deep breath.

"Keep it together, Jasmine," she chided herself.

She turned back to the maintenance cover, keen now to move more quickly. The tire iron she held was partly for personal protection, but also because she had anticipated needing to lift the cement cover again. She hadn't anticipated it being out in the open like this, but she had no choice now. Working quickly, she jammed the flat end of the bar into a small hole at one end of the cover and leaned her weight into it. Having been moved recently, it offered little resistance. Hooking the tire iron through a belt loop on her jeans, she took out a small flashlight and flicked it on, then went down the ladder into the curved tunnel. Some quick answers, some more photographs, maybe even a sample of... well, she didn't know. Something. She had some plastic sandwich bags stuffed into one pocket in case. Whatever, she intended to get anything she could and get out again quickly.

She moved through the section of tumbled down wall and stopped, mouth falling open.

"No!" she breathed. "This can't be."

She shined the flashlight up and down, left and right, unable to believe her eyes. Everything was gone. Every bone, every scrap of clothing, every bit of debris, every speck of dust. The space was entirely empty, like nothing had ever been there.

CHAPTER 13

Crowley followed Rose through the corridors of Bellevue Hospital. Rose had told him it was the oldest public hospital in the US, so on the way he'd done more research. It had been founded in March of 1736, and traced its origins to the city's first permanent almshouse, a two-story brick building on the city common, an area now known as City Hall Park. Then, in 1798, authorities purchased a property near the East River several miles north of the settled city, called Belle Vue Farm. The farm had been used to quarantine the sick during a series of yellow fever outbreaks. Apparently, First Avenue was so named because when the city grid was established, the hospital and its location had to be accounted for, so that's where they started. The place was then formally named Bellevue Hospital in 1824. Now it handled nearly half a million outpatients and over a hundred-thousand emergency visits every year. Crowley marveled at the stories that would have been told inside its walls.

As they walked, he smiled to himself. So much for enjoying a quiet holiday, a few days off. He and Rose were more alike than he would care to admit, he supposed, both absolute workaholics, driven to be active. He tried to imagine lying on sun loungers in some tropical idyll, sipping cocktails and reading trashy novels. The picture was so incongruous he laughed out loud.

Rose looked back, frowning. "You okay?"

"Yeah, just thinking dumb thoughts. Look." He pointed to a door marked Records Office, which is what the front desk had told them to seek out.

Rose knocked on the door and went in, Crowley close behind. Behind an old scratched desk sat an equally old woman. She had deep brown skin, wrinkled like a walnut, and a cloud of bright white hair. Her eyes were tired, but her smile was wide and genuine.

"Good morning. How can I help you, my dear?" she greeted in a heavy, nasal voice.

It never ceased to amuse Crowley that a New Yorker could take a simple word like "dear," drop the consonant at the end, and still manage to turn it into a two-syllable word.

"Hi," Rose said. "I was wondering if you could help us look into something from a long time ago." She gestured vaguely back over her shoulder. "At the front desk, they said you might be able to look up some records for us."

"Now what kind of accent is that?" the old woman asked.

"English. I'm Rose, and this is Jake. We're both from England."

Crowley waved.

"I'm Marion, good to meet you. You don't look English!"

"My mother is Chinese."

"Oh? Have you visited Chinatown yet?"

"No," Rose said flatly.

Crowley wasn't sure if she was bothered more by the stereotypical question or the thought of all the knockoff watches and handbags that were sold there. Rose found those sorts of cheap imitations highly offensive.

After a moment more, the old woman let her smile out again. "English. Well, isn't that just fine? You're a gorgeous girl." She looked over at Crowley. "In fact, you're quite the handsome pair. Just imagine the beautiful babies you'll make."

Color rose swiftly into Rose's cheeks, and Crowley laughed. He stepped up next to Rose, thinking maybe he should push the conversation back into some kind of useful direction. "We're working on a story and wondered if you could tell us about the situation in the early 1900s, when a doctor was fired for questionable medical practices. The doctor's name was Michael Prince."

Marion pursed her lips, doubling the wrinkles and adding to their depth. "I know a little about that. Even before my time, of course, and I'm older than the hills." She laughed, but it was brittle, and Crowley hoped she wouldn't break right there at the old, scarred desk. Then he thought perhaps he ought to give her credit for being tougher than she looked. She still came here to work every day, after all. "Just a minute," Marion said.

She stood, moving with more energy than her frame implied, and disappeared into the shadows between the racks of shelving behind her. She re-emerged a couple of minutes later, carrying a manila folder. "There's not much, I'm afraid."

Crowley and Rose opened the folder, held it between them to skim through the contents. It listed Doctor Michael Prince, his term of service at Bellevue, an address not far from the hospital. It also listed his termination and cited "Unsound medical practice" and "Bringing the Bellevue Hospital into disrepute" as the reasons. That was largely it.

Rose handed the envelope back. "Thank you, Marion."

"Sorry there isn't more."

"Anyone on staff who might know more about it? Or someone else who might have a more detailed knowledge of the hospital's history?"

Marion shook her head. "You're talking about over a century ago. A whole lot can happen when we're talking about that much time. I'll tell you what though, there is one person here even older than me and he hears all kinds of gossip. That's pretty much his job description."

"Really?" Crowley asked, trying to think who might fit that description.

"That's right. Father Damien Jessup. He's the chaplain here and has been since the 1950s. He's not a hundred years old, but I'm guessing he's not far from it!"

Rose smiled warmly, her eyes glittering, presumably with the possibility of another lead instead of a dead end. "Thank you so much for your time."

"You're quite welcome, child. You have a lovely day."

The Bellevue Hospital Chapel was a small, but warmly inviting space. A floor of small square tiles led between two rows of dark wooden pews to a basic altar. Behind it, three arched windows let in diffuse sunlight. On the right-hand side, a large wooden cabinet reached almost to the ceiling, a board listing the hymns of the day hung on the side. Fleur de Lis wallpaper circled the room high on the walls, while dark wooden vertical boards covered the lower halves.

As Crowley and Rose entered, they saw two people sitting with their heads bowed in prayer or contemplation, one on either side, a man near the front left and a woman halfway back on the right. An old man, presumably Father Damien Jessup, saw them enter and came up to greet them. He was indeed ancient, like a withered branch, bent and knobbly with age. His skin was pale, thin blue veins tracing maps across the back of his hands in between dark liver spots. His head was almost entirely bald, just a few defiant white wisps of hair around the backs of his large, pendulous ears. A small man, but with a confident presence nonetheless, his blue eyes rheumy but friendly.

"Good afternoon," he said softly.

"Do you have a moment to chat about some of this

hospital's history?" Crowley asked. "We were chatting to Marion over in the records department, and she suggested you were the man to know such stuff."

Jessup inclined his head and gestured back out the door. In the corridor outside there was a recessed area with several armchairs and small tables covered in tatty magazines, probably almost as old as Jessup himself. The three of them sat.

"I think dear old Marion and myself are the last of the old guard at this place," Jessup said. "It's all different nowadays, but I can try to help you. What would you like to know?"

Crowley was pleased the old man didn't seem to care why they were asking. He was probably just happy to chat about anything.

"Back in the early 1900s there was a doctor fired from his position here," Rose said. "Unsound medical practice, among other things."

Jessup smiled, nodded. "Doctor Prince. Yes, Michael Prince. Quite a story, that one."

"Do you know his story?" Rose asked.

"Well, he's one of the more infamous ex-employees here, even after all this time. But I don't know a lot for certain, I don't think anyone does really. Even then I imagine it was a need-to-know situation, so only a handful of people in charge would have really had the details. Obviously, I wasn't around when the experiments were conducted, but I've heard a few stories. Probably unreliable, they were handed down for many decades before they reached me, of course. And people do love a story, so it's no doubt grown in every telling, like a minnow caught in the mountains that's a giant salmon by the time the yarn reaches town. And a story like his? Well, nothing like a scandal, eh?"

"Can you share some of what you have heard?" Crowley asked.

Jessup pursed his lips, sucking a long breath in through his large nose. He stared up at the ceiling for a moment, presumably gathering his recollections. "There were several different versions," he said at last. "But they tended to carry a similar theme. People like to inject a little fantasy, I think, when the truth is often entirely more mundane, and the cruelty of men often has no greater reason to it. People always look for some greater truth, but often the folly of men is simply that and nothing more."

Crowley thought it a little ironic that a priest would suggest truth injected with fantasy was something reserved for cruelty, but he chose not to mention that in this instance. "Go on," he said instead.

"Well, some say the man fancied himself a new Frankenstein, trying to reanimate the dead. Others that he was a vampire, himself the reanimated dead and that he tried to make more like him. Rather than the Hollywood idea that one vampire bites a person to make another, some stories suggested he was a lonely creature of the night, desperate to make more in his image, to spend eternity with, and he fancied a medical procedure might provide his answers. Other stories still suggest it was some kind of witchcraft, and that he was trying to save a woman he loved through black arts. Details varied, but in all the stories, the man was looking for a way to extend human life, or cheat death, or raise the dead. Or perhaps continue to live even after physical death. Macabre, eh? Back in those days, I think there was a lot more mysticism intertwined with medicine, so these things might seem ridiculous now, medical science advanced as it is, but then? I think it wasn't so strange. Still, they're good stories nonetheless."

Crowley exchanged a glance with Rose and saw she wore an expression that no doubt mirrored his. The stories, while wildly varied at first consideration, did indeed all share a thread of similarity. Based on their previous researches into all kinds of mysteries, Crowley knew not to ignore those kinds of coincidences, especially coupled with the recent discoveries at Washington Square Park.

"Have you heard of any other rumors?" Rose asked. "Similar experiments being conducted since, even in recent decades."

Crowley knew she was thinking about the bodies in Washington Square Park too, and their freshness, recent decades right up to recent days. He had thought her line of enquiry entirely fruitless at first and was simply humoring her, but now something tingled at the base of his neck. A sense of something serious and dangerous. They were edging into something, and he thought maybe it would turn out to be darker and more dangerous than they had previously considered. Despite himself, he was a little excited by the thought. "Any copycat sort of stuff?" he said, to back up Rose's question.

"Here?" Jessup said. "Not a chance. Even after all this time, Bellevue has strong observation policies of the activities of its staff. All modern hospitals do, but perhaps this place is more vigilant than most given what happened back then." He paused, thinking, staring at some distant spot above and behind them. Crowley and Rose both sat quietly, letting the old man have his thoughts. Crowley thought they both probably hoped for something, anything, the old man might recall that would give them something to follow up. The trouble with any kind of investigation was that when leads ran dry, it was over. They couldn't conjure knowledge from thin air. But the tiniest, however random, might be all they needed, like the one thread that comes loose and unravels the entire garment.

"I did hear of some crazy stuff, though," Jessup said eventually. "And now you're asking me these questions, I wonder if it's not perhaps quite similar to Prince's madness. I heard about a secret facility on an island in the Hudson River, and some similar scandalous accusations. Same kind of things, like raising the dead or cheating death. Of course, those things are not unusual, people have been trying to crack those secrets as long as there have been people. I don't recall the name of the island." He gave them an apologetic smile. "My old brain loses more than it retains these days, I'm afraid. Something about fruit, maybe? Not sure why I think that... But I heard there was a secret lab there, contained in a literal dungeon."

A little over two hours later, they sat at a small table inside Tom's Restaurant. The iconic Upper West Side diner at the corner of Broadway and West 112th had provided the exterior shots for *Seinfeld's* fictional Monks' Café. It was now crowded with students from Columbia University.

As they waited for their meals, Crowley and Rose looked at the notes they'd written up between them. Crowley sat back and shrugged. "I guess that's the best guess then."

Rose nodded. "Plum Island. The old man remembered fruit!" She laughed, shook her head.

"It does seem the most likely. But it's a long way away."

Crowley looked over the notes again. Plum Island was in Gardiners Bay, east of Orient Point, off the eastern end of the North Fork coast of Long Island. That made it more than a two-hour drive just to get to Orient Point, let alone the island some mile or so off that pinnacle of land. The island was quite large, about three miles long and a mile across at its widest point. Now the site of the Plum Island Animal Disease Center, established in 1954, it was also the site of the former U.S. military installation of Fort Terry, built around 1897, and the historic Plum Island Light from around 1869. Now that lighthouse had an automated replacement.

"The real problem," Crowley said, "is that Plum Island is owned in its entirety by the United States government, specifically the Department of Homeland Security."

"Check out this guy," Rose said and turned her phone for Crowley to see.

A grainy black and white photo showed a man with a huge white beard sitting on a grassy slope in front of the old stone building topped with the original lighthouse. He wore a large dark hat, and pants held with suspenders halfway up his chest. "Quite a character," Crowley said.

"George Bradford Brainerd," Rose clarified. "Lighthouse Keeper from 1845 to 1887."

"That's some career."

"Originally called 'Manittuwond' by the Native American Pequot Nation," Rose said, slowly scrolling. "Then named 'Pruym Eyelant', which is Dutch for Plum Island, because of the beach plums that grow along the shores."

Crowley smiled. "Which is all very interesting, but doesn't get past that key point I made before."

Rose looked up from her phone. "Sorry, what was that?"

"Department of Homeland Security!"

"Hmmm." Rose looked back at her phone. "There's no mention of any dungeons, but I guess there wouldn't be, given the military presence since before the turn of the century. But given that the main installation there is the Animal Disease Center, I suspect that's quite recent. We'd be better off looking around the remains of Fort Terry. I'm guessing the dungeons would be under the fort, don't you think? We should try to investigate those remains. It says here that 'During the Cold War a secret biological weapons program targeting livestock was conducted at the site, although it had slowly declined through the end of the century. This program has, for many years, been the subject of controversy.' Sounds interesting."

Crowley raised his palms. "Once again, Homeland Security!"

Rose laughed. "I know, I know. Maybe we should contact Agent Paul from the DHS. He helped us out after the Anubis

Key business."

"Agent Paul had no real incentive to help us now, other than general kindness," Crowley said. "And he wanted us out of America, don't forget. I think he'd probably be unhappy if he knew we were still in the States."

Rose sighed. "So what do we do?"

Crowley smiled. He'd been slowly leading her around to this. "We? Nothing. But it's something I can do on the sly."

CHAPTER 14

Jazz refused to quit. Whenever she caught a whiff of a really good story, she became a dog with a rope, clamping down tight and , refusing to let go. It was the thing that made her a damned good investigative reporter, and it was also the thing that caused her a lot of problems in life. Often at the same time. She was okay with that.

Despite LaGuerta trying to shut her down, despite the city wiping the site clean, she was determined to find out more. Pressure on her editor was one thing, and it was entirely possible the woman had genuinely decided there wasn't a story and resources were limited. So be it. But the entire crypt cleared out as if nothing had ever been there? That was something else. The kind of organization and resources that would take, in just a few hours, belied a deep concern on the part of whoever had orchestrated the removal. Where had all those bodies gone?

Jazz sat hunched before her computer monitor, slowly clicking through the photos Rose had taken. She'd been through them half a dozen times already, but something had to be there. Some clue she could follow up.

She zoomed in on the freshest two corpses, the redheaded young man and the blonde woman. Their clothes were nice, the kind of things the comfortably off middle classes would wear. Certainly not the rags of vagrants or the well-worn wardrobe of travelers. The man's sleeve was pushed up to his elbow, and she saw the colors of a tattoo on the back of his forearm. She zoomed in further, starting to push the resolution, but it was still clear enough to see the tattoo was new, the ink raised up in smooth scabs that had yet to drop off. The design was quite distinct, she recognized the three looping swirls of a pagan triquetra behind the solid lines of a pentagram. Between each point of the five-pointed star were softer designs in smooth colors, green leaves, blue waves, white clouds, red and orange flames, and the purples and blues of a night sky. The design took up most of the man's forearm and was neat, artistic work. She framed it up and printed out a close-up. A new tattoo was something tangible to research, maybe it would give her the lead she needed.

She moved the view to see if the blonde woman bore any similar ink, but her clothing covered her almost completely, just half her face and one hand visible. But there was something on her wrist. Jazz frowned, looking more closely. The woman had what appeared to be a home-made beaded bracelet, with each bead an intricately carved symbol. Again she pushed the image's resolution to get a better look. She saw an ankh, a pentacle like on the man's arm, a crescent moon. Each symbol could easily be associated with Wicca or paganism, and that matched up with the young man's new tattoo. She was definitely finding an angle here. But it was more than that. Her heart sped up as she considered the bracelet, certain she'd seen the exact item, or one identical to it, on the wrist of a coworker not too long ago.

CHAPTER 15

Crowley had enjoyed the two-hour drive in a rented car, heading out along the North Fork coast of Long Island. He'd listened to the radio turned down low and been alone with his thoughts. It was a long while, he realized, since he'd had any time to himself or any genuine peace and quiet. He hoped the peace remained when he continued this hare-brained journey. It had taken some effort to convince Rose to let him do this alone, but there was no way he would risk it with her along. On the one hand, she didn't have the training, and on the other, he would never forgive himself if anything went wrong. So he had suggested she catch up with Jazz for dinner and a few drinks or something similar. He had chafed against the suggestion slightly, his jealousy raising its head again, but he knew he also needed to get over himself. Rose would see whatever friends she wanted to and he couldn't, nor should, chaperone her every time. He had to ignore his insecurities and trust Rose. She had seemed genuinely pleased with the suggestion too, perhaps recognizing that he was trying to be a better person, and he was pleased about that.

He found a good place to park in deep night shadow just off the road not far from the Orient Point ferry station. He had a bit of greenery to trek through for a few minutes, carrying his rented tank and gear, then it was a decent bit of water to traverse to reach Plum Island. But he relished the idea of the exertion, the exercise. He'd swim on the surface most of the way, then SCUBA the last few hundred meters to make sure he arrived unseen. He smiled to himself wryly. *Just like the old days.*

The island had a wide triangular main body, then a long, thin peninsula heading due east from the furthest point from the mainland shore. Annoyingly, Fort Terry, which he considered his best bet as Rose had mentioned, lay on the far northeast end of the island, at the start of the narrow peninsula. He planned to swim out around the south side, then come in from there. He could leave his gear on the long, thin strip of sandy beach, ready for a quick getaway he hoped he wouldn't need, and investigate the remains of the fort. The fort had two main buildings, large C-shapes, with right-angled corners rather than curves, and several smaller buildings, seven or eight of them largely still standing.

He had a sweat on by the time he reached the water's edge and began organizing his tank.

"What the hell are you doing, Jakey-boy?" he asked himself as he zipped up the wetsuit and shrugged on the tank. Then he allowed himself another small smile. Enjoying adventure and indulging the woman he loved was what he was doing. Perhaps he ought to tell her that's how he felt. He hoped the feeling was mutual. But that could wait. *Focus on the task at hand, soldier,* he thought to himself, surprised at how easily and casually he had slipped back into these habits.

He slipped into the water, hissing at the frigid temperature even at such a warm time of year. He'd soon equalize that with his wetsuit. Orienting himself in the near pitch dark, the silhouette of the distant island just visible on the horizon, he struck out, swimming strongly, kicking the long fins in deep, regular rhythm.

It took a while, fighting against strong currents, but the exercise was every bit as invigorating as he had hoped. Before long he rounded Pine Point, the southernmost tip of Plum Island, and started north-east following the beach, staying a good couple of hundred yards off-shore. When he saw the beach start to curve due east again, he put the regulator in his mouth, pulled the mask over his eyes, and went underwater. Visibility was nil, but he trusted his sense of direction, and soon enough, the ocean floor rose to meet him. Moving slowly to avoid splashing, not that he expected anyone to be around at this hour, well after midnight, he eventually emerged and walked carefully up the beach, watching all around for any signs of movement.

To the right of him, fifty yards or so north-east of Fort Terry, the island was heavily wooded. He made his way into the shadows of the first trees and slipped out of his SCUBA gear. He kept the wetsuit on, the dark charcoal grey of it a good color to conceal him in the night, and slipped on thick rubber reef shoes to protect his feet. His tank, fins, and mask he placed in the shadow of an oak tree and then crept out towards Fort Terry. He emerged from the trees onto a narrow asphalt road but stayed to one side in the shade. Finding a dungeon among the ruins of Fort Terry seemed like a fool's errand, but given the stuff he and Rose had discovered in various other places recently, he wasn't about to write off the possibility.

To his right was a cement foundation of a building long gone, then a little further on to his left a building still stood. Broken and run down, it had a grey roof and nothing but shadows inside. He quickly jumped in through a window that had long since lost its glass and paused while he eyes adjusted. After a moment he scouted around and came to the swift conclusion there was nothing under the ground here. More solid concrete, no trapdoors. He made his way to the other side, planning to go over to the biggest building, the largest square C-shaped structure on the southern side of Fort Terry.

As he stepped up to a window, bright beams of light swept through the broken opening. Crowley froze, even held his breath, then quickly flattened himself against the wall inside. A moment later he heard to purr of an engine. Sealed roads crisscrossed between the buildings of Fort Terry and in places tire tracks had worn other roads across the grassy areas around the whole installation. As Crowley allowed himself to peak out of the window, he saw a pick-up slowly cruise towards him, right between the building he was in and the square-C structure he had been planning to move on to. The pick-up slowed, and he heard two men talking to each other, but couldn't make out the words. He pressed himself back into the shadows. Was this a coincidence or had he been spotted? Was there CCTV he hadn't noticed? He had a trained eye and had been watching out for any kind of security measures but had seen none. Perhaps it was something new that he didn't know to recognize.

"Are you slipping, soldier?" he whispered to himself.

The pick-up engine revved gently, then Crowley heard the tires crunch over dried grass and dirt. The car went past the south side of the building, then turned north again to rejoin the sealed road. Flashlight beams swept left and right from the car windows, but they seemed lazy and cursory, simply scanning rather than searching. Perhaps it was only a routine patrol. Crowley hurried back across the building to watch the pick-up turn left and pass back westwards toward the other end of the island. He watched its red tail lights disappear down the road and then waited another couple of minutes. Nothing happened. Convincing himself it was indeed nothing more than a routine patrol, he resumed his plan and ran over to the other, biggest building.

It took another thirty minutes or so, thankfully without any further interruptions, for Crowley to decide he was a dog barking up the wrong tree. There were no dungeons here, not even any basements. Despite their best guesses, this idea was a bust.

He stood in the night-darkened street, hands on his hips, frustrated. Then he turned to look to the west. Was it possible there might be something worth investigating at the Animal Disease Center? His conspiracy-minded thoughts made him consider that it was an ideal cover for something Homeland Security would want to keep secret. It was about a mile to walk along the asphalt road to reach the center. Having come all this way, it was surely worth a look. Again using the cover of the trees for shadows to stay concealed, he set off.

When he reached the high fencing some twenty minutes later, he realized immediately there was no chance of looking inside. Security was far too tight, and besides that, Rose had been right when she suggested it was too new an installation. Unless it had been built over extant dungeons, which seemed incredibly unlikely, this entire venture had been a waste of time and energy.

"There!" a voice yelled, and lights swept across him.

Crowley dived for cover as an engine revved hard and the pick-up he'd seen before roared up the asphalt toward him. Idiot! So busy staring at how secure the place was, he'd left himself out in the open for the security patrols to spot.

He bolted into the cover of trees as the pick-up hammered towards him, its engine revving hard, and then he quickly jack-knifed back on himself, hoping to come out behind the vehicle. The plan worked, but now he was running in the wrong direction, away from his gear and toward more fencing. He sprinted hard as the pick-up screeched to a halt, then white lights lit up on the back of it and it reversed hard. Crowley heard someone yelling directions, so they were clearly calling for backup. The pick-up did a neat bootlegger reverse and then drove straight for him as he ducked around behind a large building, maybe a garage or guard house. Thankfully it was dark and closed up, but surely the place would be crawling with people soon.

"Stop or we shoot!" a voice boomed over a loudspeaker, presumably a handheld megaphone, then a bullet whined into the asphalt right behind where he had been a moment before.

"What was the point of the warning if you were going to shoot anyway!" Crowley said to no one in particular as he ran.

But he saved his breath and didn't shout it. It was painfully obvious that these guys were already beyond the conversation stage of proceedings. Gun-happy Americans on an island with little recourse to the mainland and law enforcement suddenly made Crowley feel distinctly vulnerable.

A small jeep-like vehicle stood around the back of the building, open-topped, no doors, more like a beach buggy or a mini-moke than anything else. Crowley threw himself into the front of it, curling up on the floor between the front seats and the dash, hoping the deep shadow would hide him. The pick-up came around the corner and roared past, lights bright, the passenger shining a flashlight left and right from the window. They sailed by and Crowley knew he had a couple of minutes at best, but to do what?

He pictured the layout of Plum Island in his mind, memorized from studying it extensively before he left. A number of thin roads looped around the trees and grassy areas, and there was more than a mile between him and his gear. He couldn't remember the exact layout of all the small roads, but he supposed he didn't need to. Perhaps it was time for a little cat and mouse.

He dug at his belt and pulled out a universal tool, quickly using it to crack open the casing below the steering wheel. He heard the pick-up slow and then the engine grew louder as it came back around. From his left he heard another engine approaching. Or as that two more? Either way, the back-up had arrived.

He swiftly selected wires, tracing with rapid eyes the connections to the ignition. More old skills coming back to him without a problem. In moments he had what he needed and stripped the wires free, and then touched them together. He hissed in pain as an electric bolt shocked through his fingers, where he'd been careless with the wire's insulation, but the little car revved into life. Leaving the lights off, he sat up into the driver's seat.

The first pick-up came rapidly towards him, and another car, a black four-wheel-drive, sat waiting as the main gate to the complex slid open. No time to waste. He revved the small car and shot forward, catching the first pick-up entirely by surprise as he suddenly flew past. Their tires screeched as they braked and made a quick U-turn. Though the small vehicle he had hotwired had little in the way of power, it was light and maneuverable. Trusting his senses and luck, leaving the lights off, Crowley shot down a small road between trees. As soon as he reached the first junction, he turned hard right, almost heading back on himself. As the pick-up came up behind him, he made another right, knowing this thin road simply looped around some scrubby ground where a building had once stood. That much he remembered from the maps and Google Earth. He turned again, sharper than the pick-up could manage, and just in time as more gunshots rang out. He had no idea where the bullets went, but not into him or his vehicle and that's all that mattered in the short term.

The pick-up shot past as Crowley careened along a gravelly road in the other direction, almost skidding into unforgiving trees as he made a left onto the bigger road leading back towards Fort Terry. More bright headlights lit up the night behind him. No way was that the pick-up again already, so the other security car had obviously made a good guess and was right on his tail.

"Dammit!" Crowley gritted his teeth and prayed for luck as he hauled hard left on the wheel, broad-sliding into another narrow track. His bones rang as the tiny car clipped a tree trunk and slewed the other way, nearly throwing him clean out of the seat, but he refused to relinquish his grip on the wheel and wrestled back control. The big shiny black SUV shot past, smoke from its tires as it tried to brake in time.

Crowley hoped he was remembering correctly that another dirt track led eastward in a couple of hundred meters, just two tire ruts in the dirt. Thankfully he was correct and turned onto it, bouncing on the seat like a dried pea on a drum as he thrashed the weak suspension of the small vehicle. He only needed it to hold together for another half a mile. If he ended up in a drag out straight race with either of his pursuers, he wouldn't stand a chance of getting away, but if he could stay ahead of them for another thirty seconds or so, he'd come out again on the main road back to Fort Terry with not much space left between him and the relative safety of his gear.

He came to a T-junction and cursed. He'd remembered it wrong. The dirt track ran parallel to the sealed road. He hauled left anyway, sliding and fishtailing along the gravel, a thin line of trees preventing him from getting back onto the road he wanted. He dared a look back over his shoulder and saw brightness painting the trees behind him. Gritting his teeth, he pushed harder still, wincing as something metallic twanged and snapped under the small car. It began to whine and slow as he reached a loop of track that rejoined the sealed road.

"Come on, little hero!" he shouted at the car, followed the loop and then turned left again, zooming between the buildings of Fort Terry, leaving smoke and oil in his wake. Halfway through, the car quit and died, slowing quickly with a fatal grinding sound.

Crowley cursed, leaping from the vehicle and running for the same gap between buildings where he'd first seen the pick-up on patrol. As he ducked around the corner, lights bathed everything as both the pick-up and the SUV roared down the road side by side. They skidded to a halt, the road blocked by the broken car Crowley had just abandoned, but they'd know he couldn't be far away. There was about a hundred yards of open grassy area between the last building and the start of the trees where he's stashed his gear and Crowley bolted for it, running zig-zag, crouched low, his back crawling with the anticipation of a bullet any moment.

He'd made it maybe seventy-five yards when someone yelled, "Stop!" and a gunshot rang out. Then another, then two more.

Crowley instinctively ducked and rolled. He had no idea where the bullet went, but it didn't hit him and that was all that mattered. He came up on to his feet and sprinted the last twenty yards, zig-zagging again as three more shots rang through the night. A moving target in the dark was a tough thing to hit. None of the shots got him, and the shadows under the trees swallowed him up.

But he didn't pause, knowing his pursuers wouldn't be far behind. He grabbed his tank, fins and mask and ran directly out across the beach, heading for the water. As he waded out, he crammed the regulator into his mouth and dived under as soon as he was beyond knee-deep. He thought he heard two more shots buzz over him as he went, shrugging into the straps of the tank awkwardly as he held onto the rest of his gear. Then he reached back, hauled a fin onto each foot, and paddled hard, blind. He just needed to get away, and stayed low to the sand, fingers trailing in it to be sure he didn't inadvertently rise up again. He kept going until he was sure he'd got a good couple of hundred yards from the beach, then slowly rose to the surface. In the gloomy distance he vaguely made out four people looking up and down the beach, gesticulating wildly at each other. A couple waded knee-deep in the ocean, straining to see out over the water. But Crowley knew distance and the night concealed him. He slipped the tank more comfortably onto his back, settled his mask, and turned west, paddling for the mainland and his waiting hire car.

Exciting though that had all been, it was also a completely wasted night's effort.

CHAPTER 16

Jazz headed out to Hell's Kitchen and *The Illustrated Dragon Tattoo* studio. The shop had a large front window with bold-colored designs on it, the name in cursive calligraphic script across the top. Inside she saw several couches for waiting customers, large books of designs for people to choose from, and the sales counter. All the tattoo studios for the four or five resident tattoo artists were curtained off out the back.

She pushed the door open, triggering a ring like an old-fashioned candy store, and walked in. The walls were covered with designs, dragons and skulls, daggers and hotrods, Celtic and tribal patterns. Jazz walked to the counter as a young woman with a shaved head and multiple piercings came through the curtain from behind the counter. She had colors writhing up both arms, visible under the black singlet she wore. Jazz guessed there was a lot more ink under the clothes.

"Help you?" the young woman asked.

"Yeah, is Carlo in today?"

"He is, but he's with a client. Can I take a message?"

Jazz chewed her lip. "I just need to run something by him. Can you let him know Jazz is here? I only need a minute."

"I'll ask."

The young woman disappeared behind the curtain again and Jazz scanned the walls while she waited. Hard rock music piped in from somewhere, not too loud, but she nodded along regardless, wondering where the speakers were.

"Jazz! Too long, girl!"

Carlo came around the counter and scooped her up in a huge hug, massively muscled and tattooed arms as thick as her legs. He stood well over six feet, broad as a bull. His head was shaved, but a dark, oiled plait of pony-tail hung from the back of his head to halfway down his back. His cologne and the sweet smell of his hair oil triggered memories instantly.

Jazz laughed, returned the hug. "Put me down, you oaf!"

"Been too long, where you at?"

"Just busy, working, you know. It's kind of why I'm here, I don't want to keep you from your client."

Carlo grinned. "It's cool, he could use the break. He's

perishing under the needle in there, and only been at for three hours. What do you need?"

"Well, I know this is a long shot, but is there any chance you might recognize a tattoo?"

"If I did it, sure. I remember all my work. Photograph it too."

"Sure, but what if it was someone else's work?"

Carlo shrugged. "That depends. Some people have a really distinctive style, others don't."

Jazz pulled the printout from her bag and handed it over. "Any idea who did this?"

Carlo smoothed out the paper on the counter and leaned forward for a closer look. "Pretty unique design," he said. He pointed at the pagan triquetra behind the solid lines of the pentagram. "This stuff here could be anyone, really." Jazz deflated slightly, but he carried on quickly, tapping the softer designs in smooth colors between each point of the star. "This stuff though, the way it's shaded, is more nuanced. There are two people in New York I know about who are into this pagan stuff and have that kind of touch for color. Doesn't mean it was either of them, but it might be. Seamus over at *Celtic Tattoo* in Queens, or Ahiko K at *Cherry Blossom Ink* in Brooklyn. You could ask either of them. Of course, it could also be any of a hundred other artists anywhere in the world. This was definitely done in New York City?"

Jazz thought about how fresh the tattoo was and how dead the owner, and figured it was most likely, but she didn't want to tell Carlo he was looking at a corpse's arm. "I can't be certain, but I think so."

Carlo tapped the picture. "This ink is new, you know that, right? Still raised, still healing. So if this photo is recent then so is the ink."

"Yeah, I was thinking the same thing." But it was new when he died, and she didn't know how long ago that was. Of course, given the freshness of the corpse, it couldn't have been too long. She had to hope it was done in New York, or that trail was a dead and cold as the poor guy whose arm bore the design.

Carlo grinned. "Investigative journalist superstar hot on another trail, huh?"

She returned his smile. "I hope so. Thanks, Carlo, I owe you one."

"You owe me nothing, but let's not leave it too long before

we hang out, yeah? Call me for drinks soon. Carly still works here, and she asks you sometimes." His look was sly.

Jazz laughed. "Carly is a pretty lady."

"She sure is, so you come by again soon."

"I will."

"Or I'll call you!"

Jazz laughed. "That a threat?"

Queens was a lot further out than Brooklyn, so Jazz headed to Cherry Blossom Ink first. The shop was in most respects a replica of Carlo's place of work, but with a distinctly East Asian vibe added in, bamboo screens in place of curtains, lots of calligraphic Chinese script and watercolors on the wall hangings. Behind the counter sat a beautiful young woman with long black hair and prominent cheekbones. She smiled as Jazz entered. "Hi."

"Hi yourself." Jazz immediately had a variety of carnal thoughts about the woman and pushed them quickly aside. She needed to focus on business. But she also filed the thoughts away for another day. "I'm looking for Ahiko K?"

The woman's smile was radiant. Jazz couldn't help wondering if her initial thoughts about the tattooist were mutual. Maybe she wouldn't be catching up with Carly any time soon after all.

"That's me," the woman said. "What can I do for you?"

Jazz pulled the printout from her bag again and handed it over. "Carlo at the Illustrated Dragon said I should ask you if this is your work."

Ahiko nodded. "Sure is, I remember it. Only a couple of weeks ago. Ginger dude, a bit flaky but very nice."

Jazz's heart raced and she smiled. Bingo! She was glad she'd come here first instead of heading all the way out to Queens. "I know this is probably not usual procedure, but I'm really trying to track this guy down."

Ahiko's smile faded slightly. "Oh, really?"

"Not like that. I don't play for that team anyway." The heat was immediately back between them. She again didn't want to let on that the man was dead, but she needed an angle. "I'm going to be straight up with you. I'm a journalist and I really need to talk to this guy, so if there's any way you can help..?"

"What's in it for me?"

Jazz smiled, looked down at the counter. There were several little plastic holders with business cards in them. She found the one for Ahiko K and took a card, held it up. "Maybe I'll give you a call sometime soon, when I'm not working. And when you're not working? I got a pretty good expense account we can abuse and then… who knows?"

Ahiko dipped her head, not breaking eye contact. "Interesting. Okay, I'll tell you what. Clients all have to sign a release form, and there may be some info on that you could use, I don't know. Folks often fudge it, of course, and we don't chase it up, but I'll check."

She went to a filing cabinet and began flicking through. After a couple of minutes, she came back and dropped a hanging file on the counter, opened to a single page filled in with scrawling handwriting. "I can't give out confidential client information, but if I happened to have left a file on the counter while I went to the bathroom, who knows who might see it." She winked. "Don't forget to call." Then she stepped out of sight behind a bamboo screen.

Jazz looked at the form on the counter. Ricky Gallagher, and an address in Ridgefield. That was over in New Jersey, right on the other side of the Hudson. It would take ages to get out there, but Jazz was smiling all the same. A genuinely solid lead, an actual name. She closed the file and put one of her own business cards on top, then quietly left the shop, slipping Ahiko's card into her pocket as she went.

The address turned out to be a decent-sized white brick, two-story house on a leafy street. A low chain link fence ran around the small garden and six steps led up to a white wooden front door under a deep, red-tiled porch. Jazz took a deep breath and trotted up the steps to knock. The door was soon answered by a well-dressed middle-aged woman, maybe somewhere in her 50s. Her skin was pale, her eyes a soft blue that was almost gray. She wore tan slacks and a pale green blouse, her feet were bare.

"Yes?" she asked nervously.

Jazz considered the age of the woman, the address, the fact that Ricky had been a young corpse. She wasn't entirely sure how to proceed, but decided to feel her way with ignorance. "I'm looking for Ricky Gallagher?"

The woman's face crumpled slightly, then she quickly regained her composure. "We don't know where he is. Why are you looking for him?"

Don't know? He's a missing person! Jazz thought. "You're his mother?"

"Yes."

Jazz nodded, smiled as kindly as she could manage, thinking fast. "I'm sorry to bother you. I'm a journalist and I'm working on a large feature piece about missing people in New York. I'm sure I don't need to tell you that it's a huge problem. So I'm following up on a few specific cases to get a kind of snapshot on the sort of person that goes missing."

"The sort of person?" Ricky's mother's eyes narrowed in suspicion.

"Well, I'm starting the piece by pointing out that anyone, from any walk of life, can end up missing," Jazz said quickly, trying to put the woman at ease. "I want to break down the clichés and stereotypes first and foremost, then try to find a way to suggest positive changes, to prevent it happening so much in the future." Despite her subterfuge, Jazz realized her suggestion would actually make an interesting feature and she mentally logged it away for future use. She might try it out on LaGuerta once this current stuff was out of the way.

Mrs. Gallagher's smile turned soft and sad. "Well, that's very decent of you. Sadly, I think perhaps Ricky might only reinforce your stereotypes though, much as we'd wish things were different. He was a troubled young man. Barely graduated from high school, and struggled with addiction. He never really wanted for anything, you know, he had a good life. We're not rich, but we have all we need. Ricky was never left wanting, but he got tangled up with people who did drugs and they took him down with them. I think it all started a bit casual and harmless, but it's a pernicious and dangerous road. Easy for young people to get lost."

Jazz wondered how true that was, and how much Ricky might have been left wanting despite their relative wealth, but it wasn't her place to judge another person's parenting. "I'm very sorry to hear that," she said. "So you have no idea where he might be? You've followed up with all known associates, I imagine?"

Mrs. Gallagher nodded and she suddenly looked a lot older. "We did, the police did. He's still listed as a missing person and the case is open, but we have little more left to do but wait and hope he comes home."

Jazz knew he wouldn't ever do that. Was it better to give this woman closure? She had no proof, except the photo of Ricky's corpse back at work. She chewed her lower lip, wondering if maybe she should show that to his mother. She'd need to think long and hard before making a decision there, it wasn't something to worry about right now.

Mrs. Gallagher filled the silence between them. "He was a good boy. He would vanish for months at a time, but he'd always check in eventually. We can only hope he will again. Recently he'd seemed to be doing better, and the last time we spoke he said he was going to the city for a job interview. But we didn't hear from him again, and can only assume he's fallen off the wagon again. He obviously didn't get the job."

"How long ago was that, Mrs. Gallagher?"

"We last heard from him a little over three months ago. That was when he told us about the possible job. Then nothing. The police followed it up, but the company say Ricky never showed up for the interview."

"Well, I'll be sure to let you know anything my investigations uncover," Jazz said. "Say, do you happen to remember the name of the company where he was supposed to be interviewing?"

"Just a moment." Mrs. Gallagher went back inside and Jazz waited uncomfortably on the steps, listening to birdsong and enjoying the warmth of the afternoon sun. Ricky would never hear birdsong or feel the sun again.

"Here you are." Mrs. Gallagher handed Jazz a scrap of paper. It said *Mr. James Burton, SaleMed*.

CHAPTER 17

Crowley and Rose enjoyed a late breakfast in the hotel, Crowley's head muggy from lack of sleep after spending most of the night out on his fruitless mission. The two hours of sleep he'd managed on his return somehow made him feel worse instead of better. He told Rose all about it and enjoyed reliving the adventure. "But regardless, the whole thing was a bust," he finished. "I'm sorry, but I think we've hit a dead end here."

Rose stared into her coffee cup as if answers might be divined from it. Maybe if it was tea and she could read the leaves, Crowley mused. "There must be more we can do," she said eventually. "This is too interesting, don't you think?"

"It is intriguing, I'll give you that. Is this how we unwind now? We're not the rest and vacation kind, are we."

Rose grinned at him. "No, I guess we're not. I need to do more research."

"Do you think we're clutching at straws?"

"Maybe we are," she said. "But think about it! A whole crypt of corpses, some of them really fresh. Secret experiments and crazed doctors doing witchcraft or trying to be the new Frankenstein or something. Underground dungeon labs! Even if it's all nonsense, it's better than a lame guided ghost tour, isn't it? I'm enjoying the search. It's what I do, after all."

Crowley laughed. "But aren't we supposed to be taking a break from what we do?"

"No, Jake! We're taking a break from weird artifacts and my psychopathic sister trying to kill us. Getting back into hard research and historical weirdness is my comfort zone."

He had to credit her with that. She made a good point. "Well. I want to go and catch up with Matthew Price again, so maybe I'll do that while you research more."

Rose scowled. "I wish you wouldn't."

"I know you don't like him. I'm still not really sure why, but I think he's an interesting guy. And besides that, he's entangled himself in my aunt's life, which means he's in my life now too. I need to get to know him."

Rose sighed, swallowed the rest of her coffee. "I suppose so." She caught his eye then looked quickly away.

"What?" Crowley asked.

"I had Jazz look into him," Rose said, not meeting his eye again.

"Why? He's not a criminal!"

"Well, I just have my suspicions about his best intentions, that's all."

"I'm pretty sure he's independently wealthy and not just hanging around to gouge an old lady's bank account, Rose!"

She met his eye at last and her gaze was hard. "I know, but it's not that simple. I just don't entirely trust him, okay? Will you simply accept that and bear it in mind? For me?"

He saw that she felt strongly about this, more than a hunch. He'd be an idiot to completely disregard it, no matter how much he thought her concerns misplaced. "Okay, sure. But I think you're over-reacting. What did jazz find out anyway?"

"I don't know yet, she didn't get back to me. I'll try to catch up with her again today. If you're off to see Price again, I might as well."

They kissed and hugged when Crowley set off half an hour later, so he figured there were no real hard feelings between them, but Rose was still clearly annoyed he was going to visit Price. It bugged him how suspicious she was, and that annoyance put him on edge. Overtired, he told himself. But the nagging sensation of wrongness wouldn't go away.

Price's apartment building was really something else. It was maybe no Dakota Building, but not far from it. Four blocks west of Central Park on the Upper West Side, Crowley first had a small chuckle at the address. 666 West End Avenue. The devil's apartments! The building was called The Windermere and that gave Crowley pause for a moment, remembering enjoyable trips to Windermere in the Lake District in England. He made the snap decision to take Rose there for a proper restful holiday whenever they finally returned to Britain. It was easy for her to find distractions in a big city like New York. In the sleepy English countryside, she'd be forced to rest and join him on pleasant strolls through the woods. And he'd be forced to rest too. He had a feeling they both needed it, despite their shared urge for adventure.

The Windermere was a tall, pale beige-brick building on a three-story limestone base, built in the 1920s. Exclusive and fancy in every way, it towered up into the bright blue sky, twenty-two stories high. Relatively small in contrast to New

York's genuine skyscrapers, but imposing and impressive due to its stylish architecture, occasional balconies and terraces, canopied entrance, decorative terracotta façade features, and its even, symmetrical window placement. Crowley smiled. Classy place.

He approached the doors and a concierge smiled and waved him in.

"I'm here to see Matthew Price," Crowley said.

"Certainly, sir. And you are?"

"Jake Crowley."

The concierge whispered into a telephone, then turned a hundred-watt smile back to Crowley. "The elevators are around that side. Go on up to the twentieth floor. Mr. Price is expecting you."

"Thank you."

As Crowley emerged on floor 20, Price was standing in his apartment doorway. "Good morning, dear boy. How are you?"

"I'm well, thanks. Good to see you."

"Come in, come in."

The apartment was epic in scale, and breathably open-plan. A large square window in one wall had breath-taking city views and let in plenty of natural light. There was no TV in the large living area, but two walls were floor-to-ceiling bookcases jammed tight with hardcovers and paperbacks of every kind.

"Drink?" Price asked. "It's a little early, perhaps, but I trust it's after noon somewhere in the world."

Crowley paused, thinking perhaps a drink was the worst thing given his lack of sleep the night before. Then again, if he was already thick-headed, what more damage could a drink do? "Sure, but just a small one."

"Single-malt scotch? I have an excellent Balvenie here."

"Lovely, thanks."

While Price poured the drinks, Crowley walked slowly along the bookshelves, running his gaze over the titles. Lots of non-fiction, all kinds of historical and geographical tomes. Several sets of classics – Dickens, Shakespeare, Bronte, and more. Near the end of one shelf was a book turned face out on a small mahogany stand. F. Scott Fitzgerald's *The Great Gatsby*, in hardcover and absolutely mint condition. In fact, it looked almost brand new. The dustjacket was midnight blue, stylized female eyes and mouth over a brightly lit city, the title and author name in white text. Crowley had the feeling it was an old book, despite the incredible condition, but he couldn't recall when it might have been published. He leaned in for a closer look, trying to remember when it was popular.

Price appeared beside him and handed over a cut glass crystal tumbler. Crowley took the drink and gently tapped glasses with his host. "Cheers."

"Quite the treasure, that one," Price said, looking at the old book.

"First edition?"

"Indeed. It wasn't a best-seller when it was released, back in 1925. Only about 25,000 copies had sold by the time of the author's death in 1940. But a genuine first edition with the dust jacket is a valuable item, especially in good condition. Firsts are always worth more, especially in the top bracket of condition like this one, but there's another interesting facet to this book. There's a typo on the back of the dust jacket. It says "jay Gatsby" with a lowercase j. It was corrected by hand with ink or a stamp wherever possible, but some sold without being fixed."

"This is one of those?"

"It is. It also has quite a romantic history, this particular volume. The original owner bought it for his wife when it was first published, to read aloud to her as she was dying. Fitzgerald was her favorite author. He read it to her just that once, and she died soon after. It's never been touched again in accordance with his will, except for being moved to this new shelf when ownership transferred after I acquired it."

"It should be in a vault somewhere," Crowley said quietly, touched by the tale. "Or at least in a protective case."

"My apartment is well-sealed and climate controlled. I couldn't bear to have the thing actually locked away. But it's cared for, don't worry about that."

"Have you ever opened it, just to peek inside?"

Price smiled, shook his head. "It wouldn't be right."

They stared in silence for a moment, feeling the weight of history emanating from the simple object. Simple, Crowley mused, yet altogether magical as well. There was something touching about Price using his wealth on a thing so whimsical.

"Would you like to see the Golding?" Price asked.

"I would."

Price led him to another set of shelving, with one section covered by glass doors. On a display stand inside was the book. Price opened the door and gestured for Crowley to take a look.

"You sure?"

"Your hands are clean and dry?"

Crowley grinned. "I think so, yes."

"Then be my guest."

Crowley gently lifted the book from its stand, marveling at the cover of long-leafed jungle vines. He loved this novel so much, the way it enthralled and disturbed him at the same time. He opened it carefully and sure enough, it was signed. The title page was simple enough. LORD OF THE FLIES across the top, then a stylized graphic, with

a novel by
WILLIAM GOLDING

beneath it. And under that the man's signature, a clear cursive rendering of his name in pale blue fountain pen ink. Crowley stared, stunned by it. Golding had really held this very volume, put pen to it before he could ever have known how far-reaching this novel would become, what an impact it would have. School children around the world would read it and discuss its meanings, films would be made of the story.

He sensed Price beside him and looked up to see the man smiling warmly. "Quite something, no?"

"Astonishing," Crowley said, reverently pacing the book back on its stand.

Price closed the door again as Crowley sipped his scotch.

"Would you like to own such a thing?" Price asked.

Crowley laughed. "I would, but I'd be terrified it might come to harm. I don't think I'm responsible enough."

"Do you have a 'Holy Grail' book you'd like to own, other than that" Price asked. "If money were no object?"

Crowley thought about that, then said, "I'd love to have the pages of Carrie that Stephen King's wife famously rescued from the garbage. Do you know the story? He'd been rejected several times, decided he was done with it, and threw the book away. But she took it back out of the bin and urged him to continue trying, to continue writing. And look where he ended up!"

"So many men are all the better for the women who support them," Price said quietly.

"What about you? What's your holy grail book? I'm guessing with you, maybe money is no object?"

Price smiled softly. "I'm comfortable, certainly, but I'm sure there are plenty of things I can't afford. But for me, with books, it's not a matter so much of cost, but of scarcity. I would love to have Edgar Allan Poe's *Masque Journal*. Most people have never even heard of it, but it's the journal Poe used while he was working on *The Masque of the Red Death*. Do you know his work?"

"I do. And I've read that several times. I have a couple of compendiums of Poe's fiction at home. Nothing rare, of course, modern editions."

Price pursed his lips, nodding subtly. "Hmm. Well, this journal reportedly contains his original ideas, research notes, early drafts of the story, and random free-form thoughts. It would be entirely fascinating, don't you think?"

"I've never even heard of it," Crowley said.

"Very few have."

Crowley thought back to when he and Rose had first arrived in New York. He hadn't ever heard of the journal Price referred to, but was it possible he'd seen it? Was it possible the very thing Price desired most in the world had been recently unearthed and Price had yet to hear about it? "You know, Rose and I saw a Poe journal a few days ago," he said.

Price's eyebrows rose. "Is that so?"

"We visited the Poe house on West 3rd Street, do you know it?"

"Of course."

"Kind of lame, really. Bit of a letdown all around, but they'd just put a new journal on display a few weeks ago. A small, tatty leather-bound thing. They found it during repairs to an older part of the foundations below the house, bricked into a basement wall." Crowley squinted, trying to remember the details, and realized Price was looking at him with undisguised intensity. "The university, I think," he went on. "They uncovered a metal lockbox containing several items including the journal. But they said it was mostly indecipherable."

Price chuckled and sipped at his scotch, though Crowley noticed his hand was trembling slightly. "Well," he said after a moment. "Wouldn't that be something?"

CHAPTER 18

Rose refused to give up on her suspicions about Matthew Price, but she decided to hold them a little closer to her chest in the future. She had to agree that if the man was insinuating himself into Great Aunt Trudy's life, it was in Jake's best interests to get to know Price as well as he could. It would be doing his aunt a great disservice to ignore the relationship. She just wished he would treat their new friendship with more caution.

But with this position in mind, she had met back up with Crowley after his visit and they enjoyed lunch together and laughed and joked. She told Crowley that her research had turned up another likely spot for the secret dungeon laboratory, and he had humored her. They decided the following day, they would visit Bannerman Island and its ruined castle. She felt it might be the last chance to unravel this mystery, and hoped it wouldn't be another dead end. The rest of the day had been spent pleasantly relaxing and sightseeing, simply enjoying the chance to spend time together as if they really were tourists. That had been Crowley's price for continuing her search and she had gladly paid it.

The next day started gray and overcast, a light drizzle making everything in the city dark and glistening, but it wasn't cold. A light jacket was enough and they ignored the damp as they headed through the streets after breakfast. They picked up another hire car and Rose drove, following the Hudson River north out of the city up the Croton Expressway. They marveled at the sign for Sleepy Hollow along the way, Crowley wondering if it was the same one as the famous headless horseman tale. Further north they passed Peekskill and some fifty miles out of the city they stopped at Cold Spring where Crowley rented a canoe for the day, and strapped it to the hired SUVs roof rack. He took over the driving for the last bit past the Hudson Highlands, along the alarmingly named Breakneck Road. As they neared their target, Rose read from her research.

"It says here that the ruins on the island are the remnant of a Scotsman's fortress called Bannerman Castle, which he built as an arsenal for his immense collection of weapons rather than as somewhere to live. There's a sentence I never thought I'd say aloud. Public access was briefly permitted, but curtailed by Native American and Dutch settler's fear of resident spirits and goblins."

"Goblins?" Crowley asked with a laugh. "That'll be a new one for us."

Rose grinned, pleased they were having fun. "Fingers crossed, then. Maybe we can get a goblin familiar to help us out."

"With what exactly?"

"No idea, but goblins must be useful for something, right? Anyway, access has been restricted since 1900 for more contemporary safety reasons."

"Well, they could hardly admit to still being scared of goblins in this day and age."

"Jake, will you forget about the damn goblins."

He smiled, enjoying the absurdity. "You started it."

"Okay, now I'm finishing it." She scanned through her research a little further. "Apparently there's a trust working on stabilizing the ruins now, with the hope of reopening the island to the public. It's officially called Pollopel Island on maps. Six and three-quarter acres of mostly rock, about a thousand feet from the eastern shore of the Hudson. It says here to watch out for the current and make sure to put in north of the island when the current is flowing south."

"Okay," Crowley said. "We can do that."

"The castle was built by Frank Bannerman VI, a Scottish patriot, proud of his descent from one of the few Macdonalds to survive the massacre at Glencoe in 1692."

"It's a hell of a story, that one," Crowley said. "You know it?"

"Not really."

"Well, in short, during the 1690s, the King of England demanded allegiance from the all the Scottish clans. Supposedly the Macdonalds were not too keen and delayed in giving the English their oath of loyalty. So on behalf of the Crown, the Campbells, a rival clan, set upon the McDonalds and slaughtered all the able-bodied men. Anyone aged between twelve or fourteen or something, and seventy. So pretty much every male past puberty."

Rose remembered the story vaguely from history lessons and tapped away at her phone for a minute to check, then nodded. "You're right. And it says here that one McDonald escaped the massacre and ran to the hills with the clan banner. From that day on, his family name was Bannerman."

"Well, what do you know!"

"The Bannerman family emigrated in 1854, when Frank was three, and settled in Brooklyn. Frank joined the Union army during the Civil War, when he was only thirteen! But after the war, the U.S. government auctioned off military goods by the ton, mostly for scrap metal. Young Frank came to realize that much of what was being sold had a market value higher than scrap and Bannerman's became the world's largest buyer of surplus military equipment. Enterprising lad! Their storeroom and showroom took up a full block at 501 Broadway, and was opened to the public in 1905. According to the New York Herald, 'No museum in the world exceeds it in the number of exhibits.' Subsequently, Frank Bannerman married an Irish woman and they had three sons. After the Spanish American War, Bannerman bought 90 percent of all captured goods in a sealed bid, and he needed a secure place to store a large quantity of volatile black powder. His son, David, saw Pollopel Island in the Hudson, and Frank Bannerman bought it in 1900."

"Imagine buying an island," Crowley said. "Just like that, because you needed some space. It would be pretty cool!"

"Right? During the next seventeen years, Frank Bannerman personally designed the all island's buildings, docks, turrets, garden walls and moat in the style of old Scottish castles, almost all of it without professional help from architects, engineers, or contractors. He's quite the over-achiever, huh? It was elaborately decorated, with biblical quotations cast in all the fireplace mantles, and a shield between the towers with a coat of arms. The family sold Bannerman Castle to New York State in 1967. They ran tours for a short while, but on August 8, 1969, a fire destroyed all of the buildings. Since then, the Taconic State Parks Commission has declared it off limits. It says here people should not attempt to visit the island as it a full of buried hazards and unsafe walls, despite a lot of scaffolding trying to prop things up. It suggests taking a Hudson River cruise if you want to see it, and enjoying it from the safety of the water."

"Well, we're not going to spot dungeons from a river cruise, are we?" Crowley said with a grin.

Rose shared his excitement. Despite the dangers, she loved these adventures with him. "Let's just be damned careful, okay?

Pay special attention to where we step and stay away from the walls wherever we can."

It turned out that parking the car out of sight and picking a good spot to enter the river far from prying eyes was easier than they thought it would be, and before long Crowley was hauling the canoe up on to the shore of Bannerman Island, breathing hard from the exertion of rowing against the current for the last few yards to make a good landing.

"Well done, soldier," Rose said.

"Phew! I need to work out a bit more often. I've been lazy as hell lately."

Rose wondered if he meant that or was genuinely unaware of the shape he was in. "Didn't you recently swim a mile to an island?"

He laughed. "Sure, but I was puffed out."

They paused while Crowley caught his breath, then set off through the thick undergrowth toward the castle ruins.

The day had improved as they traveled and while it was still overcast, the light rain had stopped. The gray plastered red bricks of the remains towered over them like broken teeth, long struts of scaffold braced into them in several places, their other ends jammed into the ground and braced with iron spikes and fallen brickwork. Vines and poison oak had encroached well inside the boundaries of the buildings and they stepped carefully, watching out for wildlife as well as the irritating vegetation and any potholes. It didn't take long to establish that while the ruins were interesting in their own right, despite the massive degradation, there was nothing else of interest to see. Rose stood back and sighed, disappointed.

"Another bust," Crowley said, putting an arm around her shoulders. "I'm sorry, love."

She shrugged. "At least we're getting to see parts of the country we wouldn't have known about otherwise. And you're not being chased by armed guards this time."

"Yet."

"Well, here's hoping. I guess we head back? The current will take us a fair way down river and we'll have to hike back to the car carrying the canoe. Or maybe you can hike back while I wait with the canoe and then you can bring the car back to me?"

Crowley didn't respond and Rose turned her head to see why. He was looking intently at something off to their left. A rill of nerves fluttered in Rose's gut as she quickly looked the same way, wondering if maybe guards or police had arrived. But he was looking at a plain wall.

"What is it, Jake?"

"Wait here a moment, yeah?"

Without waiting for an answer he stalked off between two bulging clumps of tangled vines and ran his hand over the wall. Rose watched as he looked closer, then stepped back and checked above. Her brow knitted as he lifted one leg and before she could yell out for him to stop he'd driven a front kick hard into the bricks. He leaped back as the bricks all crumbled in and bits of mortar and showers of dust rained down from above.

"Jake, you idiot!" she yelled. "What are you doing? Get away from there before it all comes down."

He jogged backwards, not taking his eyes off the wall. Rose held her breath. The dust settled and Crowley turned, smiling at her. "It's a bricked up doorway!"

"That's you being careful, is it?"

"As careful as I could be kicking in a wall, yeah. Just as well the mortar was compromised by the damp."

"Just as well the mortar above it wasn't!" Rose shook her head, amazed at his foolhardiness. But he had got a result. "Where does it go?"

"Don't know. Let's find out."

They carefully approached the dark aperture he'd made and looked in. Stone steps led downwards, underground.

"That's the right direction, at least," Crowley said.

Sharing a quick smile, they both pulled out pocket flashlights and flicked them on, then Crowley started down. Rose kept close behind.

The darkness was damp and cold, instantly different to the dreary but temperate day above. The steps went down about twenty feet, then leveled off. They both shined their flashlights around and saw only a large open basement, maybe fifty feet square, with brick walls and brick support columns every ten feet or so. The space was otherwise featureless, but for dirt and cobwebs.

"Aw, man," Rose said, genuinely deflated. "For a moment there I let myself hope we'd found something."

She watched as Crowley paced a circuit of the basement, then return to her, his lips pressed into a flat line. "Sorry. We tried."

But now it was Rose's turn to stare. "What's that?" she

asked, pointing at an area of ground near the far wall.

The floor was packed dirt, hard and dry despite the overall dankness of the cellar. The dirt she looked at seemed to be slightly sunken, which wouldn't have seemed so strange in and of itself, but it was sunken in an almost perfect square.

"I missed that. Hold my light," Crowley said.

She took his flashlight and held one in each hand, trained on the area of ground, while Crowley grabbed a half brick from the bottom of the steps where he'd kicked the wall down. Using the corner of the brick he scraped at the dirt and quickly revealed a hollow, wooden sound. He redoubled his efforts and in no more than a few minutes had cleared a trapdoor. It was featureless, with no ring to hold and lift it, or any other means of shifting it.

"Maybe I can just jimmy it out?" Crowley mused. He took his universal tool out of his pocket and opened the small metal prong on one side, then began running it along the edge of the wood, clearing the gap between it and the packed earth.

"What the hell is that thing for?" Rose asked. "All multi-blade tools and penknives have one, that metal thing with a hole in it."

Crowley paused, held it up. "This? It's an awl. You can make holes with it, or put twine through the hole to pull it through leather for field repairs, that sort of thing."

Rose's eyebrows raised. "Well, you learn something new every day. My dad said he reckoned they were for removing stones and mud from horse's hooves, but I always thought that was nonsense."

Crowley looked at the tool for a moment, then shrugged. "Well, you could use it for that, I suppose." He grinned and went back to work. Once he'd cleared it all away he began gently digging the tool under the edges. At first it appeared to be stuck tight, but then shifted just slightly.

"It's loose but I can't get a grip to lift it," Crowley said, frustration evident.

"Wait there!" Rose ran back up the steps, remembering something she'd seen nearby. It took a moment to reorient herself, but she soon spotted it again. A flat piece of metal about eight inches long, with a hole in each end. It was a kind of bracket for connecting some part of the scaffolding, she assumed, perhaps dropped and lost during construction. She ran it back down to Crowley. "Try this."

He grinned. "Perfect!"

It took a little more digging, but once he could get the metal strip in beside the wood he used it like a crowbar and the wooden cover levered up easily. He lifted it free and revealed a square hole about three feet to a side, and more steps leading down. Rose stood beside him and shined the flashlights down. The stairs were wooden and the walls below them stone. At the bottom they saw a pale gray flagstone floor.

They went down into the dark and shone their flashlights around, each making a noise of shock. But Rose also felt a rush of excitement. Metal mortuary tables filled a space almost as large again at the basement above. Around the sides were metal cabinets, bone saws and clamps and calipers lay forgotten, rusting and dust-covered.

"Well, this is clearly evidence of some kind of surgery and no doubt experimentation," Crowley said.

"And it's pretty secret. It would qualify as a lab, I think, don't you?"

"I guess so. Certainly before it was abandoned, you can imagine there would have been a lot more stuff here. It's well fitted out, just left to go to ruin now."

Rose took her phone out and used the flash to record as much of the space as she could. They returned to the basement above and made a record of the access point, then retraced their steps again and photographed the spot where Crowley had kicked in the wall and the area around it. But the excitement of the discovery waned the more Rose thought about it. While they had certainly uncovered something, it had been left well alone for a long time. There were no fresh leads here.

"I think we need to look into Bannerman and his history a lot more," Rose said. "What we learned in the car seems to be only most public of his activities."

"Possibly," Crowley said. "Or someone else used his space, perhaps without the knowledge of the Bannerman family. This was a storage facility, don't forget. Not a home."

"True. We've certainly got more research to–" Rose was interrupted by her phone coming to life in her hand, ringing. The number was unknown. She frowned, but answered. "Hello?"

"Is this Rose Black?" a man with a broad Brooklyn accent asked.

"Yes, who's this?"

"This is Sergeant Tony Palmetto from the New York City Police Department, ma'am. I'd like you to brace yourself as I have what may come as bad news to you."

Rose's stomach clenched. "What is it?"

"Would you know a woman by the name of Jasmine Richards?"

"Yes! Jazz. She's my friend."

Rose heard the police officer suck in a breath and swallow hard. "Ms. Black, I'm very sorry to inform you that your friend has died. She appears to be the victim of a robbery."

"What? No, that's not possible!"

Crowley moved to her and put his arm around her shoulders, his eyes creased in concern. Rose had the wherewithal to pull the phone from her ear and tap it onto speaker.

"I'm afraid it's true, Ms. Black. Miss Jasmine Richards was found in her apartment early this afternoon and there's evidence she disturbed a robbery in progress. We're ringing you as she had a slip of paper with your name and number on it in her back pocket, so we wanted to know why that might be. We're following up any leads we find I'm very sorry, Ms. Black. Would you be able to come to the station and help us with our enquiries?"

Rose felt as if a dagger of ice had been plunged into her heart. She shared a look with Crowley, aware that tears were rolling over her cheeks. "Yes, of course."

The Sergeant gave her an address, apologized again for the imparting such terrible news over the telephone, thanked her, and hung up.

"Rose, I'm so sorry!" Crowley said, gathering her into a hug.

She cried into his chest for a moment, her mind a whirlwind. "I'm sure Matthew Price has something to do with this," she said, before second-guessing the wisdom of the statement.

Crowley gently pushed her back, looked into her eyes. "Come on, now. Why? What possible reason could there be for that?"

"Because I asked her to look into him. Perhaps I caused this! Maybe she got too close and poked a hornet's nest."

"He's just an old man, into pharmaceuticals, for goodness sake."

Rose realized anger was battling inside her with grief, a dangerous combination, but she couldn't hold her tongue. "You never liked Jazz from the outset, anyway, Jake! I think you're threatened by her."

Crowley's mouth fell open and his eyes darkened for a moment, then she saw him mentally check himself. He pulled back some kind of control. "You know what? I was a little threatened. I'm only human, I guess. But that's not why I'm questioning your accusing of Price."

She opened her mouth to berate him further, but he held up a hand to forestall her, then placed his palm on her cheek. "But! Your friend has just died and that's awful. And who knows, maybe you're onto something and I can't see it. I've been wrong about stuff often enough before. Let's get back to the city, and I promise to keep an open mind."

CHAPTER 19

Rose was grateful Crowley had allowed her to have suspicions. And she harbored them still. But Jake was a good man and she was grateful for his support. She needed it. They had spent the majority of the late afternoon at the police department answering questions, but had really had no answers to give. Driving back from the Bannerman Island they had discussed what information they might give out. Crowley had cautioned against letting on too much about the crypt they'd found or the locations they'd been to without permission. Better to avoid any scrutiny on themselves, or possibly besmirch Jazz's memory. While he was happy to entertain the possibility that Jazz may have run afoul of Price, she was equally likely to have run afoul of any number of other adversaries. Given her profession, perhaps danger was never that far away. Crowley insisted it was something they could check into themselves, and he promised they would do that. If they uncovered anything, they would tip the police off somehow afterwards. Rose thought maybe his caution was right.

So they had told the Sergeant only the most superficial details. They were on vacation in New York City, enjoying the sights, visiting Crowley's great aunt. Jazz and Rose were old friends and they had caught up a couple of times and had every intention of doing so again before Rose returned to England. That's probably why Jazz was holding her number, Rose told the officer. Maybe she was about to call and plan their next catch up. Rose admitted she had been trying to reach her friend for the last couple of days and always going through to voicemail. She also told the sergeant that Jazz was usually good at returning online messages, but that she'd been unusually quiet on that front as well over the previous 48 hours or so. Rose put it down to Jazz being busy with work. The police seemed happy enough with all that.

"Do you think Jazz was planning to call you to catch up?" Crowley asked, as they walked back to their hotel.

"Maybe. Or call and tell me some juicy information about Price or the crypt or something else," Rose said, her voice husky with emotion.

"Possibly," he allowed.

"Juicy enough to get her killed maybe." Rose swallowed, refusing to let tears flow again. For now she wanted to maintain her rage at the injustice of it all. There would be time enough for grief later.

Crowley had asked a few probing questions of the Sergeant, about what had been stolen, had the door been forced or did it look like Jazz had opened it to let someone in, maybe someone she knew. Sergeant Palmetto had been friendly, but his eyes narrowed at Crowley's questions and Jake wisely clammed up. It had been smart to try for some details, but pushing too far would only seem suspicious coming from a couple of English tourists. The officer had finally warned them off, punctuating it with a muttered comment. She'd caught "civilians" and "crime shows are bullshit." Rose thought maybe that was true, but it didn't mean there wasn't more to this crime than met the eye. It was New York, so she had to accept it was possible Jazz had fallen foul of violent burglars, but she wouldn't trust that possibility until every other avenue of enquiry had been exhausted. Now who sounds like they watch too many crime shows on TV, she thought wryly.

Sitting over breakfast the following morning, after a somewhat restless night, Rose was cranky and over-tired. The loss of Jazz was a hole inside her that was equal parts grief and guilt. What if it did have something to do with Jazz doing research into Price? Would that make Rose almost directly responsible for her friend's death? She voiced her concerns to Crowley.

"It could have had something to do with her digging into the stuff about the bodies in the crypt too," Crowley said. "Maybe we should head back there and see what's happening. Or it could be any number of other stories she may have been working on that we don't know about."

"So you think it is suspicious then?"

He shrugged, sipped coffee. "I don't know. It's entirely possible that it's as simple as a botched robbery like the police think. Horribly mundane, but if we take an Occam's Razor point of view—"

While that echoed Rose's own thoughts, she still didn't want to accept it. "If someone deliberately killed her, they would certainly make it look like a botched robbery."

"They would," he agreed. "If there is something more

suspicious about this, it makes sense to put the police off like that."

Rose scrolled through the news on her phone, partly looking for any mention of Jazz's murder. Nothing yet. Maybe in a city this size, a bungled robbery and a dead reporter didn't make the news cycle. Then the word Poe caught her eye and she scrolled back.

"Huh," she said, skim-reading the article. "You remember that Poe house we visited when we were first here?"

"Yeah, of course. Lame as it was, it's hard to forget."

"It got broken into last night apparently. Fair bit of damage and a bunch of exhibits stolen. They're asking for people to come forward if they know anything or might have seen anything."

When Crowley didn't answer, Rose looked up and had a moment of shock at his pale face. He looked like he'd seen a ghost.

"What is it?"

Crowley shook his head slightly, as if in disbelief. "Can't be."

"What, Jake?"

"When I went to see Price yesterday we got to talking about books. He had an impressive library, lots of rare and valuable stuff. He has a first edition of *Lord of the Flies*, signed by Golding. It was amazing. More than that, he has this one book, a first edition *of The Great Gatsby*, in mint condition that he really treasures. I looked it up afterwards and it's worth nearly two-hundred-thousand bucks."

"Holy hell!"

"I know, right? That particular copy has quite a romantic story attached too, I'll tell you about it later. Anyway, looking at this stuff we got onto the subject of what our holy grail book might be. You know, the book we'd love to own more than any other. And Price said he'd dearly love to have Edgar Allan Poe's *Masque Journal*. It's a one-off, obviously, apparently the journal Poe used when he wrote *The Masque of the Red Death*. Price said it contains Poe's original ideas, research notes, early drafts of the story, and random free-form thoughts. I thought that was a strange turn of phrase at the time, random freeform thoughts. But Price was quite wistful about it. Anyway—"

"You told him about the Poe house," Rose interrupted, realizing where this was going. "And the old journal they'd recently turned up."

Crowley nodded. "I did."

"And so Price broke in and stole it!"

"Well, we don't know that…"

Rose gave him one of her sternest stares and he had the decency to look away from her. "Come on, Jake. It's too much to be all coincidence, surely. Something is going on here and I think it's all connected. Price and the break-in at the Poe house, the journal, Jazz's murder. Even the crypt, the mass burials, and the bodies, the crazy trepanning experiments. It's all connected somehow, I can feel it!"

Crowley frowned. "I don't know. I grant you there's a lot of suspicious stuff going on here but you're drawing a long bow."

"You said that before, but I still maintain I'm right. Just a minute." Rose tapped up the details for the Poe house and rang the number. She held up a hand to stay Crowley's questions while it rang, then a woman answered. "Hi there," Rose said. "My name is Claire Cowans and I'm a reporter for the New York Herald. I just wanted to ask you a few questions about the break-in last night for a write-up we're doing."

"Okay, sure. But there's really not much to tell."

"Well, we have most of the police report details, I just wanted to ask what items in particular were stolen."

The woman made a thoughtful noise and then said, "Well, there's a register here and that was broken open but no cash was in it. They also broke into a couple of display cabinets, and they pried open the drawers of the writing desk that was on display. We're still trying to figure out all that was stolen, but definitely a couple of old books."

"Old books, really? Was one the journal that was recently put on display? The one they found in the basement walls not long ago?"

"Oh, you know about that?"

"Yes," Rose said, thinking quickly. "I visited there quite recently, which is why I've been put on this story. I just remember that as one of the exhibits."

"Well, interestingly, one case that was broken into was the one that held the journal you're asking about," the woman said. "But it wasn't in there. It's on temporary loan to the Grolier Club for an exhibit they have starting tomorrow evening."

"Well, I suppose that's fortunate, at least," Rose said. "Say, while I have you on, did anyone read that journal? When I was visiting I was wondering what it was about."

"All I know is it was a writing journal for one of his stories, but I don't recall which one, I'm sorry. Mind you, the people at the Grolier Club were very excited about it."

Rose smiled. "Thank you so much for your time."

CHAPTER 20

Despite his suggestion that Rose was drawing a long bow by connecting all the strange things they had encountered since arriving in New York, Crowley had to admit his own curiosity was piqued. He couldn't deny that Rose was onto something, but at the same time he couldn't put his finger on what that something was. So they had decided to snoop a little further. Rose went off to the offices of the *New York Sentinel* to ask around there, and Crowley found himself outside Jazz's apartment door. He was nervous, knowing that if he was caught here it would put him and Rose deeper in the frame for whatever had happened to Jazz. Right now they were safely distanced from it. But it wasn't in his nature, or Rose's, to walk away.

Marks on the top right of the doorframe and the floor on the bottom left, showed where a single strip of black and yellow plastic crime scene tape had been. Now that it was taken away, Crowley assumed the police were done with the place. Perhaps they were done with the case too, if they'd written it off as a botched robbery. The file would stay open, they'd be happy to catch the killer, but probably wouldn't waste a lot of resources on it. Or maybe he was doing the NYPD a disservice by assuming that. He didn't know. Either way, he hoped there was something left here that the police had missed. Something to give him a chance of learning more.

He slipped on a pair of surgical gloves he'd picked up at a pharmacy on the way over and tried the doorknob, but it was locked. There was a deep gouge in the wood beside the door handle where the door had been forced open and Crowley wondered if that was after the killing or before. It would make sense for a killer to do this and back up the robbery story, to draw the attention away from the possibility of a deliberate, premeditated murder. The police had either repaired or replaced the fixture as the door was locked again now, despite the remaining damage to the frame.

Crowley looked furtively left and right to ensure he was alone in the hallway, then crouched in front of the door and set to work with his new customized lock picks. It was startling the kind of thing you could pick up an at Army Surplus store if you knew how do co-opt one tool's use for a more nefarious purpose. It took a couple of minutes and a high heart rate, but thankfully no one appeared to catch him until a soft click inside the door told him he was in. Crowley turned the handle, slipped inside, and quickly closed the door behind him.

The place was tiny, a true city studio apartment. Immediately on his left was a small kitchenette, with a bar fridge, microwave and two-burner stove top, all clean and well-kept. Next to that a tiny metal sink, one coffee-stained mug sitting in it waiting for rinse it would now never receive. On his right was a bathroom with toilet, tiny sink, and shower stall. He thought perhaps he'd have trouble turning around in there, let alone washing comfortably. The rest of the room in front of him was filled with a bed at one end under the window, a desk against one wall and a bookcase against the opposite wall. Next to the bookcase was a clothes rack overloaded with outfits in a kind of barely-managed jumble. But otherwise the place was neat. Not much space remained in the center between these few items of furniture.

The desk hand two drawers in it, side-by-side above where a person's knees would be. Both were broken, forced open with a crowbar or something similar. Crowley pulled them out again and saw they were empty. There was some mail on the desktop, bills and coupons, but nothing else. He'd hoped to find some evidence of what Jazz had been working on, but nothing seemed apparent. He thought the place was too clean. He supposed he could put that down to a robbery, they would have taken any laptops or tablets or anything else of value, but working on the assumption it wasn't a robbery and only made to look like one, he'd hoped to find something, even if the perpetrators had taken electronic items to back up the robbery story. But there were no calendars or diaries either, no notebooks, post-its, nothing. Maybe Jazz kept all that stuff on her phone like so many people did these days. The crooks would have taken her phone too, after killing her, he didn't doubt that.

He turned and looked at the bookcase and noticed for the first time a dark stain on the thin, dark carpeting by the bed. Dark brown now, about two feet in diameter, it was clearly dried blood. He let out a slow breath and swallowed. Poor Jazz.

He went to the bookcase and started rifling through the books, checking inside the covers of the dozen or so hardbacks, shaking out the paperbacks, checking behind the books themselves. Jazz had quite a diverse and eclectic library, including a variety of thrillers kept in among non-fiction books covering everything from autobiographies to flight mechanics. But despite Crowley's rigorous searching he found nothing.

Under the clothes rack, overhung by several pairs of jeans, he noticed a small, three-drawer cabinet and checked that. Underwear, activewear, the usual. Nothing of interest. The same in the bathroom, just a normal selection of make-up and day-to-day medications.

Crowley sighed, returning the center of the room. He was becoming tired of missions turning out to be total busts. Then again, they'd found that sub-basement on Bannerman Island, so there was something going on. Or there had been, a long time ago. He was beginning to share Rose's view that there was definitely more to uncover here, he simply needed to start looking in the right places.

He spotted a wastepaper basket tucked into a corner at the end of the bed and went to it. Nothing but a few packets, a shopping list, some tissues. A small, red, plastic basket stood in the narrow space between the foot of the bed and the wall. It held a bunch of crumpled up clothes, no doubt Jazz's laundry ready to be taken downstairs and washed. He had a quick look, checked the pockets of a pair of jeans in there. Tucked into the back pocket was a crumpled scrap of paper with names and notes scribbled on it. Crowley smiled. The police had missed something after all. Ironic, given they found Rose's number in the back pocket of the jeans Jazz had been wearing, but hadn't checked these ones too.

The list didn't make too much sense at first glance, but could be something to follow up. He really hoped it was, because it was their last chance for a lead. He smoothed it out and was about to read it more carefully when someone rapped sharply on the apartment door. Crowley started, looked quickly around. There was no other way out of the apartment except a fire escape through the window above the bed. As soon as he saw that, he also saw the window had a lock on it and he had no way of knowing where the key might be. He was trapped.

CHAPTER 21

Rose took the elevator to the fourteenth floor and the offices of the *New York Sentinel*. She wasn't sure what she had been expecting, maybe rows of wooden desks and typewriters with green-glass shaded desk lamps. Of course, that might have been the case decades ago, but the reception she stepped out into was clean and bright. The reception desk itself was a simple curve of silver-topped white wood, bearing nothing but a computer monitor and a complicated-looking landline phone. A receptionist was tapping animatedly on her cell phone and barely gave Rose a glance as she walked in. Through the open door behind the desk was a large open plan office full of more modern desks and desktop computers, several people in casual office attire, some working, others milling around.

Rose decided to be brazen and take a chance. She strolled casually past reception and the young woman on the phone, and through the open door. The receptionist didn't even look up. Rose thanked the gods of social media and the inattention of the young.

She wandered around the large space, trying to look like she belonged. Several people sat at their desks working keyboards or phones didn't look up, or didn't acknowledge her if they did notice. Others stood in pairs or small groups chatting. Several single offices, with large glass fronts and closed doors, stood all along one wall, windows beyond looking out over the city.

Rose spotted a framed photo of Jazz and her mother on one desk and headed for it. Her stomach clenched as she picked up the photo for a closer look. Her friend was really dead. Jazz's mother looked young in the photo, barely even 40. Rose remembered the stories from Jazz, how her mother had been a teenage mom. Jazz had said she almost grew up together with her mom as much friends as parent and daughter. They were close. Did her mom know what had happened? She could be barely out of her forties and Rose remembered Jazz was an only child, the poor woman would be devastated. Rose made a mental note to try to track down Mrs. Richards and offer her condolences at least.

The computer on Jazz's desk was on, a screensaver of

tumbling neon lines rolling on forever repeat across the screen. Rose spared a quick glance over her shoulder and she was still remarkably unnoticed. Perhaps it was pretty normal for people to come and go from these offices. Either way, she would take advantage of it as much as she could. She shifted the mouse hoping to get a look at Jazz's files. A dialog box popped up asking for a password. Rose silently cursed.

On a whim, eyes narrowing, she tried *blackrose*. Black Rose had been Jazz's somewhat tongue-in-cheek nickname for her, and perhaps her return to New York had made Jazz think of it. Who knew if she even changed her password often. It was a long shot, of course, but... The screen unlocked.

Heart racing, barely able to believe her luck, Rose quickly opened the browser and looked at the search history. Nothing. Everything had been erased. So had all the bookmarks. That had to be a deliberate cleansing. After the murder? She opened up the Recent Documents box and there was a list of items, mostly Word documents. At the top was one file called "Price-Missing". What might that mean?

Rose clicked on it, but the computer informed her the file could not be found. Also deleted. This was all too convenient and more than a little worrying.

Wondering where on the hard drive to look for other files, Rose glanced over her shoulder again and barely suppressed a startled jerk. Coming in her direction was a tall Latina with thick dark hair pulled back in a loose ponytail, clearly heading directly for a confrontation. Rose quickly re-evaluated, trying not to let guilt color her perception. The woman was imposing, but her face was relaxed, even kind-looking. Rose remembered Jazz talking about her boss, the editor here. LaGuerta, that was it. Jazz had a lot of respect for the woman and often talked about how lucky she was to have that kind of boss, especially in the media industry where so many places were still run by old white guys and their rusted-on prejudices.

Rose quickly closed the file window she had opened, and picked up the photo of Jazz with her mother, as if that was what she had been looking at all along.

"Can I help you?" the tall woman asked as she got nearer.

CHAPTER 22

The heavy knocking came at the door again and Crowley tried to think fast. No exit, no way of knowing who they were or what they wanted. One thing was certain – there was no situation where he should be inside Jazz's apartment. Whoever it was wouldn't be happy to see him.

He ran to the kitchenette and pulled the biggest knife from a wooden block next to the microwave. It was a decent-sized carving knife, a broad eight inches of sharp steel. Then moving on soft feet, he crept up to the door and chanced a glimpse through the peephole. A large man stood outside, his face dark. Crowley ducked back, mind racing. He knew that guy. Where had he seen him before?

"Come on, come on!" Crowley whispered to himself. "Who is that guy?" It seemed important.

Then it came to him. The broad-shouldered and thick-limbed fellow was even still wearing the same charcoal suit, but he'd taken off the dark sunglasses. His mop of dark brown curls and pale skin were unmistakable though. It was the same man Crowley had spotted in Washington Square Park after they first discovered the mass burial site. The one who had surreptitiously snapped a photo of Rose and Jazz. And now here he was, outside Jazz's apartment. Could he even be the killer, returning to the scene of the crime? But why?

Initially Crowley had hoped that whoever was knocking would go away, but now he thought maybe he needed to have a chat with this guy. But a big, angry dude like that? It wouldn't be easy.

Crowley moved to take another look out the peephole and saw the man back up a couple of steps and drop his right shoulder. He was about to barge the door and ram it in. Subtlety was clearly not this guy's style.

Crowley quickly reached out and turned the doorknob just as the big man ran, then whipped the door open. He stuck his foot out as the poor fellow barreled at full speed into nothing and over he went, crashing hard into the floor and sliding up against Jazz's bed. The crash was enough to shake the entire studio and Crowley winced at the thought of how that impact must have felt. *Better him than me*, he thought. The man deserved credit, he was rolling and almost up onto his knees before he'd even stopped sliding, but Crowley was quicker. He dropped to one knee, cracked an elbow into the man's temple to stun him, then grabbed him from behind, one arm across his chest, the other holding the knife blade against the thick meat of the man's neck.

"Don't move, or you'll slit your throat!"

"What the hell?" the guy asked in a tight voice, frozen still against the blade. "Who are you?"

Crowley laughed. "I'll ask the questions. First of all, hands behind your back."

Grudgingly, the man complied. Crowley grabbed a bedside lamp, cut the lamp from the cord with the sharp knife, and used it to tie the man's hands together securely at the wrist. He pulled it painfully tight, but he wasn't about to take any chances.

"Back against the bed."

"You'll get nothing out of me!"

"We'll see." Crowley remembered a pair of pantyhose were in the laundry basket, so he grabbed those and tied the man's feet together, again pulling the knot as tight as he could. "What's your name?" he asked.

The man used a colorful word that certainly wasn't a name.

Crowley smiled. "Fair enough. I'm going to call you Jerkwad. Feel free to correct me any time. So, Jerkwad, what are you doing here?"

Jerkwad kept his mouth closed, tipped his head and kept a disdainful expression in his face. His eyes betrayed the speed of this thoughts as he seemed to be sizing up his options for escape.

Crowley wasn't about to give him time or opportunity. "Silent type, eh? I saw you in Washington Square Park, and I saw you take a picture." The man's cheeks twitched as he ground his teeth. "Why are you following Jasmine Richards?"

The man's eyebrows twitched slightly this time, relaying an altogether different emotion. First it had been anger, now it was surprise.

"Did you not know her name? Or were you not following her? Were you following me, Jerkwad? Or my friend?" He was careful not to mention his or Rose's name. He could hope this guy and whoever he worked for didn't know yet who they were, though maybe that was naïve. And he was sure this fool worked for someone else. He had the look of a minion, not the brains of an operation.

"Okay, Jerkwad, let's see what your pockets tell me."

Crowley reached forward and the big man thrashed, tries to head-butt forward. But he was big and slow and tied up, and Crowley was no mug. He sent a pair of knuckles in a swift clip across the point of Jerkwad's chin and the big man grunted and went partially limp, eyes crossing. Not out cold, but disoriented. He dragged in breath, getting his equilibrium back as Crowley rifled through his suit pockets. He found a set of car keys and a phone.

He put the keys aside and held up the phone. "What have we here?"

"I ain't giving you the passcode." The man sneered, one side of his mouth curving up, pleased with himself.

"I probably won't need it. The facial recognition feature on these new gadgets was a big mistake, don't you think?" He held the phone in front of the man's face, but nothing happened.

Jerkwad grinned, but Crowley wasn't finished. He stood up and drove a knee into the big man's shoulder, tipping him over sideways. Then he grabbed the meaty tied hands and pressed one thumb pad to the home button on the phone. This time it opened right up.

"There we go," Crowley said. "When one technology fails, there's always another to try."

Jerkwad said some unkind things about Crowley's mother. Crowley ignored him and had a quick look through the phone, quickly realizing it was must be all business. "All the calls to a single number, all the emails to the same address, eh?" he said. "This is clearly your boss you're talking to. I knew you had to be a monkey, not an organ grinder." He went into settings and changed the passcode. Much easier than cutting the guy's thumb off and carrying it around with him. "I can see from a quick scan that there's enough dirt here for me to easily convince your big boss that you've betrayed him."

Jerkwad's eyes went wide.

"Oh yeah," Crowley said. "I play dirty. I'll set it up so your boss will have you wiped out in no time at all. I imagine he's known for that." It was a gamble, but a fairly safe one, Crowley thought.

"Don't do that, man! I'm just trying to get by, right? You know how it is, don'tcha?"

"So now you're more talkative," Crowley said. "Well, fine by me. Tell me everything you can about the man you work for."

CHAPTER 23

Rose sucked in a deep breath to calm her nerves as the tall woman closed the gap between them. As she approached, she smiled and reached out a hand.

"Elena LaGuerta."

Rose took the offered hand, found it warm and smooth. "Rose Black. Good to meet you."

"You're looking for Jazz? For Jasmine?" LaGuerta's eyes were calculating, but also a little wet. Rose saw the conflict there, the sadness coupled with the need to protect Jazz. Or her memory, at least.

Rose shook her head. "I know I won't find her. I've heard the news."

LaGuerta's mood immediately softened. "Oh, thank god. I thought maybe I was going to have to break the news to someone I didn't know. You're that friend of hers. The English girl. Lily, is it?"

"It's Rose. And yes, we're old friends." She was proud she'd managed to remain calm. Of all the names LaGuerta could have landed on, the name of Rose's sister? It couldn't be a coincidence. Had Jazz and Lily remained in touch? With one of the two dead and the other most likely in the same condition, the emotional baggage surrounding that imagined scenario was more than she could unpack right now.

LaGuerta misinterpreted her silence, reached out and put a hand on Rose's shoulder. "I'm so sorry. It's truly awful. How did you guys know each other?"

"We met when I was in New York before. I'm here again, on vacation with my boyfriend, so I called Jazz. We caught up a couple of times, and then…" A slight frown danced across Rose's face as she heard herself refer to Jake as her boyfriend. It was the first time she'd done that verbally, or even internally for that matter. She didn't mind how it sounded. Funny how life went on even in the face of the worst tragedies.

"She was a good person," LaGuerta said. "And a fine reporter too. The office here, we're all still in shock. It's hard to fathom, you know? I mean, this is New York, there's awful news every day, but not usually so close to home. We report the news, we don't usually become the news."

"What was Jazz working on?" Rose asked, trying to sound as casual as possible.

LaGuerta drew a breath, shook her head gently. "A few things. She'd been putting together a feature on corporate property scandals, she was enjoying that. She loved to expose the rats and crooks. She also had a piece going on a young girl, only fourteen years old, who's just joined Juilliard, playing violin. The kid is an absolute prodigy and Jazz had been building a great human interest piece, following her story. Jazz is a great features writer." LaGuerta swallowed. "Well, she was."

Rose nodded, thinking what else she could ask. LaGuerta hadn't said anything about missing persons, or Matthew Price, or even the discovery of the mass burial site. Perhaps Jazz had been keeping all that to herself until she had more to go on.

"You have any clues about what Jazz was doing in the days before her death?" Rose asked.

"No," LaGuerta said, eyes narrowing. "Not outside usual work and life. I thought Jazz was the victim of a burglary gone wrong, that's what the police told us. And they seemed pretty convinced of that. Do you know something else? Are you really just a friend?"

Rose sensed this woman might be mostly friendly, but was unlikely to be her ally. LaGuerta would be keen to protect her paper and its reputation as much as anything else. And Rose didn't want to give away anything that might compromise what she could learn later. "No, no, I'm sorry. I'm just her friend. I guess I'm having trouble dealing with the situation. I'm looking for something more. Trying to find some reason in it all, you know? It's just so bloody senseless."

LaGuerta softened again. "It is, yes. Absolutely tragic. Sadly, so many deaths are."

"Well, look, thanks for talking to me. I won't keep you."

"If you need anything, and you think I can help, you can give me a call, okay?" LaGuerta handed over a card.

Rose slipped it into the pocket of her jeans. "Thank you. I really appreciate that."

LaGuerta smiled, but stood waiting. She wanted to make sure Rose left, perhaps, so Rose made her way back between the desks towards the office's main door. From the corner of her eye she saw LaGuerta watch for a moment longer and then head back towards her office.

As Rose walked out the doors and headed for the elevator, she sensed a presence across the hall and turned. Someone ducked out of sight, behind a closet door marked CLEANER. Rose watched the door and saw a shadow move behind it.

The hairs on the back of her neck stood up. She had learned to never ignore her intuition and suddenly she wanted to be out of the place as soon as possible.

She imagined the elevator arriving and someone leaping in just as the doors closed, trapping her in the small box. Trusting her gut, Rose turned and went quickly to a door marked STAIRS and pushed it open.

The stairwell was cool and gray concrete, and smell chalky and unused. She quickly ran down, her feet echoing as she rapidly descended. As she turned onto the level below, the stairwell door she'd come through opened and a large shadow came through.

Rose cursed and started to run. She jumped down steps three or four at a time, hand gripping the railing to swing around at each landing. Heavy footsteps from above increased with hers, a grunting breath of a large man not used to running down stairs echoed over the slapping of her own feet.

Well, I'm fit and fast! Rose thought. *I'll outrun you, buddy.*

She passed a large sign on the wall with a 1 on it and then hurried down one more flight, before bursting through the doors, expecting the lobby on the ground floor. She found herself in a long cement corridor, air-conditioning tubes and electrical conduits running along the ceiling. A basement? She cursed again. Of course, in America, 1 meant the ground floor. In England the ground floor was marked with a G and 1 was the first floor up.

Too late to worry about that now, and she couldn't go back up. Surely there would be another way out. She ran along the corridor and came to a T-junction. As she randomly chose left, the door she'd come through banged open. She had a moment to glimpse a large man with thick dark hair, then she was running again. The new corridor had no more features than the last, but it did end in a double gray door.

Rose sprinted to it and slammed the bar to push it open. Nothing happened. She hit it again, drove a shoulder into the door, but it didn't budge. Locked tight. She was underground in a dead end.

The big man got to the junction and looked down to see her

standing there, panting for breath, back pressed to the wood. He smiled.

CHAPTER 24

"Okay, man, it's not worth all this hassle, okay?"

Jerkwad was talking happily enough now, Crowley noticed with amusement. Clearly he was scared of his boss.

"I'll decide what's hassle and what's not," Crowley said. "Just tell me about your boss. Who is he, and why are you here?"

"I'm private eye, okay?"

Crowley was getting annoyed with how often this guy said "okay". Maybe it was a nervous habit. "Tell me all about your work, then."

"I don't work full time for anyone, usually. I've always been just a gumshoe for hire. But a few years ago I was contacted by this one fella. He wanted someone with my skills and contacts and he wanted me to work for him and no one else. He said I needed to commit to his payroll, and ask no questions, and I'd be very well compensated for it."

"You didn't think that was a little suspicious?" Crowley asked.

"Of course it is! But do you know how hard it is to make a living in this town? Especially in this business? I used to celebrate whenever I'd get a gig that would put me on retainer for two weeks. This guy? He wanted me on retainer permanently. And it was a good retainer at that. I ain't never been paid so well before in my life. So I can look away from the occasional less than honest request now and then, okay? What are you, an angel?"

Crowley shook his head. "I don't think anyone would ever call me that. But I have morals. So who is this guy you work for, asking no questions?"

"I ain't ever met him in person, never seen his face. He keeps it that way. And I don't know his real name, before you ask. He calls himself the Witchfinder, and that's what we call him too, officially."

"We?"

"There's a couple other guys around. They're his underlings that he sends to me with messages or payments, stuff like that. Like I said, I never met the guy in the flesh."

"And you all call him something different from the

Witchfinder?"

"Naw, man, I call him what he wants to be called. But these underlings, they're sycophants, you know, they creep and scrape around. But they don't show much respect. They think they're getting something over on him because they secretly call him the Revenant. They think it's funny, maybe, I dunno. I have no idea where they got it from."

"Okay, sounds all very cloak and dagger." Crowley pursed his lips in thought. "So what does he do, this Revenant?"

"The *Witchfinder*," Jerkwad said, emphasizing the correct name, "he spies, snoops, gathers intel. I rarely have a clue why I'm being told to get things I'm sent for, or learn the things he wants to know. He's a complicated guy, you know? This is just another job, like hundreds before it. I have no idea why the Witchfinder is interested in this Jazz Richards lady, but he sent me to find out anything I could from her apartment. I didn't expect anyone to be here."

"Do you know anything about how she died?" Crowley asked.

Jerkwad licked his lips like he was about to answer, then grinned as the apartment door banged open. "What kept you?" Jerkwad said to the man in the doorway.

The newcomer swung up a semi-automatic pistol and fired it at Crowley.

Chapter 25

Rose drew breath to scream, her only thought to bring anyone in hearing distance running to her aid.

The big man shot up both hands, palms out, and said, "Please don't! It's about Jazz!"

The scream stuck in Rose's throat like a rock and she stared, heart-racing, adrenaline making her thoughts slippery. "You stay back there, okay? Keep your distance."

The man had started forward again, but he stopped, nodded. "Okay. I'm sorry, I'll stay here."

He was huge, maybe six and half feet tall, broad as a barn, with rounded shoulders belying a powerful physique. But under his mop of thick brown hair, his face was soft, kind. His eyes, even in the dim lighting of the basement corridor, were warm.

Rose found herself relaxing slightly, but remained a little on edge. The man stood awkwardly, moved a bit from side to side as if embarrassed about something. Maybe the guy was just weird, or not altogether neurotypical, but anxiety seemed to wash off him. "Why were you chasing me?" Rose asked. "Why not just call out to me?"

"I'm sorry, I wasn't sure how to get your attention, and then you ran away. I'm not supposed to fraternize with the staff." He stumbled over the word 'fraternize', making it into four or five syllables, and Rose thought perhaps she was right about his mental state. But was he scared or always this way?

"Okay, let's start again then," she said, trying to keep her voice calm and level. "What do you have to tell me?"

"Can we go somewhere private? I don't want to be caught talking to you. And I don't want anyone to overhear."

Rose narrowed her eyes. "Where?"

"I'm the janitor here. My room is just back that way." He gestured over his shoulder, right from the T-junction where Rose had turned left.

Staying alert, she nodded. "Lead the way then."

Just a few yards along the passage, they came to a door marked JANITOR, so he wasn't lying about that much, at least. He went in, held the door for her, then closed it quietly behind them. He had the decency to hurry past her and stand a good distance away on the far side of the room. Rose had the feeling that perhaps this guy lived his life constantly aware of his size and how just being himself maybe intimidated people. A wave of sorrow passed over her for that, but she remained nervous. Was she foolish for letting him shut her away in a room like this? Her body was wound tight, muscles tensed ready to fight or run again if she had to.

The room was like a large supply closet, with steel shelving holding all kinds of cleaning chemicals, rolls of toilet paper, hand towels, and more along two of the walls. A rack of mops and brooms filled one corner, and tiny scratched and battered desk was shoved into another corner. Beside the desk was a set of three tall metal lockers, like the kind that might be found in a gymnasium. It was dim inside, one low wattage bulb bare in a cage of wire fixed into the cement ceiling. The big man leaned against his desk.

"I'm sorry for scaring you."

"It's okay. I'm Rose, by the way."

"My name is Derek."

"And what do you know about Jazz, Derek?"

He took a long breath, then looked down at the cold cement floor. "Jazz was my friend." He stopped there and his shoulders moved in a way that made Rose think perhaps he was crying, or at least suppressing tears. She wanted to hug him, but wasn't feeling safe enough for that yet.

"She was my friend too," Rose said quietly. "And we're both going to miss her fiercely."

Derek nodded without looking up. "She was always real nice to me. She treated me like a colleague, not like some slave or something. Or worse, like I wasn't even there. Most folks act like I'm invisible, or as if they're embarrassed to notice me. But not Jazz, no way. She always had a smile and took time to have a chat."

"She was a good person."

Derek nodded again. "Anyway, I heard you talking to her boss, and I thought maybe you'd be interested in what I know about her. You see, I know Jazz was researching witch covens, but I don't think she'd told anyone else. She used to chat to me about stuff she wouldn't tell other people. She said I was good for bouncing ideas off of."

"Witch covens? Really?" Rose felt as though this small piece of information was important, that it carried weight. She had been learning about the possibility of witchcraft herself, after all, and how it might be related to the experiments, to the bodies under Washington Square Park. But why was Jazz looking into witches? Did it have anything to do with the bodies they'd found? Or with Price?

"Yep," Derek said. "Witch covens. And the night she died, she was supposed to visit one. But I don't know if she did."

Rose was momentarily lost for words as she processed the information, wondering how it might be relevant to anything. The lab under the Bannerman Castle maybe? Would a coven meet there? Some people had said those experiments were somehow connected to witchcraft back in the day, but could that be ongoing? It seemed a little far-fetched, but she had recently learned that far-fetched things were rarer than a person might think.

"This all just seems so..." She wasn't certain how to finish the sentence.

Derek turned to his desk and pulled open its single small drawer. "This might be helpful," he said. He moved closer and held something out at arm's length.

Rose stepped forward to take it and saw it was a phone message pad. As she opened her mouth to thank him, there was a sudden sharp knocking at the door.

"Derek, you in there?"

Rose and Derek exchanged a surprised look, both clearly recognizing LaGuerta's voice. "What's she doing down here?" Rose whispered.

"I don't know! I have more to tell you. Hide somewhere while I talk to her."

Rose paused for a moment, wondering where in the small space she could possibly hide, then saw the lockers. She could maybe squeeze into one. Derek opened the door and slipped out as Rose quickly moved to the locker and opened it. The inside of the door was plastered with dozens of pictures, all of them various shots of Jazz.

Rose gasped, quickly put a palm over her mouth to stifle any noise she might make. The weirdness level, which had been easing, ratcheted right back up again. She moved cautiously back to the door and listened, and heard the voices of Derek and LaGuerta moving away. She'd had enough, and while the big man might have more to tell her, she felt all her trust had evaporated the moment she saw his freaky picture gallery. She slipped out and headed back to the stairs, desperate for the fresh air of the street.

CHAPTER 26

As the stranger's gun boomed, Crowley was already moving. He dived over the tied man he had been interrogating, snatching up the bedside lamp as he moved. He'd cut the cord off to tie up Jerkwad, and now the lamp was easily thrown. He twisted and launched it through the window above the bed, shattering glass raining over the fire escape and no small amount all over the bedclothes. He knew the shooter would be tracking him, so the moment he had let go of the lamp, he flipped back over, enjoying the crack of his knee into the tied man's cheek as he went, an unexpected bonus. The gun boomed again and the carpet where Crowley had been burst upward. Crowley grabbed the laundry basket as he went over and swung it hard at arm's length directly as the shooter. The basket itself tipped over and a shower of clothes filled the air between him and his assailant. The man grunted more in annoyance than anything else, but he was momentarily blocked and blinded.

Crowley was unlikely to have any more luck when it came to not getting shot, but that moment of distraction was all he needed. He stamped onto Jerkwad's lap, savoring the man's grunt of pain, and launched himself up over the bed and through the window, landing in a forward roll on the fire escape outside. He huffed air out as the hard metal impacted him, praying he didn't get any bad cuts from the broken glass, but didn't pause. He twisted and slid on his side down the first few steps as another bullet *spanged!* into the metal railing behind where he'd been a moment before. The guy was a good shot, but a target moving as erratically as Crowley was hard to hit. But his good fortune wouldn't last for long.

"Get him, Blackwell!" he heard Jerkwad yell, then he bolted.

As Crowley swung around the narrow black metal steps he heard the shooter land on them outside Jazz's window. Hunched against potential shots, he held onto the central railing and leaped down the stairs three at a time, then jump over onto the next landing every time he was close enough. The clang of shoes on metal above told him Blackwell was close behind. And he assumed Jerkwad would cut himself free before too long and make chase as well. He needed to get away, he would lose a fight if even one of them caught up. Only the element of surprise had kept him alive this long, and that never lasted long.

Crowley didn't have time to lower the ladder at the end of the fire escape, so simply dropped off the last landing, caught the edge with both hands for a second to slow his fall, then let go. He hit a dank alleyway floor with considerable impact, grunting as his knees sank and absorbed the shock. He let the momentum continue, ducking forward and tucking one shoulder, chin to his chest, and rolled before his legs snapped. Then he was up and running. He zigged and zagged as he went and two more bullets chipped up pavement with inches of his feet, but he managed to avoid getting shot and ducked out of the alley into a busy street. Surely they wouldn't shoot blindly into crowds of pedestrians.

He didn't pause to think about where he was or where to go. He knew Blackwell would be on auto-pilot, intent only on running him down, so he simply sprinted along the sidewalk, ducking left and right around surprised people.

Shouts of "Hey, slow down!" and "Where's the fire, buddy?" and the like followed him. He risked a glance back and saw the crowded footpath separating like water around a rock, faces wide with shock, as Blackwell came charging through, gun held up in plain sight. He wasn't shooting, but he was making no secret of his intent either.

The man was fast, and while he might not shoot through these crowds, he clearly wasn't worried about being seen and obviously had no intention of giving up. And the man was plainly athletic enough to not only keep up, but actually gain on Crowley. He was tall and thin rather than bulky, but with a wiry strength apparent even through his tailored suit. And a long stride, despite the crowds. He had close-cropped dark hair, a narrow face with dark eyes a little too close together, and a look of steely determination. Crowley was briefly reminded of the T1000 in *Terminator 2* as Blackwell pumped his arms in resolved pursuit.

All this Crowley took in during the half-second that he spent looking back, then he focused on nothing but flight. He ducked sideways down the next street, and almost immediately into the front doors of a large department store. He ran between displays of dresses and silk blouses, vibrant colors all around as his shoes squeaked on the polished marble floors. He'd barely made it twenty paces inside before he heard shouts and screams that must be in response to Blackwell barreling in behind, gun in hand. Damn, the man was relentless.

Crowley ran to the left around a sales counter, then immediately dropped to the ground. A shocked woman looked over at him, and Crowley winked. Blackwell was barely ten paces behind and as the tall man leaned into the corner in pursuit, Crowley was there, crouched low. He shot out a leg and took Blackwell's feet from under him. The tall man was immediately airborne, mouth falling open in surprise for one stretched moment of hang-time in mid-air, then he hit the hard floor with a slap and slid along, crashing into a display rack of light cotton jackets that came down over him like a collapsing tent.

Crowley was about make good on the surprise attack and hammer the guy before he could regain his focus, but a pair of store security guards came running in from the other side, yelling and demanding to know what was happening. Cursing, Crowley leaped up and ran back the way he'd come. He couldn't afford to be detained, he needed escape more than answers.

As he ducked through the doors again, out onto the street, he heard a shot and screams. Something told him it was Blackwell who had fired. Hopefully, only a warning shot to get moving again, but that meant he would be back in pursuit.

Sucking in a frustrated breath, Crowley tipped his head and sprinted again. More screams sounded behind him and he glanced back to see Blackwell emerge from the department store, gun leveled and braced in both hands, arms extended straight. Everyone on the street between Blackwell and Crowley dropped as if in practiced synchronization, and Blackwell fired.

Crowley ducked to one side and heard the whine of the bullet as it screamed past his left ear. The fool had resorted to shooting in public. This had got about as bad as it could.

"That was too close!" Crowley yelled to no one in particular, then hurtled down stone steps into a subway station. He had no idea if it was a wise choice or not, but he could only hope the subway would be more crowded than the street, and prevent Blackwell from getting off any more shots. The man couldn't shoot everyone.

He reached the bottom of the steps, jumped a turnstile, ignoring shocked faces all around him, and ran along the first platform he came to. Muffled shouts and screams echoed down the stairs, indicating Blackwell not far behind. Deciding to take his chances with the dark and machinery over the relentless gunman, Crowley leaped down beside the tracks and sprinted in the tunnel.

Shouts of "Hey, are you crazy?" and "What are you on?" followed him into the gloom, and then he just kept running.

A rumbling began in the distance and air started to rush past him, pushed along by an oncoming train. "Great timing, Jake!" he berated himself, and increased his speed, looking for anywhere to hide. A bright light not far away began to swell around a long bend, glistening off the curved wall of dirty bricks. It got brighter and brighter, the rumbling becoming a hard vibration, the wind a gale.

The train was like a dragon swooping down to swallow him, then the driver must have seen him as brakes began to screech and a horn blared loud enough to make his ears numb. Then an archway of blackness on his right was highlighted by the train's headlight and Crowley dove into it.

He wasn't sure what he expected to find in there, but he had imagined it would be a small space. Instead, as the train barreled past in noise and dust and wind, Crowley went head over heels down a narrow flight of steps. He barked out cries of pain as his shoulder, then his knee, cracked painfully into the edges of the stairs, but it was far better than being flattened by a train or shot by Blackwell.

After the train had passed, Crowley lay at the foot of the short stairway, breathing hard and gritting his teeth against a variety of aches and pains. The timing of the train might have been a blessing, it would have stopped Blackwell from following him into the tunnel, at least for a short time. But he couldn't go back that way and had no idea how far it might be to the next station. He didn't want to risk playing chicken with another train.

He pulled himself to his feet and felt around in the darkness. He had finished falling in a small brick area at the foot of the steps and a wooden door was closed right in front of him. He didn't want to risk discovery by making light, so he felt around, hoping for a handle. He found a strip of cold metal and, not expecting much, pushed it down. To his pleasant surprise, the door opened.

"Finally something going my way," he muttered, and stepped through.

Once he'd closed the door behind him, he fumbled out his cell phone and used the camera flash as a flashlight to see where he was. An arched brick passageway stretched away from him. It was that or go back the way he'd come, so he set off. Hopefully, Blackwell would never find him down here, so Crowley decided to see if there as another way out and, if not, retrace his steps hoping Blackwell would have given up and gone by the time he got back.

At the end of the short passage he came to a T-junction and looked both ways. No particular features drew his attention to either side, so he went left. He'd walked about fifty paces, wondering where he might find himself if he stayed underground for too long, when he heard a sound behind him and stopped. The sound continued a fraction of a second longer, then stopped too. There was a moment of light scraping and shuffling, the sensation of soft breathing. Over his own labored breath and hammering heart it was hard to tell what it might be, but images of Blackwell standing right behind him, gun raised, flashed through Crowley's mind. But He had nowhere to go and sprinting away seemed foolish.

Slowly, he turned around, lifting his phone up to shine it back the way he'd come. In the passage were five or six people, grimy faces and dirty, tattered clothes in several bulky layers, eyes squinting tightly against the harshness of his light. They were all armed in one way or another, holding knives, lengths of pipe, home-made shivs. They held the weapons out in front of them and their faces were hard and mean. As one, they moved forward.

CHAPTER 27

Rose tried again to call Crowley, but again his phone went directly to voicemail. That meant it was either switched off or out of a service area. She couldn't imagine anywhere in New York that didn't have cell phone service, so why would his phone be turned off? Unless he was in the subway, she supposed. Maybe underground he couldn't get a signal. But it had been a long time and she was beginning to worry.

Then again, Crowley had proven time and again that he was resilient and resourceful, so she decided to defer her worry for the time being. She did have one thing to distract herself with in the meantime. The woman from the Poe house had said the journal they had seen was on temporary loan to the Grolier Club. That was something she could investigate.

She looked the place up and it was quite something, with a rich history. According to the Club's website, it was founded in 1884 and was America's oldest and largest society for bibliophiles and enthusiasts in the graphic arts.

Rose smiled. She liked it already. Named for Jean Grolier, who had died in 1565, and was a Renaissance collector renowned for sharing his library with friends. The Club's objective was apparently to promote "the study, collecting, and appreciation of books and works on paper." She was surprised she hadn't heard of it before.

It had quite some reach, with an international network of over eight hundred men and women involved in a wide variety of bookish pursuits. Not only book and print collectors, but antiquarian book dealers, librarians, designers, fine printers, binders, and other artisans. The Grolier Club reportedly pursued its mission through its library, its public exhibitions and lectures, and its long and distinguished series of publications.

If she and Jake had learned so easily that the journal was on display there, then surely Price would have as well. And Rose thought maybe it was worth checking the place out sooner rather than later. No doubt Price would be snooping around it too. If he wanted that journal badly enough to break into the Poe house for it, he would surely have no qualms about breaking into the Grolier Club either. She decided head over to East 60th Street and have a look around. By then, Crowley would surely have got back in touch and they could plan their next move. Whatever that move might be, she wanted it to be before Price's attempt to get the journal.

It didn't take long to get across the city and Rose found herself standing under wide black scaffolding outside an old building. The building itself had a gray stone base and then pale red bricks above with tall arched windows evenly spaced. The entrance was a black double door under a carved stone archway nestled under the edges of the heavy scaffolding. There was obviously some major work going on in the surrounding buildings, though she couldn't be sure exactly what it was. It seemed to be mostly concentrated a couple of addresses down, but the scaffolding extended all the way along this side of the block. She wasn't sure if that would be a help or a hindrance to someone attempting a break-in.

She tried the doors and they were locked, with no apparent bell or intercom. They were heavy, almost medieval looking, and had no feature at all to invite someone in. She wondered if they were even used any more, or was this simply an old entry left for aesthetic purposes?

Rose frowned, looked around herself in frustration. The Club was built right behind Christ Church on Park Avenue, so Rose walked around to the other side. The church itself was only three or four stories high, dwarfed by the surrounding towers. It had a row of arched stained glass above its red wood door, then a rose window above that, surmounted by a smaller story and more narrow arches. Rose walked a little along Park Avenue, past the front of the church, and found a small area set back from the main sidewalk right beside it. She went in for a look and found a side entrance to the church and another entrance to the Grolier Club. This one had a more inviting double wooden door, far less obstructive in appearance, up a small flight of three stone steps with an access ramp laid over them. But these doors were also locked, and again no bell or obvious means of entry or attracting attention.

An exclusive club, Rose thought. Perhaps they only opened their doors and accepted any visitors when something particular was happening. They clearly weren't interested in casual visits today. Rose stood for a moment, chewing softly at her lower lip. She really wanted to have a look around, especially at the journal on loan from the Poe house. In truth, she badly wanted to steal it herself, hold it against Price's desires. But it seemed she would have to wait. She'd come back with Crowley later, maybe do more research on the Club's opening hours first. *Where are you, Jake?* she thought to herself, worry gnawing deeper all the time. She wished he'd call. Meanwhile, she wanted a coffee.

She went back around to East 60th Street and headed west, remembering from her earlier perusal of a map that Central Park was only two blocks that way. She crossed Madison Avenue and saw greenery at the end of the next block, marking the start of the Park. Across the road was a restaurant called Avra, with tables on the sidewalk covered with bright white cloths. The place looked a little fancy, but it wasn't busy and she figured she'd be able to sit quietly and enjoy a coffee there even if she might have to pay double the going rate.

While she waited for her order, enjoying the comfort and the pleasant aspect towards the trees, Rose got online and started searching the recent names and numbers on Jazz's message pad that Derek had given her. She still felt quite discomfited by her run-in with Derek the janitor, unsure what to make of his obsession with Jazz. The man was clearly not entirely balanced, perhaps his love of Jazz, while obviously unrequited, was harmless enough. But on seeing those photos, Rose's first and only instinct had been to get away, and she had long since learned to trust those instincts. But he had said he had more to tell her. What might that have been? Whatever else she had missed out on this time, she was genuinely grateful for the pad he'd given her.

A waiter brought her coffee, put it down with a smile, breaking her reverie.

"Thank you!" she said.

He nodded, smiled, but said nothing and slipped quietly away. Rose returned her attention to her phone and her searches. The first name she tried came up with connections to an accounting firm, and it didn't take a great deal of digging to find a connection between it and Matthew Price. Rose sat and stared, her heart rate a little elevated. Was this something, or coincidence? Of course, that one detail alone didn't mean anything in particular. Big firms had many clients. But Jazz had been looking into Price and perhaps this accountant was a link Rose needed to follow up. She made a note and carried on searching.

The next two numbers were each listed with two names,

with the same surname. Married couples presumably, or siblings perhaps. The former seemed more likely. Rose did more searching, thinking on all the things Jazz had been looking into. By the time she'd finished her coffee, she had learned that both couples were the parents of missing persons. Again, it had the ring of relevance to it, but she couldn't put her finger on what, exactly. Or why. She felt as though she were looking into murky water, trying to see something in its depths. But every time she spotted something and reached for it, she only muddied the water more and lost what she might have seen.

Frustrated, she checked every message going back to the date she and Jake had met up with Jazz at the site of the mass burial in Washington Square Park. Nothing else was pertinent, nothing triggered that sense of connection.

Disappointed, she dropped the pad to the table and was about to get up when she saw a couple of little tags of paper caught in the spiral binding. Looking closer, she realized a page had been torn out. The most recent one, after all the messages she'd already checked. She scrabbled in her bag and came up with a pencil. Feeling like James Bond in an old movie, she turned to the following page and did the pencil rubbing trick, brushing the side of the pencil lead lightly over the page to highlight the dents from whatever had been written above.

The first line of whatever had been written there was illegible, but beneath that Rose clearly made out a phone number. Below the number, a word had been written in block letters: REVENANT.

"Anything else, madam?"

Rose jumped, then smiled, looking up at the waiter. "No, thank you. Although… My cell phone doesn't work here. I'm from England."

"Yes, I noticed your accent."

"I really should sort out the roaming or something, but I haven't got around to it yet and I need to contact my friend. Is there a phone here I can use. It's a local call and will only take a moment. I'd be happy to pay, of course."

The waiter raised an eyebrow and Rose switched on her best one thousand watt smile, dipped her head a little coyly. "I know it's cheeky to ask," she said, emphasizing the English accent. She'd heard some Americans found it alluring.

The waiter softened, smiled a little crookedly. "There's a landline on the counter inside. If you're quick."

"Thank you so much, you're a life-saver!"

Rose paid for her coffee then picked up the landline the waiter offered and dialed the number she'd revealed. It rang three times, then someone picked up. Rose braced herself to respond carefully to what might be said, trying to think of something nondescript to start a conversation, but the line remained silent. She waited a moment more, wondering if the line were dead, but she heard a soft, relaxed breathing at the other end.

Not knowing what else to do, she said quietly, "Revenant."

After a moment, a deep man's voice replied. "Tonight. Midnight. The park. Behind Jacob's Witch."

CHAPTER 28

Crowley stood ready to fight, wondering if he could outrun the half a dozen rough-looking people blocking the way back. In truth, he was getting a little tired of running away from people.

The group paused. One man took a step forward. He was thin, baggy clothes hanging off his wiry frame. He had dark skin, smudged with dirt, but his eyes were bright, narrowed. "You okay, man?" he asked.

Crowley frowned. "I'm not sure. Am I?"

A woman stepped up next to the man who had spoken, brown hair matted and ratty, but her eyes as bright as his. "What's a British fellow doing running around down here?"

"I'm Clyde, this is Sarah," the first man said. "You in trouble?"

"My name is Jake. And yeah, I was in a spot of bother, but I think I outran it."

There was murmuring among the group and then Clyde turned back to Crowley. "There's been some sketchy looking characters down here." He flashed a self-deprecating grin. "Some of ours have disappeared. More than usual, I mean. We're kinda on the defensive." He slipped his knife away in one oversized pocket of his coat and the others lowered their weapons.

"S'why we don't go near the tunnels under Bellevue anymore," said one man at the back.

"The hospital?" Crowley asked. "There are tunnels under there?"

"Anyhow," Clyde said, deliberately interrupting. "You say you outran your trouble?"

Crowley decided to log that mention of Bellevue for later consideration. He hadn't considered before what might lurk under the old hospital. "Who are you people? I mean, are you a group or something?" he asked instead.

"Topsiders call us mole people, because we live underground."

Crowley looked around, wondering where to find the best way out. But curiosity burned. "You said some of yours had gone missing?"

Clyde turned to the others behind him and there was more whispered conversation, then they headed off back down the passage. Only Clyde and Sarah remained. "Want us to lead you back topside? We can talk on the way."

"Sure, thanks."

Clyde moved to walked alongside Crowley, with Sarah falling into step beside him. "We lose people for lots of reason," he said. "But lately it's been a lot more than usual. It's got us on edge."

"Understandable. What do you mean by lately?"

"The last year or so. Usually it's drugs, booze, jail or..." He drew a finger across his throat. "A few just go. But then a bunch started disappearing. We had to find out where they were going."

"So where did they go?"

Clyde flashed Crowley a dark look. "Dead. Murdered."

"By whom?"

"The Revenant."

Crowley's heart pulsed an extra beat. His conversation earlier with Jerkwad on the floor of Jazz's apartment came back in technicolor. The man talking about his boss. Snatches of conversation echoed in Crowley's mind.

I ain't ever met him in person, never seen his face... He calls himself the Witchfinder...

But these underlings, they're sycophants, you know, they creep and scrape around.

But they don't show much respect... they secretly call him the Revenant.

"You okay, man?" Clyde asked. "You look like you saw a ghost."

"The Revenant?" Crowley asked. "That's what he's called?"

"Yep."

"And he's real? Not just an urban legend or something?"

"Oh yeah," Clyde said. "He's real."

"Too real," Sarah added.

"So who is he?"

""No one really knows who or what he is," Clyde said.

"But we hear stuff," Sarah said. "We hide, we listen. We talk to each other."

Clyde sighed, nodded softly, and dropped back a little to let Sarah speak.

She licked her lips, then said, "They say he's some sort of vampire or soul-sucker. Not like monsters from the old movies.

He's the real thing. And he's old, been coming and going since New York was called…" She scratched her chin.

"New Amsterdam?" Crowley prompted, the school teacher in him unable to resist.

Sarah nodded eagerly. "Every time he comes back, the dying starts again. They say he wants revenge for his lost love."

"That's not the reason," Clyde said.

"Is he a serial killer?"

"More like an evil sorcerer," Clyde said. "Or a mad scientist. He wants to be immortal. That's what this is all about."

"Can anyone describe him?"

Sarah shook her head. "Clyde follows him some times and spies."

"From a long way away, and he keeps his face covered. If I went topside I could pass him by in the street and never know it. And that would be fine with me."

Crowley's mind whirred. Surely this was all urban myth, it rang like a campfire tale. He tried to think of anything that might connect Jazz to the Revenant, why the man's cronies were at the reporter's apartment. He didn't really believe all the stuff Sarah had told him, but there were always seeds of truth in legends, even those of the modern urban variety. There had to be some connection. Two things Jazz had been investigating were Matthew Price and the bodies in the crypt under Washington Square Park. An unexpected piece dropped into place, but Crowley wasn't certain if it actually fit or if he was clutching at straws. Clyde had said the disappearances started about a year ago. Wasn't that when Price said he'd come back to New York from travelling around the country?

Every time he comes back, the dying starts again.

Crowley shook his head. He couldn't write it off, but it was also easy for confirmation bias to put things together when they didn't actually mesh. He decided to file that possibility away for later. But he was beginning to think that perhaps Rose had been right all along. So what about the crypt? Lots of bodies, some of them very fresh, several others less than a year old, maybe.

"You guys live underground," he said. "Do any of these passageways connect to old crypts? Washington Square Park for example.""

"Haven't heard about that one," Clyde said. "But could be. A lot of times, topsiders dig down to the underground by mistake. Other times something opens up on its own, like a crack in the old rock finally busts open."

On a hunch, Crowley pulled out the scrap of paper he'd found at Jazz's apartment. "Tell me if you recognize any of these people," he said, reading by the light of his phone.

They didn't react to the first couple of names, but when Crowley read out 'Ricky Gallagher', both Clyde and Sarah said, "Ricky!"

"You know him?"

"Ricky was a good kid," Clyde said. He really wanted to get clean. Tried hard. He lived down here a year ago, maybe more. One day he just disappeared like most do. We figured he was dead or in jail. But then he showed up about four months ago."

Crowley drew a deep breath. The coincidence was too much to ignore. "You remember the name of the company?"

Clyde shook his head. "I don't, sorry."

"Sale something?" Sarah offered.

"SaleMed?" Crowley asked, remembering the name of Price's company.

"That was it!" they both said together.

"How did you know that?" Clyde asked.

"Let's just say you guys are joining some dots for me."

"Is that why you were running for your life and ended up down here?" Clyde asked.

"Yes, my friend, I believe it does. Can you remember anything else about the Revenant? No matter how far-fetched or insignificant it might seem."

"I reckon Sarah told you all of it," Clyde said.

"There's one thing." Sarah scratched her head, the lines of her brow furrowed. "Some say his brother stole something from him and he's trying to get it back. He can't be immortal until he does."

That sounded like fairy tale nonsense but Crowley nodded in thanks. "Fair enough. So any idea where I can find Ricky."

"Maybe he's working at that SaleMed place," Clyde said. "But last we saw him, a few weeks ago, he was going to a meeting. I don't know where, but if you like we can show you where Ricky went back topside."

"Okay, that would be great."

Crowley thought maybe he needed to check out SaleMed in more detail. And he owed Rose an apology too. He didn't expect to find Ricky Gallagher working happily in his new job. If anything, he suspected he'd already met the poor lad briefly, the top-most corpse of that pile under Washington Square Park. But the more he could learn about him, the better he might be armed with information.

It didn't take too long going through a bewildering series of old passages before Clyde stopped and said, "This is the place." He pointed up to a rusty set of iron rungs buried in the bricks that led up to a maintenance cover similar to the one above the Washington Square Park crypt. "You can head up there, but be cautious when you open it up. Make sure no one's around, they tend to freak out, you know? Or you might trip someone."

"Okay, I'll be careful. And thank you, I really appreciate your help."

"Our pleasure. Best of luck to you."

Clyde smiled and Sarah dipped her head briefly in farewell, then the two of them slipped away and were quickly swallowed by the darkness. Crowley marveled at their life, their intricate knowledge of these underground passageways and their ability to navigate them in the blackness. His phone was quickly losing charge where he'd been using it as a flashlight and he couldn't wait to get back above ground.

He climbed the ladder and carefully lifted one edge of the maintenance cover. He looked out and his eyebrows shot up in surprise. "Bloody hell!"

CHAPTER 29

Crowley laughed to himself, staring at the ostentatious gold marquee that read TRUMP TOWER. Of all the places in New York to emerge. Then he saw a heavily-armed security guard staring at him with wide eyes and Crowley's amusement fled. The guard started toward him.

Well, he was seen, so he might as well own it and make like he had every right to be there. He pushed the cover the rest of the way aside and climbed out, then turned and put the cover back in place. As he stood up straight again, the security guard was right beside him. Assault rifle held level with Crowley's gut, casual but threatening.

"What the hell are you doing?" the guard asked.

Crowley put on his best smile. "Well, I was lost, but now, as they say in the old hymn, I am found."

"Spend a lot of time in the sewers do you?"

It hadn't been the sewer, but the man's words gave Crowley the excuse he needed. He'd noticed a van earlier that day, and the name emblazoned on the side had entertained him. He used it now. "As a matter of fact, yes. I work for the Bureau of Water and Sewer Operations. I was inspecting a system down there and got turned around, lost the way I'd come down. Now, of course, I can see exactly where I am. I should be one block that way." Crowley pointed back over his shoulder and started taking a few steps backwards. "Have a good day now!"

He turned and strode off, his back itching at the thought of the security guard's weapon trained on him. But there was no challenging shout and Crowley kept walking then quickly turned the corner. It seemed he had bemused the man enough to slip away. Now he needed to call Rose.

"Where the hell have you been?" Rose's voice was exasperated, but her relief was also evident. "I've been trying to reach you for hours."

"Sorry about that. It's a long story and I'll fill you in when we catch up. Where are you?"

"I'm in a café not far from Central Park. And I've got news for you too."

They met on the corner of Park Avenue and East 60th

Street, outside the Christ Church, only a couple of blocks from where Crowley had emerged from underground. They hugged, Rose's tight grip betraying her concerns. He was saddened he'd caused her such worry.

"This way," Rose said, and led Crowley around to a pair of dark double doors.

"Before you tell me why we're here," Crowley said. "I just wanted to say, I think you're right about Price."

She gave him a look and he weathered it, knowing it was one he thoroughly deserved. "I know," she said.

"I should have listened to you."

"You should." She stared hard at him for a moment, then her face softened. "Thank you." She leaned forward and they kissed, Crowley savoring the immediate thaw in her.

"That's the Grolier Club," Rose said, pulling away and pointing at the doors. "It's locked up tight right now, but it's relevant. Let's take a walk and compare notes."

They headed down East 60th and into the southern end of Central Park, enjoying the greenery and birdsong. Crowley marveled that such a place could exist in a city as dense and packed as New York. They strolled along East Drive, past Central Park Zoo, then turned left and walked past the Carousel. As they went, they related their respective stories, and all they had learned.

Once the tales were told, they walked on in companionable silence for a while, both digesting the news. After a moment, Crowley said, "Hang on, I need to make a call. Check on Gertie."

His aunt answered after only a couple of rings, sounding in good spirits. "How are you doing?" Crowley asked.

"I'm well. Are you two lovebirds enjoying the city?"

"We're having quite a time, I'll tell you that." Crowley remembered running for his life, bullets flying behind him, and suppressed a smile.

"Well, that's wonderful, dear. When are you going to come and see me again? Shall we have dinner tonight?"

Crowley looked at Rose. "Dinner with Gertie tonight?"

"Sure." She smiled. "But not too late, yeah? An early dinner and early to bed?"

Crowley turned back to the phone. "Sure thing, Auntie, we'll come over about five? We don't want to be out too late tonight."

"Wonderful, I'll see you then?"

"Will Pr... Matthew be there?" Crowley asked before she could hang up.

"I'm not sure. He's been a little absent the past couple of days, actually. Caught up in a lot of work stuff, apparently. I'll be sure to let him know you're coming, but I don't think he'll make it. When he gets into these work things, it usually occupies him totally for however long it takes."

I'll bet, Crowley thought to himself, but was relieved to hear Price probably wouldn't be around. "Okay, well we can see him again later. It'll be nice to have just the three of us together."

They found a bench and sat down to investigate the phone Crowley had taken from Jerkwad. He'd switched it to flight mode, partly to preserve the battery and partly in paranoia against it being traced. All the emails on it were cursory, no details of anything specific or helpful. The one number it had been used for was unlisted, but Crowley had no doubt who was at the other end. Everything added up too neatly.

"So Price is the guy they call the Revenant," he said quietly, shaking his head. "This is all a little frightening."

"Do you think it's possible that he really is... immortal? Ish?" Rose asked. "Remember the photo I found in that book on witchcraft?"

Crowley scoffed, shook his head. "Come on, that's impossible."

Rose's eyebrows shot up. She held up one hand and began counting off on her fingers. "The blood eagle, the hammer, the Anubis key–"

"Okay, okay, point taken. You're right. There's weird stuff in this world, but really? My aunt's boyfriend is an immortal witch?"

"I have more." Rose took out her phone and tapped up the photo gallery. "This guy here is the doctor who conducted the Bellevue experiments."

Crowley pursed his lips. It was undeniable. The man was a dead-ringer for Price.

Rose swiped across to the next photo. "And this one is of Francis Bannerman, a few years before he began construction on the castle."

"He looks a little bit like Price," Crowley said. "But that's not him."

"Shut your hole," Rose snapped. "You know better. Don't

be so obstructive. This is Bannerman on the day they broke ground." She swiped across to the next photograph, a much less grainy and aged image. It was undeniably Price. Not someone similar, maybe related. It could only be Matthew Price himself.

"I think that from now on, just to be on the safe side, we ought to assume everything is true," Rose said. "Price is the Revenant. He's been alive for at least a few centuries, and whatever he's doing to keep alive involves killing people. He uses the underground tunnels of New York City to transport the bodies unseen when he's here. Who knows what else he does when he travels elsewhere."

"And the vault uncovered in Washington Square Park was one of his hiding places," Crowley said.

Rose nodded, chewing one side of her lower lip. "I think Jazz died because she was looking into it and looking into Price himself. We have to be very careful. Especially as it looks like he's on the verge of becoming truly immortal."

"I wonder what his secret is," Crowley said. "What his formula involves, why he has to kill people to get it."

"Whatever it is, its effectiveness must be limited, thus the regular killings. The frequency of them. Look at all the bodies in that crypt under Washington Square Park. The two on top were fresh, but the stack of them went back several years. How many, do you think? Two killings a year? More? And what about elsewhere, outside New York?"

"The cost is high, obviously," Crowley agreed.

"He said he just moved back to New York," Rose said. "I'll bet he has to move around a lot if he's regularly killing people."

"And traveling for his business is a good excuse." Crowley paused, then admitted the thing that had been on his mind for some time. "I think Poe's *Masque Journal* must be the thing Price is looking for. The second half of the immortality formula must be in that book. I don't know why, but why else would it be the one thing he wants more than anything else? And I told him all about it. He might have gone on searching for weeks or months otherwise, but I think I've accelerated everything quite considerably."

"That's not really your fault," Rose said, putting a hand on his knee. "Then again, if you'd trusted me when I said we shouldn't trust Price, you wouldn't have been cozying up to him so much and you wouldn't have had the chance to spill the beans."

Crowley glanced up sharply, cut a little by the accusation. Probably because it was accurate. But Rose was smiling softly. He smiled too. "You're right."

"But I meant it when I said it's not really your fault," Rose said, and gave him a soft kiss on the cheek.

"But I do need to fix it," Crowley said. "He'll know it's at the Grolier Club now. Of course, security is tight there, as you found out."

"Price might be tempted to wait until it's returned to the ghost house," Rose said. "After all, he's waited this long. It would be much easier to lift from there."

Crowley shook his head. "I doubt it. I can't see Price being that patient, can you? Not when he's is so close. And not if he's onto the fact that we're onto him."

"So what do we do?"

Crowley grinned. "Isn't it obvious? I'm going to steal it first."

CHAPTER 30

Crowley felt bad for once again refusing Rose's offer of help, but knew this mission was best tackled alone. He had spent the rest of the day researching and planning, then he and Rose left the hotel for dinner with Aunt Gertie a little after 4.30pm. They'd enjoyed a pleasant evening, taking the opportunity to talk about mundane things and pretend they weren't deep into investigating a potentially immortal witch. Some things, Crowley thought to himself, were best put on the back burner now and then so a soul could enjoy a good meal and a fine wine. But he had restricted himself to only a couple of glasses of wine, given his later plans. It was slightly awkward every time Gertie mentioned her boyfriend, but he and Rose had both done a good job of quickly diverting the conversation each time. He was comfortable his aunt hadn't noticed anything amiss.

Once dinner was finished, they had chatted until around ten and then excused themselves. Rose had been upset Crowley wouldn't take her along and tried again to convince him to let her join him on the mission, but he insisted he go alone. It would be hard enough for one person, he said. Sometimes more hands didn't make for lighter work. Besides, she needed the rest, he firmly believed that. So did he, for that matter, but the opportunity wasn't there for him. So reluctantly Rose had returned to the hotel while Crowley shouldered his small backpack and headed over to Park Avenue and East 60th Street, and the large stone Christ Church on the corner there.

His research had led him down a maze of city planning and blueprints. It was remarkable the kind of information a determined person could unearth, and he had discovered one fatal flaw in the Grolier Club's defenses. At least, he hoped it was a flaw. And just why the Grolier Club was so tightly secured was a mystery he chose not to dwell on too deeply. Maybe it was merely the value of its collections. There was a wealth of books in there, after all.

The flaw he'd discovered had to do with the Club's adjacency to the Christ Church. At nearly midnight, the street outside wasn't completely deserted, he assumed nowhere in New York ever was, but the sidewalk was mostly empty, and the shadows of the arched doorway afforded Crowley the concealment he needed for a few moments with his lock picks. He slipped inside the church and closed the door behind him. He paused for a moment, and there were no shouts from outside, no alarms flashing inside. Good. Stage one was a success. But it was also the easiest part.

The interior was ostentatious, even by church standards. A black and white checkerboard floor stretched away from him between wooden pews. The walls were mostly gold, the ceiling black tiled with gold grouting. Two large white-veined, black marble columns stood sentinel to either side. At the far end, a great domed arch stood tall, filled with murals. Crowley only paused a moment to take it all in, then moved quickly through the church and down the right-hand side. On the other side of the black marble column, he headed for a door. It was open, and he slipped through, a penlight flashlight piercing the darkness beyond.

The corridor ahead was narrow, and Crowley followed it, then slipped through a side door and up two narrow flights of stairs. "Come on, come on," he whispered to himself, gritting his teeth against a possible end to his mission right here. Then he saw a small wooden door in the side wall, about three feet square, and let out a suppressed, "Yes!" of triumph. The maintenance hatch hasn't been marked on any of the plans he'd studied, but he had bet it would be there, as there was no other access to the ducting otherwise.

He crouched at the door and set to work on the small padlock pinning the hasp closed. It only took a moment to pick that lock, and he was in, crawling through a service space behind the large, arched end of the church, and, if the blueprints he'd found were to be believed, above the Grolier Club itself.

As he moved further through the crawl space, a dim light began to illuminate the area ahead of him. He got closer and saw it was leaking up through the edges of ceiling tiles off to his left. This was it. Crowley carefully shifted himself into position and gently pried up the nearest tile. It was about two feet by three feet, old-fashioned pressed metal instead of the more modern particle board new buildings might have had. It was heavy and scraped across its mountings, the sound harshly loud in the silence. With it halfway off, Crowley paused, teeth gritted. There were no other sounds. He slid it the rest of the way, then leaned forward over the gantry he sat on to see. The light came from soft, concealed nightlights around the edges of the ceiling, a couple of feet below where he squatted as if suspended above the large room below. The wooden floor seemed an awfully long way away, and Crowley swallowed down a moment of vertigo. It would be an ignominious end to fall through a suspended ceiling and die on the floor of an exclusive book club.

There was a camera mounted in the corner, only a few feet from where he sat, that seemed to take in the whole room. Its fish-eye glass stared forward and down. He checked, and saw no other cameras in the large room and thanked his luck that his first attempt had put so near to it. He replaced the tile, shifted carefully back, and levered up the tile he estimated to be right above the camera. Dust drifted down in a soft rain, vanishing from sight as it fell. He paused a moment, but nothing more happened, no alarms triggered. Holding his breath, he lay on his stomach and leaned down to reach the camera.

Two wires went into the back of it, and Crowley reached forward, balanced precariously, and tugged at the nearest. It popped free of its socket, and Crowley let it lay almost but not quite connected. It was ample to ensure the signal was interrupted. With any luck, someone would put it down to a wandering rodent or something similar rather than deliberate sabotage. He only hoped no one was looking at a security screen at that moment, who may then come and investigate. Regardless, he needed to move fast, just in case.

From his backpack, Crowley pulled out a coiled length of knotted rope. It was thin, but incredibly tough nylon, designed for climbers. Lightweight but able to support a considerable load. He looped and fixed one end securely to a metal stanchion set into the stonework behind him and was about to drop the rest down when something caught his eye.

Set evenly around the walls, maybe ten feet apart, were small black boxes, each with a dark lens in the center. Frowning, Crowley dug in his backpack and found nothing to help. Cursing, he looked around. Then he smiled, remembering the soft rain when he had moved the tile. The rarely used maintenance space was very dusty. Gathering a small handful of fine dust, he sprinkled it through the hole in the ceiling and watched it tumble through the air, enough this time that he didn't lose sight of it. As it passed in line with the small black boxes, it sparkled red briefly. Lasers. This place was serious about security.

Crowley gathered more dust, blew it gently forward, and watched it fall. It took about ten minutes, which felt like ten hours as he expected a security guard to appear and look right up at him every moment, but he eventually had the crisscross pattern of security lasers figured out. He'd been forced to remove two more ceiling tiles in the process. Now he'd found a spot he could use to drop into a laser-free diamond area, then he could crawl below the lasers to get to where he needed to be. He replaced the other two tiles and re-tied his rope at his new chosen point of entry. He lowered the line with excruciating slowness, desperate that it did not swing and interrupt any beam of light. Once it was down, he lowered himself through the hole in the ceiling and painstakingly went hand under hand down to the floor. His arms were trembling with the effort by halfway down, going so slowly, but his strength would hold out. He knew his limits. Once his feet hit the wooden floor, he immediately dropped to his belly and crawled forward. From his vantage point high in the ceiling, he'd seen the cabinet he needed. At least, he hoped he had.

On the floor by the correct cabinet, he turned onto his back and mentally tracked all the small black eyes around the room and their invisible beams of light. Nodding once he'd chosen the space to stand up in, he slowly rose to his feet. No alarms. At least, none he could hear. Silent alarm systems were common, but he had to hope against that.

With his surgical gloves in place, and his face covered with a bandana in case he'd missed any cameras, he quickly went to work on the lock at the side of the glass display case. Now he was close enough to read the small cards placed next to the exhibits, he confirmed the small, black journal he'd seen from above was indeed the Poe journal on loan. His heart raced with excitement and nerves, but he forced himself to work slowly and calmly.

The small sliding lock took no real effort to open, and Crowley slid the glass front carefully aside. He reached in and took the journal, his hands trembling with tension. If he and Rose were right, he was holding all he needed to pin Matthew Price to the wall.

He slipped the book into his pocket and removed a small black book of similar design. It wasn't entirely a lookalike, but it wasn't bad. He'd found it in a book store not far from their hotel, roughed it up to make it appear aged, and smeared it with road gravel. Once he'd brushed that off again, he had been quite pleased with his handiwork. It looked interesting enough to put off the casual eye. Placing it on the small glass display stand now, it didn't look out of place at all. With a soft smile, he slid the glass door closed again and re-locked it.

Making sure he'd left nothing behind, he commando-crawled back to his hanging rope and climbed slowly hand over hand back up again. It was slow going, ensuring the end of the rope didn't swing back and forth with his motion, and his biceps were burning as he neared the top.

He crawled in through the gap where the ceiling tile had been removed and began to carefully bring the rope up, coiling it slowly over his arm. He was awash with relief when the end of it lifted above the level of the crossed lasers. Then a sharp beep made his heart stutter. He froze.

Nothing discernible had changed. What had beeped? Then the door at the end of the large room rattled. Crowley held his breath as the door opened slowly. A large man, his dark skin reflecting the nightlights softly, entered the room and looked around. He wore a navy blue security guard's uniform, with a black peaked cap bearing a logo Crowley couldn't quite make out. Tufts of gray hair curled out from the edges of it. The guard shone a flashlight left and right, lips pursed.

Crowley's rope hung in the air maybe ten feet off the ground. If the man's gaze rose even a little bit, he was sure to spot it. Then that gaze would rise up the rope to the hole in the ceiling and Crowley framed by it, wide-eyed and breath held. He was tempted to haul the rope quickly up, but surely the guard would see the movement. Or perhaps he could drop it and run, but then the guard would definitely see him, and they'd know there had been a break-in.

Like a rabbit in headlights, Crowley squatted, his legs cramping from the precarious position he held, his arms trembling from the climb and then being held so still, holding the rope out in front of him like he was fishing for something in the room below.

The guard swept his flashlight around the room once more. Then once more.

Crowley gritted his teeth. *Don't look up! Don't look up!*

Then the man turned and left, closing the door silently behind him. Crowley's relief was so complete that for a moment his vision crossed and he thought he might pass out and fall through the hole back to the hard wooden floor below. He sat back, legs muscles screaming, and quickly coiled up the rest of the rope. That was way too close for comfort. Heart racing faster than if he'd run a mile at a dead sprint, he replaced the ceiling tile and quickly retreated the way he'd come.

CHAPTER 31

Rose tried not to be too angry with Jake for not letting her come along to the Grolier Club. On the one hand, she understood how breaking and entering a place like that wasn't something you did with tourists tagging along. But she was capable and had got Crowley out of trouble on several occasions. She didn't like being sidelined. "It's just that it's really a one-person operation," Crowley had said.

Well, Rose thought that was bulldust, but she'd given in. Mainly because she knew there was something else she could be doing while Crowley was crawling around the Grolier Club like a ninja. The last number in Jazz's message pad had given her a lead. When she'd rung it, and on a whim had simply said, "Revenant," the concise reply she'd received was mysterious.

Tonight. Midnight. The park. Behind Jacob's Witch.

She'd had no idea what any of that meant. But while Crowley had been studying city plans for his great heist, Rose had been doing research of her own. She thought she had discovered what it meant when she came across the story of George Jacobs Sr, who had been hanged in Salem Village, Massachusetts, on August 19th, 1692, a victim of the infamous Salem Witch Trials. Among his accusers were his granddaughter, Margaret, who implicated him through an attempt he had made to save her life. His daughter-in-law also accused him, though she was thought to be mentally ill and suffering from a brain tumor. Others were said to have fits at his trial, caused by his witchcraft. Rose reflected on the collective madness that had infected that terrible time and thought the stain of it might never be washed away. But George Jacobs story was a dead end with regards to "the park."

So Rose searched using the only park she thought the message could mean, Central Park, and she discovered a stone carving of a witch that had been made in the 1800s by an architect called Jacob Wrey Mould. It was a strong possibility this was what the cryptic message had been referencing, though she had no idea how it might be of any use. Regardless, as Crowley had gone off adventuring without her, she intended to check it out all the same.

New York never slept, so the story went, and the streets were indeed far from deserted, but there was a weight of nighttime over Rose as she walked from the hotel to Central Park. Once she left the streets behind and moved into the much quieter green space, her senses were on alert. She watched everywhere, checked the shadows. It would be foolish to stumble into an assault or mugging while wandering around at nearly midnight as she was. Then again, let them try, She was a fighter, had beaten men bigger than her before and would again if necessary. But it was always better not to fight, so caution was the preferred course of action.

The Bethesda Terrace, leading to the Bethesda Fountain overlooking The Lake, was about dead center of the park between 5th Avenue and Central Park West, only a quarter of the way north from the park's southern boundary. The start of the terrace was on the road above, sandstone pillars and balustrades intricately carved in a variety of designs. A person could walk either side for a higher view, or take stone steps down through a gallery, with arches at either end, that passed under the wide roadway and led to the fountain at the lake's edge.

Rose searched and found that several of the square pillars had a bas relief design carved deep into them, each within a clover-shaped indentation. An owl on a branch with a bat flying behind, an open book lying atop a lectern, a sun rising over rocks and flowers, and then she found Jacob's witch. The design had the classic fairy tale witch astride a flying broomstick, a jack-o-lantern below her and a house, or maybe a stone church, in the background. It was an artistically rendered carving, somehow both cartoonish but also imbued with a weight of meaning. Or perhaps that was simply because it was late at night and Rose had been reading about witch trials.

Looking around to ensure no one was watching, Rose reached out and ran her fingers over the carving. She pushed and pulled, wondering if there was something beyond the mere sandstone that she might discover, but nothing happened. Frowning, she stepped back. Was she being foolish, wasting her time? Or maybe she just needed to wait here, and someone would come to her, but that option seemed fraught with danger. And the message had said *Behind Jacob's Witch*. But there was no behind really, it was a square pillar in the open.

The scuffle of footsteps, someone hurrying along, made her

nervous. "Come on, we're late!" a voice said urgently. Rose quickly ducked around the low stone wall and crouched in shadows across the bridge from the witch carving. Two young men jogged up to where she had just been standing, their faces concealed in the pulled-up hoods of sweatshirts. They didn't look around, and she was thankful for that. Her hiding place was rudimentary and wouldn't have passed even cursory scrutiny, but it sufficed for these young men in a hurry. One of them trotted straight up to the witch pillar and put his thumb against the carved jack-o-lantern half concealed by the witch's flapping cloak. He pressed hard, and the pumpkin sank back. With his other hand, he took hold of the witch and twisted anti-clockwise. There was a deep click, and the man stepped quickly back as the ground at his feet, right at the base of the pillar, sank two or three inches, and slid back. The two men hurried down the stone steps it revealed and disappeared into the darkness. Almost immediately, the stone trapdoor slid closed again.

Rose shook her head in wonder. Would she have figured it out? It didn't matter now, she knew she was onto something. More voices. This time Rose moved further away, chose a better hiding place, and waited. Two more people, a man and woman of early middle age, checked quickly around themselves to ensure they were alone, and then copied precisely what the two young men had done, and disappeared below the bridge.

Rose waited a few more minutes, but no one else came along. Maybe that was the last of them. The first two lads had said they were late, so perhaps anyone coming was already inside. Whatever inside was. Crowley would go in, she knew that. If she were with him, she'd most definitely go along. The question was, did she have the courage to go alone? Well, if Crowley would go, and he definitely would, Rose could summon the courage too. Hurrying over, before nerves got the better of her, she pressed the pumpkin, twisted the witch, and stepped back. The ground slid open. The steps led down a fair distance, disappearing into gloomy shadows. But orange light, flickering like flames, leaked up, so it wasn't pitch dark down there. Taking a deep breath, Rose started down, and the bridge closed over the top of her.

The steps led down to an arched tunnel, and she heard voices, a kind of monotone chanting. The passageway went along a short way, then grew brighter as it opened out. There were steps at the end leading down to a vast open space, brick walls, and an arched ceiling. Flaming brands stood on poles all around the edges of the walls. Above the brands, a narrow gallery, a kind of thin mezzanine, encircled half of the room, accessed from either side of the tunnel she stood in, instead of taking the steps down.

Rose moved as quietly as she could to one side of the gallery and squatted in the deep shadows there, watching between thick stone balusters. In a semi-circle around one side of the large room were a couple of dozen people, their voices providing the chanting, all wearing long masks that concealed their features completely. She spotted the two hooded lads among them.

Before them stood a raised dais, on it an altar covered in a black silk cloth. Atop the cloth were eight tall, thick black wax candles, burning brightly. A man in a heavy black robe, lined with red silk, stood at the altar, his arms raised as if accepting their worship. The hood of the robe was up, the man's face lost in shadow. The voices seemed to be speaking a form of corrupted Latin, but Rose couldn't quite pick out the phrases. Either way, this wasn't some pagan ritual or modern Wicca. This was black magic, surely. Modern Wicca was a fairly benign belief system, but this had the feel of something entirely more malevolent.

Then someone started screaming. The voices chanting rose suddenly over it, in volume and passion, the delivery fevered. A man was dragged out, shouting and hollering, his eyes wide in terror. The masked men holding him either side lifted him roughly and slammed him face down onto the altar, his scream ending sharply in a whoosh of air. He began babbling, shouting "No, no, no!" over and over as the two men held him down by pulling his arms out to either side and leaning their weight into them. A third masked man stepped up and leaned over the unfortunate man's thrashing legs, pinning him to the altar. His protestations continued.

The leader, his hood still up, moved around to the man's head and held up a large silver tool of some strange design. It looked like a hand drill, but with a broad, serrated bit. The chants of those who had congregated in this dark place increased pitch and fervor again. Rose clapped a hand over her mouth, eyes wide in horror. Surely this couldn't be happening. What could she do about it? Against this many people, she was impotent.

The high priest, or whatever he was, pressed one hand hard into the top of the prone victim's head, squashing his face into the altar. With the other hand, he placed the disturbing metal instrument just at the base of the man's skull and squeezed a trigger-like control. The toothed bit spun, and the man screamed, high and long, in pain and terror. Rose realized the priest was coring out a section of the man's skull. She felt dizzy with shock and disgust. The drill punched through, and the man's scream ended abruptly. Blood flooded from the hole. The chanting continued as the hooded man extracted something from his victim's brain with a syringe, his own voice rising over the chant, claiming, "The brothers will be reunited again!"

He repeated the phrase over and over as he took a small silver knife and slipped it into the hole in the skull. With a deft movement, he cut a chunk out of the victim's brain and ate it right off the shining, blood-soaked blade. Rose gasped, despite her hand pressed over her face, her body shaking. This practiced ritual was so efficient, the priest-like man had obviously done it dozens, maybe hundreds of times before.

The man threw back his head in ecstasy, his hood falling away, and Rose saw Matthew Price's face clearly. Even though it confirmed all her worst suspicions, it was a shock that made her heart skip a beat, the breath lock in her throat.

Price looked right at her and Rose stilled as if frozen instantly. His dark eyes flickered in the torchlight, then his gaze moved on. He must not have seen her in the shadows, but for a second, it had been as if their eyes locked. Taking no more chances, Rose scurried away and ran back up the tunnel as fast as she could. At the end, she ran up the stairs, and a new panic struck her. How did she get out? How did the ground open from the inside?

She scrabbled around the stone walls, doing her best to suppress sobs that threatened to burst out of her like a flock of startled birds. Her hand brushed over something, and she turned to look. A simple lever, cold metal in a narrow slot in the wall. She yanked down on it, and the deep click sounded, the stone above her sinking down and sliding back. Gasping in the fresh air of Central Park, Rose ran up the last few steps and out next to the pillar with Jacob's Witch carved into it.

She jerked as a heavy hand grasped her shoulder.

CHAPTER 32

Crowley headed back to the hotel, first along East 60th Street, heading for the south end of Central Park. The road wasn't too busy, the foot traffic thin. He passed a woman with a shopping cart, muttering to herself, wrapped up in three or four coats. He offered a smile as she passed, and the woman gasped, stopped to stare. Her dirty face was intense, dark eyes glittering in the streetlights.

"What is it?" Crowley asked. "Are you okay?"

"Oh, yes, I'm just fine. But you're not, are you." It wasn't a question.

"I'm not?"

The woman leaned forward, gaze intensifying. Crowley felt as though she were looking not into his eyes, but through them, her gaze searing his soul. "You're marked," she said.

"What does that mean?"

"It means there are clouds about you. Shadows and clouds, darkness binding you, wrapping you up!"

Crowley swallowed, licked suddenly dry lips. He had nothing to say to that. He wasn't even sure what she meant.

The woman nodded as though he had told her he understood her words. "Watch your back, young man. And beware the knife."

"O… okay. I will. Thank you." It felt weird to thank her, but there was a weight to her warning that he couldn't ignore.

The woman continued on her way. Crowley stood on the sidewalk for a moment. He'd barely recovered from the adrenaline rush of his close shave at the Grolier Club, now this strange woman had him worked up again. He glanced back and startled slightly to see her standing on the corner, staring back at him. She lifted one hand and made a throat-cutting gesture with it, then wagged her index finger once left, once right. As Crowley's mouth fell open, she turned and pushed her cart around the corner and disappeared from sight.

"Holy hell," Crowley whispered to himself. "This is one weird night."

It was nearly two in the morning, and all he wanted was to collapse into a warm bed and nestle up close to Rose. He hoped she wasn't too cranky with him for doing this job alone. But he had been successful, so surely she would be happy about that. He carried on and was about to turn left onto 5th Avenue, right at the southeast corner of Central Park, when a man crossed the street towards him. Crowley recognized him immediately.

"Matthew Price!" he said in surprise. "You're out very late."

"Oh, ah, Jake. Well, so are you."

There was an awkward moment while Crowley tried to think what on earth he could say to the man without sounding like a fool. Price's cheeks were flushed like he'd enjoyed a few drinks, but his eyes were bright. Even his skin seemed to glow somehow, and Crowley realized it was because the man appeared to have a fewer wrinkles than the last time they'd met. Surely Crowley was imagining that.

"I went out to catch up with an old pal," Crowley said. "We ended up talking and drinking far later than I expected."

"Well, I'm sure it's not often you get to see people here, so make the most of it, eh?"

"My sentiments exactly. I hope Rose won't be too angry with me for staying out."

"Surely she's asleep by now. If you sneak in quietly enough, she need never know. She'll be dead to the world."

Crowley frowned at Price's choice of words. The man seemed gleeful in a way Crowley couldn't quite reconcile. Perhaps he was drunk. "What about you?" he asked.

"What about me?" Price asked.

"You're out late too."

"Ah, yes. Well, when one reaches my age, it's sometimes hard to sleep. I find that a brisk walk around the outskirts of the park is better than staring up at the ceiling in the dark."

"That makes sense. Nice to bump into you, but I'd better be getting along."

"And you. I've been so busy lately, which is probably half the reason I can't sleep. And I've been neglecting your aunt. I'll have to make things up with Trudy when my business calms down again."

"I'm sure she understands," Crowley said. "Rose and I had a nice dinner with her just this evening, in fact. She's well."

"I'm glad to hear that. Now, you'd better get home to bed!"

"See you soon, I hope."

Price smiled. "Oh, I hope so too."

Crowley turned and headed south along 5th Avenue,

discomforted by the meeting. He didn't buy the insomnia excuse at all. He glanced back and saw Price watching. The old man raised a hand in farewell, and Crowley returned the gesture. He continued on and glanced back again a few paces later, but Price was out of sight. Crowley paused, a smile tugging at his lips.

... a brisk walk around the outskirts of the park...

If he were making a circuit of the park, Crowley should be able to see him heading north up 5th Avenue. But it seemed Price had continued east. And if that were the case, could he be heading towards the Grolier Club, perhaps? Crowley turned back and ran up to the corner he had just left. Sure enough, there was Price, halfway along the block heading towards the Club.

Crowley pulled Jerkwad's phone from his pocket and, hiding in the shadows of the corner, he tapped to call the only number in the phone's memory. After a couple of seconds, Price patted his jacket pocket and then pulled out his own phone. The call was answered.

"Hello?" Price said into Crowley's ear. "Where have you been? Hello?"

Price pulled the phone from his ear and looked at it as if staring might answer the mystery for him. With a smile, Crowley hung up and pocketed the purloined phone again. He turned back and resumed his walk back to the hotel.

CHAPTER 33

When the heavy hand clamped down on her shoulder, Rose had sucked in a breath to scream, but another hand quickly covered her mouth.

"Please, don't scream. I'm not going to hurt you!"

"Derek?" Rose said as the hand on her mouth lifted slightly. "Don't scream?"

"Okay." Her heart raced, but she was so thankful it wasn't someone from the cellar room below the bridge that Rose was prepared to hear him out. She was released and turned to see the bulky janitor standing there, his face a picture of misery.

"We need to move away from here," he said.

He had led her away from the Bethesda Terrace, up to a hilly, wooded area of Central Park called The Ramble. There, within the privacy of night and shadows, they talked.

"We needed to get away before the others came out," Derek said.

"You were in there?" Rose asked, aghast. "You're part of this?" She had the urge to hit him as hard as she could and run, especially after he'd creeped her out so much before. That he was part of that atrocious murder she'd seen was too much. But something in his face, some measure of shame and unmasked fear, made her pause.

"Derek, I need to know what's going on here. I need to know how and why you're involved."

Derek nodded, staring the earth, his eyes as shadowed as their hiding place under the trees. "I know you don't trust me. But I promise I'm on your side."

"Derek–"

"You saw the pictures of Jazz in my locker." He looked up, met her eye, and that disarmed Rose somewhat.

"I did, yes."

"I get that maybe that's weird. I know Jazz would never have loved me, but she was always kind to me when so few others were. I loved her, though. And isn't it normal to have photos of people you admire? People put posters of pop stars or sports stars on their walls, even if those stars will never love them."

He looked at Rose for some kind of validation, and she didn't have it in her to try to explain the difference. Those stars were public figures, they made their images available, they were miles and miles away from their fans. It wasn't the same. That was hardly the point here, and not relevant any more anyway, now that Jazz was dead. "I guess," Rose said quietly instead, favoring Derek with a soft smile. "Tell me about what I just saw."

"This used to be a normal coven," Derek said. "You know, we were harmless."

"Hidden under one of the oldest parts of New York City?"

"Oh, you'd be surprised at the things that go on around this city, Rose. There are all kinds of groups and secrets and secret places. You know, there's a whole community of people who live in the old tunnels under New York? The mole people."

Rose nodded. "Actually, yes, I've read about them before. But homeless people aren't the same as a witch coven."

"They're not homeless. The undercity is their home. It's their community."

"Okay, granted. But Derek, a coven?"

Derek pursed his lips, thinking for a moment, then he said, "There are lots of different kinds of witchcraft. Wicca is modern, some other forms are older than the Salem trials. Nothing is as simple as people like to think."

Rose nodded again, wondering at the wisdom coming from this big, seemingly simple man. But while he lived a simple life, and seemed to be dealing with his own challenges, social and possibly cognitive, he was certainly no fool.

"Anyway, ours was one of the oldest," Derek went on. "We practiced our rituals, and we minded our business. But then, about a year ago, a man showed up who called himself the Witchfinder. He said he'd found us through powerful magic, and had come to show us the way. Things were amazing at first." Derek looked up, his eyes glittering in the darkness, alive with wonder. "He showed us magic that really worked. And he taught us these stories, almost prophecies. But things turned dark really fast. He told us that true power always exacts a price, and he killed a young man, right there in front of everybody. He said that was a binding act, to ensure the loyalty of the coven. Several people quit right there and then, of course. But they didn't get far. Three of them were found dead the next day, from varying causes. A failed robbery, a street mugging, one fell onto the subway tracks, but we all know he was pushed. The others? Well, we just never saw them again. So they're certainly dead too, aren't they? Maybe some got away, I don't know. But after that, everyone was afraid to leave."

Derek paused, staring at the ground again, and Rose caught the sparkle of a falling tear. The big man's shoulders were shuddering slightly. She reached out, put a hand on his forearm. "It's okay, Derek. We can do something about this. Tell me more."

"Next meeting he brought in the first sacrifice. It was one of the mole people, that's how I know all about them. I didn't help, but I didn't do anything about it. And it was so much worse than the first killing. He ate a part of the man's brain, Rose! Just like he did again tonight!" A sob escaped the big man, and he put his face in his hands.

Rose let him cry for a moment, sure this was the first time he'd told anyone and he certainly needed the release. She gave him that, one hand still on his arm.

After a moment, he sat back again, taking a long shuddering breath. "I never went back, and I was ready for an attack of some kind. Always looking over my shoulder, never taking the subway. But they left me alone. I don't think they ever really took me very seriously. Nobody does." He shrugged, a small, pain-filled smile briefly shifting his lips. "I guess that saved me. But then Jazz started to investigate things, and she was led to the coven there. I was torn. I love her, and I wanted to protect her. But I knew I could help her too. And maybe she'd expose the Witchfinder. Jazz was so strong, so smart. I thought she could bring him down. So I told her where and when to find the coven meeting. And you know what happened."

Derek slumped, spent, his weight of guilt and sorrow briefly passed on. Rose knew it would haunt him always, but none of it was really his fault. "Why were you there again tonight," she asked softly.

Tears glistened in his eyes as he looked up and met her gaze. "I went there planning to kill the Witchfinder for what he'd done to Jazz." He lifted the side of his light jacket to reveal a gun tucked into his waistband. A small pistol of some kind, dark and malevolent in the night. "But when it came down to it, I didn't have the courage. Even as he killed another person, I couldn't take a life, even his. I stood there, frozen, and when the poor man was dead, I knew what was coming next, and I slipped away. There's another exit from that place, along one side, if you how to find it. That's how I left before, and I used it again today. As I went, I glanced back and saw you hiding in the gallery. I knew I would give you away if I tried to communicate with you, so I hurried up to the bridge and waited, hoping you'd get out soon. And you did."

Rose shook her head, mystified. She'd been so shocked at the events of the ritual, and unable to take her eyes from the horror, that she hadn't even seen Derek slip in there, or noticed him slip away. It seemed perhaps no one had. For such a big man, it appeared Derek had a knack of moving unseen. She took his hand. "You can help us take him down. Tell me everything you know about those legends and prophecies."

CHAPTER 34

It was after 2.30am when Crowley got back to the Algonquin Hotel. He winced as the keycard beeped and the door clicked to unlock. He pushed the door slowly open and crept inside, then turned and closed it as gently as he could behind him. As he turned back, fear settled in his stomach. Though the lights were off and the room was mostly gloomy, he saw clearly that the bed was neatly made and unoccupied.

A hundred thoughts rushed through his mind. Had Rose come looking for him? Had she run out on him? That was insane, what kind of paranoia was that? But where was she?

The stolen phone buzzed in his pocket. Crowley took it out and stared at it. The one number it held was ringing. That meant Price. But was Price calling his man, the idiot Jerkwad, or did he know more than Crowley wanted to admit? Perhaps Crowley had been a fool all along. He stared until the phone rang out, chewing at his lower lip, trying desperately to think where Rose was, where she might have gone.

Then another buzzing started up in his pocket. His own phone ringing. He took it out and saw *Matthew Price* written across the screen. Well, he might as well take this call. He could simply play dumb.

"Matthew!" he said, trying to sound far more relaxed than he was. "Enjoying your walk still? You're lucky you caught me, I'm about to fall into bed."

"Where is it, Crowley?"

"Where's what?"

"The damn book, you know exactly what."

Crowley swallowed. Clearly, Price was far better informed than he had assumed, and all pretense had quickly fallen away. "The book?" he said anyway, trying to sound confused and relaxed now.

"Enough, you idiot. You're not fooling anyone. I don't know how you did it, but I know you've got Poe's journal. Where else would it be? I want it."

"I want doesn't get," Crowley said, dropping all pretense as well. "Didn't your parents teach you any manners?"

"Do not insult my intelligence, Jake Crowley, and do not

waste my time. You are into something deeper than you can possibly imagine, and it will kill you if you're not more careful. I want that book."

"No, can't do it, sorry."

Price breathed heavily for a moment at the other end, clearly trying to get his rage under control. "Very well. You leave me no choice. It's the book or her. You choose."

Crowley drew breath to speak, but the line went dead. Damn it! Had he already taken Rose, before Crowley even went after the book? There's no way he could have known before now, they'd only met on the street less than an hour ago. And at that point, Price still thought he was about to get the journal for himself. Had he taken Rose earlier, some kind of insurance policy? But why would he be moved to do that?

The hotel room door beeped and clicked. Crowley spun around, dropping into a crouch, anticipating the arrival of Jerkwad, here to reinforce Price's threats. The door swung open, and Rose walked in, her eyes widening in shock when she saw Crowley skulking in the darkness.

"What's going on?" she asked.

It took Crowley a moment to collect his thoughts. "He's got Trudy," Crowley said, realization flooding through him.

Rose hurried in and shut the door. "What? Who has? Price?"

Crowley nodded. "Wait a minute." As Rose turned on the light, he used his own phone to call back Price. "Come on, come on!" he muttered as the phone rang and rang and then went to voicemail.

Crowley hung up, grinding his teeth in frustration. The phone he'd stolen from Jerkwad beeped and the screen lit up with a text message.

Do you understand the situation now?

Crowley spat a curse, tapped out a quick reply. Yes.

A tense silence hung in the air as he waited for another message from Price. The bastard was toying with Crowley, letting him twist as he waited for word.

"I'm sure he won't hurt her," Rose said.

Rose! Crowley seized her and pulled her close to him. "For a moment I thought it was you he'd taken. Are you all right?" He had seen something in her eye, a dark look that disturbed him.

It took a few minutes for Rose to recount the story of the ritual she'd witnessed, how she had found it in the first place, and her talk with Derek afterward. When she had told it all, Crowley simply stood and stared. Then he gathered her into his arms and hugged her tightly.

"I'm so sorry," he said into her hair. "What a truly horrible thing you went through."

She nodded against his shoulder, then stood back, gently pushed him away. "We'll fix this."

After a few tense moments, another message came through.

In Central Park, there is a bronze statue of a Husky, dedicated to the indomitable spirit of the sled dogs. Meet me there with the journal, in three hours. Come alone. Talk to no one in the meantime. Any sign of the police, of Rose, or anyone else, Trudy dies.

Crowley *stared at the message for a long moment, Rose watching over his shoulder.*

Where is she? He typed.

Somewhere you'll never find her.

"What are you going to do?" Rose asked.

Crowley thought fast. *Somewhere you'll never find her. Where might that be?*

"He asked for three hours. Where is he that's three hours away?"

In all the running around and confusion, the excitement of getting to the journal first, and the subsequent uncomfortable encounter with Price, something had slipped Crowley's mind. Now it came crashing back. And with that memory came the beginning of a plan.

He quickly typed a reply to Price. *I'll be there.*

Rose frowned. "Just like that? You're going to trust him to return her once he has the journal?"

Crowley shook his head. "I don't trust him at all."

"So, what's the plan?"

"A rescue mission! I know where he's hiding Trudy."

CHAPTER 35

Having no better place to start, Crowley led Rose back to Trump Tower. More specifically, to the manhole cover out front. Along the way, they'd each called the police to request that officers conduct a welfare check: Crowley asked for one at Trudy's address, Rose at Price's. He held out little hope that Trudy was being held at either place, but no harm in trying.

Upon arriving at the tower, they watched until the guards in the building's lobby were busy talking to each other, then quickly slipped from the shadows, lifted the maintenance cover, and dropped into the tunnels under the street.

As Crowley pulled the cover back into place, desperately hoping they hadn't been spotted, Rose said, "It's nearly 4am. Will these new friends be awake?"

"It's always nighttime underground. Let's hope someone is up at least." Crowley flicked on a penlight and shone its sharp narrow beam left and right. "This way."

"How do you know which way?"

"Just a hunch."

They went for a while in silence, Crowley heading vaguely towards the Bellevue hospital where the presumably fake-named Doctor Michael Prince had conducted his experiments and lost his job. Michael Prince. Matthew Price. It wasn't such a leap.

Crowley froze at the sound of a soft scuff. "Hello?" he called out. "I'd like to talk to Clyde. Do you know where he is? Or Sarah?"

A silhouette emerged cautiously from a side tunnel. "Who are you?"

"My name is Jake Crowley. I'm a friend of Clyde and Sarah, and I'd really like to talk to them."

"Probably sleeping."

Crowley ignored Rose's I told you so look and said, "Do you think you can take me to them anyway? It's important. Unless you can help me?"

"Depends what you need."

Crowley took a deep breath, then dove in both feet together. Might as well lay it all out from the start. "A lot of your folk have gone missing over the last year or so, haven't they?"

The man's eyes narrowed in his grubby face. "Yes."

"Right. And I think I might know who's been abducting them. I aim to stop him. But I need help. Is there any particular place people have been going missing from more than anywhere else?"

The man pursed his lips in thought. "Well, none of us spend much time around East 18th these days."

"Why not?"

"Because everybody who goes there dies." Clyde stepped out of the shadows. "I'm glad you're here." Crowley introduced Rose. Clyde seemed vaguely surprised by this courteous treatment and managed only a nod. He, in turn, introduced the other mole man as Ted.

"What's the deal with East 18th?" Rose asked.

"There's an old abandoned subway station there. A lot of us used to hang out in it, it was a good space. But too many went missing. Any of the tunnels for a few blocks east and north of the old East 18th Street subway station are off-limits. Not by any rule, just my preference. Especially recently."

Crowley nodded. He had remembered the thing he'd meant to think about further but had forgotten for a while: the old man among the mole people saying, *We don't go near the tunnels under Bellevue anymore.*

"I thought so," Crowley said. "And just north and east of there is Bellevue Hospital, right?"

Rose gave him a sharp glance, and the mole men nodded.

"We don't come anywhere around there these days for definite. People still disappear though," Ted said.

Crowley took a deep breath, knowing that everything rested on this roll of the dice. He quickly explained the situation.

"If the two of you can help us, we can rescue my aunt and maybe even put a stop to this Revenant who has been killing your friends. And I'll pay you for your time."

"What do you need?" Clyde asked.

"First of all, I really need to get to the tunnels under Bellevue as quickly as possible."

Ted shook his head, eyes wide. "I'll take you to this side of the East 18th Street subway, but from there you're on your own. I can give you directions, though. It's not much further."

"Good enough!" Crowley said. "And thank you.:

"What can I do?" Clyde asked.

"If you're willing to take a small risk, I've got one more task that needs seeing to."

It took a while traversing the undercity of New York, but not as long as Crowley had anticipated. Eventually, Ted stopped and pointed ahead.

"Keep going down there, and you'll come to the abandoned subway station. From there, cross the tracks, and you'll find a tunnel leading out from the north end, and a few steps going down. When you get to the bottom, take the first turn each time, left, then right, then left. You'll be directly under Bellevue."

Crowley glanced at Rose, and she nodded, confirming she'd memorized Ted's directions too. She had her phone out and was tapping them into a note to be sure they didn't forget. "Thank you," Crowley said and handed Ted a twenty.

He grinned and pocketed the cash. "Be careful on the tracks. Trains still go through East 18th, they just don't stop there anymore."

"Got it, thanks."

Ted turned tail and hurried quickly away. Rose walked alongside Crowley as they headed on.

"You really think she's here?" Rose asked.

"It's a gut feeling." Crowley shook his head slightly, trying to arrange his thoughts. "There are just too many disparate threads floating around this same area. I'm convinced Price has been using the forgotten spaces under the city for decades. And I'm sure he was the doctor sacked from Bellevue. The mole people say their friends are still going missing, mostly from that area, and an increasing amount in the last year, since Price came back to New York. It's got to be there. He must have some secret area under the hospital, probably set up since he worked there. No longer accessible from above, maybe he closed it off, but still reachable from underneath. From down here."

"I hope you're right, Jake. But what if you're not? What do we do then?"

Crowley paused, looked sidelong at her, then shrugged. "We'll cross that bridge when we come to it. If we come to it."

They came out into a vast open space, and Crowley shone his light around. They stood on the abandoned East 18th Street platform, bright tags of graffiti adorning every inch of wall space. All kinds of trash littered the ground. Steps led up from either end of the platform, presumably the route back up to street level when the station had been operating, but both were blocked off only a dozen or so steps up. Cement columns were regularly spaced between the tracks. A wind picked up, pushing towards them and lifting dust and plastic packets.

"Let's get out of sight," Crowley said, and they both ducked into deeper shadows at the back of the platform as lights lit up the tunnel. In a few seconds, a train barreled through, regular rectangles of light framing bored faces, some reading, listening to music, staring into nowhere. The train rattled past for far longer than Crowley would have credited, then it passed, and everything fell into dark silence again.

"Now's a good time to cross then," Rose said. "There won't be another train for at least a few minutes."

"Right." Crowley shone his light across to an opening, cement steps going down. "There's our route."

They crossed, picking their feet up high and with great care to not touch any metal. On the other side, they quickly entered the tunnel. The steps only went down a little way, then it leveled out. They followed Ted's directions – to the end, then left, then right, then left.

Crowley and Rose turned in a slow circle, frowns creasing both their faces.

"Have we missed it?" Rose asked.

The tunnel they followed had ended in a slightly wider space that appeared to be a dead end. Two tunnels used to lead away from it, but both were bricked up, the mortar blackened and dusty. The two routes had clearly been closed for years, probably decades.

Crowley didn't answer but began shining his light more closely at all the walls. Rose shrugged and followed suit. Crowley was growing increasingly frustrated, beginning to think that maybe he'd been keen for a solution that didn't exist. Perhaps they could retrace their steps if they found nothing here and see if there were another route, a small side tunnel they'd missed or something.

"Here," Rose said. "I've found something."

Excitement built up again as Crowley hurried over.

"Look." Rose shone her light at the ground.

There was a distinct arc scraped into the dirt, like a door had been opened through it. But there was only a brick wall there. Crowley crouched, looking closely at the base of the wall where the arc began.

"There's a small gap here," he said. "This is a false wall."

After another minute or two they had found the outline of a door made of bricks, fitting so snugly it would never have been noticed if the marks on the ground hadn't given it away.

"Price getting lazy about covering his tracks?" Rose mused.

"Looks like it. I guess he figured no one came this way any longer. But how do we open it?"

He began running his fingers over the bricks, pressing here and there. One of the bricks near the edge of the fake door shifted slightly. He pressed harder, and the block went in with a solid click. The door popped open, a one-inch brick façade on a wooden board.

"Et voila!" Crowley said. "Let's go carefully now."

On the other side of the fake door, stone steps led up into darkness. Crowley shone his light up and saw another door not far ahead, closed but seemingly not locked. At least, no padlock or keyhole was visible. He crept up, Rose right behind him, and listened at the wood. Nothing. A simple, round brass knob was the only way in. He slowly turned it and opened the door a crack. A soft orange light washed out, almost like candlelight, but too steady. He leaned in and saw a few wall-mounted electric lights with dim orange bulbs. Maybe they were kept on a dimmer switch, or perhaps this was only emergency lighting.

He let his gaze roam the space and the breath caught in his throat.

"It's a lab," he whispered back, trying not to let the frustration be too evident in his voice. "But there doesn't seem to be anyone here."

He stepped in and looked around. Two metal tables like he'd expect to see in a morgue occupied the center of the room. On one of them lay a young man, clearly dead, as evidenced by the missing top of his skull, with no brain visible in the concave hollow. Workbenches lined the walls, holding all kinds of tools and jars. At least a dozen jars held liquid with human brains suspended like underwater balloons. Other body parts occupied other glass vessels.

Rose gasped. "Oh, this is horrible."

Crowley nodded. He moved closer to the dead man on the table for a closer look. It wasn't anyone he recognized. He looked to Rose, and she shrugged, shook her head.

"It's not the man he killed tonight," she said.

"How many people have died at this monster's hands?"

Crowley said through gritted teeth.

The man's eyes were empty black holes. On the end of the mortuary table stood a jar containing the brain, trailing a few inches of brain stem. The man's missing eyes floated, still attached to the brain by twists of optic nerve.

"Look at this," Rose said.

She stood by a desk littered with paper and pens and other bits of mundane administrative minutiae. But she pointed to a thick journal, that lay open on the desk's center, a pen resting in the valley of the spine. The book was thick, the pages scrawled with dense, complicated script. Maybe two-thirds had been filled already. On the open pages were a few small diagrams, some sort of biological shorthand, then at the bottom of the facing page, a phrase in angry block capitals.

DAMN EDGAR! HE TOOK HIS WHOLE BUT DENIED ME MY HALF!

"What do you think that means?" Rose asked. "Edgar? As in Allan Poe? How can he be relevant? Why is his journal so important?"

Crowley stared at the words for a moment, then nodded subtly. "I'm beginning to have my suspicions. But come on. We've discovered something macabre and interesting here, but it only confirms things we already know. Trudy is still missing, and we're running out of time."

CHAPTER 36

Matthew Price made his way to the bronze statue of the sled dog in Central Park about ten minutes before midnight. Crowley had better follow directions to the letter if he wanted to see his aunt alive again. In truth, Price had developed a genuine love for Trudy Fawcett. She was a decent woman, smart, and confident. In another life, perhaps she would have made a fine partner. But there was far more at stake and Price wouldn't hesitate to make good on his threat if Crowley tried to cross him, however much that pained him. What was one more death in the sea of murder that had been his life?

He stood on the path under the bronze statue, standing ten feet above him on a large rock, looking out over the park, tongue out, happy and panting. There was life in a well-wrought sculpture, and this one captured the nature of a good dog well.

After a moment, Price reconsidered and moved around to walk across the grass and up the shallow slope of the back of the pale gray stone to stand beside the statue. From there he had a good view all around and would see anyone approaching long before they reached him, even in the gloom of the night.

He checked his watch. Five minutes before midnight. By morning all this would be at an end. Finally, everything he needed at hand and everyone who had stood in his way irrelevant. Or dead. Both, I hope. And with any luck, he and Trudy alive and well to enjoy all the fruits of his labors.

Price became increasingly impatient as he watched the minute hand pass the twelve. How typical of Crowley to be late. Was this some kind of power play? It would do him little good.

Movement caught his eyes. A figure in a hooded sweatshirt approached along the footpath and stopped about twenty feet from Price's elevated position. Price looked carefully around and saw no one else.

"You came alone. Good."

"Well, that's what you wanted," Crowley said. "I want you to let my aunt go."

Price grimaced. How the man's English accent grated on his nerves. Crowley's face was hidden in the shadows of his hood, but Price imagined that hard, defiant expression. The man's disdain would do him no good here.

"Where's the journal?"

Crowley reached into his pocket and lifted the small, scuffed black book into view. Price smiled, a sigh escaping. After so long, he would finally gain the half he had been denied.

"Come on then," Price said, gesturing with one hand. With the other, he lifted a small gun into plain sight, moonlight glinting off the short barrel. "And don't be foolish enough to try to fight me, Jake Crowley. You may be much bigger and stronger than me, but I am not in the mood. I will shoot you dead at the first false move you make." In the dark of the night, Crowley looked bigger than ever.

"Fair enough," Crowley said. He held the book up in one hand and raised the other too, palm out. Keeping both hands raised, he ascended the sloping path beside the statue and around onto the grass. Price tracked him with his gun the whole time.

Crowley stopped some twenty feet away.

"Hand it over!" Price barked, his patience wearing thin. He would shoot Crowley dead the moment the book was in his hands, and he began to tremble with anticipation.

Crowley tossed the book forward. It fluttered in the air, covers opening like wings as the pages flickered. Price winced, terrified the treatment would damage something so old and fragile. As the journal hit the grass, Crowley ducked to one side.

Price fired, a reflex more than an intention, the gun bucking hard in his grip. The shot went wide. Crowley hit the ground, rolled, and came up running.

His hood had fallen back, and as the man ran, Price saw it wasn't Crowley at all. No wonder he had looked so large. Price recognized the great oaf from the underground. He was one of those mole people who were always skulking around. Most of them ran the other way when Price was about, but not that one. He had a curious mind. Price would have to do something about that.

Price fired again, trying to track the man as he ran. But Price had never been particularly comfortable with guns and was no great marksman. Hitting a moving target in the dark with a handgun would be a challenge for anyone, and Price missed twice more. He cursed violently, not only because he had missed, but simply because Crowley had the audacity to play these games with him. What the hell was he thinking? His aunt would die for this defiance.

Grinding his teeth, he crouched and retrieved the journal, already knowing what he would find. A fake. Crowley would pay dearly for this.

CHAPTER 37

It was near dawn when Rose and Crowley emerged from the underground. Rather than going back the way they came, they'd sought the closest exit they could find. One which brought them out a few blocks west of Bellevue Hospital at the corner of Park Avenue and 23rd Street.

"I was sure I had him figured out," Crowley said as he helped Rose up out of the manhole. He was still seething about the dead end of the underground lab.

Even at this early hour, there were a few pedestrians out and about, as well as light traffic. No one gave them a second glance.

"You were right about the lab," Rose said. "I know it's not much use now, but as things move on we know how to shut him down, right?"

Crowley half-shrugged. "If we get the chance. But if it's too late for Gertie, what difference does it make?"

Rose frowned at that. "We're going to get to her. But either way, shutting Price down will stop a lot of innocent people from getting hurt, and that's a good thing. An important thing."

Crowley glanced at her, chastised. He nodded. "Just my anger and concern talking. I hope you know that."

"I do, and I'm sorry, Jake. I know you're worried. But Price is an evil man, he's killed countless people. Whatever else happens, we have to stop that."

"And we will." Crowley took a deep breath, then blew it out in a rush. "I just hope I didn't get Clyde hurt or killed. I thought it would be the ideal distraction for Price while we collected Trudy, but she wasn't there. So now we're treading water, waiting to hear from Price." He grunted in wordless frustration.

They purchased coffees from a 24-hour coffeehouse and sat down on a bench in Madison Square Park in sight of the Flatiron Building. They had brought the *Masque Journal* along, and Rose pored over it. Crowley tried to read along, but he couldn't focus. Eventually, he gave up and sat staring at the iconic, wedge-shaped building. On any other day, he'd have found the architectural oddity fascinating, but now he wanted nothing more than to find Trudy.

Right now, he had two ideas: one involved paying a visit to the offices of SaleMed, the other to Price's home. Both involved gratuitous violence. But Price was too clever for that. Crowley couldn't risk a move unless he had better intel than what he'd been operating on so far. And he was damned if he knew where he could find that.

"I've read through all of this," Rose finally said, closing the *Masque Journal*. "It clarifies things a little bit. I mean, it's truly incredible, but it gives us a better idea of what's been happening." Evidently, she hoped the distraction would give Crowley something else to focus on even while she desperately wished for a call from Clyde too.

"Can we walk and talk? I can't abide sitting here doing nothing."

Thankfully, Rose didn't ask where they were going. She simply agreed.

"Go on then," Crowley said as they headed north on 5th Avenue. "What madness has Price been up to? And is it really Edgar Allan Poe's journal?"

"Yes. If it's read as notes for fiction, it makes little sense. But if it's all real… It seems that after the death of his wife, Poe became utterly distraught. In his grief, he began researching elixirs, desperate to find something that would ease his suffering. I'm not really sure what he thought it would accomplish, but it became his obsession. This was at the same time as he wrote *The Masque of the Red Death*. You know the story?"

"I read it years and years ago," Crowley said. "About a plague and a lord?"

"Yeah. It was originally published *as The Mask of the Red Death: A Fantasy*," Rose said. "Which seems to be a little like protesting too much to me. It's from 1842, about Prince Prospero trying to avoid a deadly plague called the Red Death. He hides in his abbey with a bunch of wealthy nobles and holds a masquerade ball, using seven rooms of the place, decorating each with a different color. While they party, a stranger dressed as a victim of the Red Death travels through each of the rooms. Prospero confronts this victim and dies after discovering there's nothing inside the costume. All the other guests die too."

Crowley forced a tight smile. "Jolly stuff, eh?"

"Well, Poe wasn't known for children's stories. But I researched a bit, and it's considered that Poe's story pretty much follows the traditions of Gothic fiction and is considered an allegory about the inevitability of death. A lot of people have tried to understand what he meant by the plague in question, but these things always have more questions than answers. Maybe he was just spinning a good yarn."

"Or maybe he was trying to understand his wife's death?" Crowley suggested.

"Sure. Maybe both. These things don't have to be either/or situations."

"But what does any of this have to do with us now?" Crowley asked. "With Price."

"Well, that's where it gets interesting. According to the journal, Poe's research led him to Price, who was working with similar aims."

"In 1842?"

Rose nodded slowly. "Apparently. And Price had been around 'for multiple decades prior to my work' Poe wrote."

"Multiple decades?"

"Yep. Poe says his work was all plant-based, and only yielding limited results. The main problem was that during all this time, Poe isn't quite right, in practice or in his mental state. He was working on his short story, recording the results of his experiments, journaling, and ranting all in this one book. It reads like he had focused in on one place and was coming undone because of it. Then he finds Price."

Crowley scratched his chin thoughtfully. He had a feeling he knew how this tale would unfold.

Rose went on.

"Poe knew Price as a scientist but had no idea who he really was, what he was, or how he did his work. But both had lost beloved wives, and they bonded in their grief, and then subsequently over their work, and quickly became like brothers. When they realized they were both looking for the same thing, they found camaraderie in that too. It became a friendly contest to see who could achieve immortality first. Finally, on a lark, Poe mixed his latest elixir with Price's latest serum and drank it. As he notes towards the end of this book, Poe could tell immediately that it had worked. The next time they met up, Price saw right away the change in Poe. He saw that Poe had succeeded."

"And that made him mad?"

Rose smiled. "No, not at first. Price was overjoyed. They were brothers in arms in all this, don't forget. So they agreed they would each produce another vial of their particular serum so that Price could do as Poe had done and also become immortal. Poe notes that it would take thirty days for him to complete his elixir. Whether it was due to joy or relief, Price let his guard down. All this time, he hadn't been entirely honest with Poe about his practices, the human cost of his experiments. As Poe puts it, 'he revealed to me then the utter depravity, the avarice, of his foul ministrations and I felt inside me the clamoring of all those murdered souls. I felt death envelop me like a shroud and knew I would wear its weight for eternity!' For all his faults, at least Poe was pretty appalled when he learned the truth."

Crowley pursed his lips, nodding slowly. "I can guess where this is going, then. He wanted to prevent Price from ever achieving immortality, thereby putting some finite end to his evil."

"Exactly. Among the last of his notes in the journal, Poes says that he realized he had to get away from Price, away from everything they had shared, and ensure Price never learned of his elixir. The journal ends there."

"But surely Poe knew that Price had been alive unnaturally long already. Multiple decades, he said it himself."

"Exactly," Rose said. "I don't get it. You'd think he would actively try to end Price, not just hide from him. And if he was so afraid of Price getting hold of his research, why did he leave the journal behind instead of destroying it?"

"And on top of that," Crowley said, "we have to assume he's still alive. I mean, if he really solved the issue of immortality, he must still be around somewhere."

"He could be in Mexico or Timbuktu for all we know," Rose said. "Or he could have died. Just because he found the answer to immortality doesn't mean he can't be killed. There are a lot of years between 1842 and now for any number of things to have happened."

Crowley opened his mouth to say something more but was interrupted when Rose's phone rang. She snatched it up and answered it quickly.

"Hello?"

"Rose? I'm really sorry, it all went badly."

Relief flooded her. "Derek, I'm so glad to hear from you. Are you okay?"

"Price took a shot at me, but yes, I'm okay. But he knows

the book I gave him is a fake, and he's absolutely furious."

His phone rang.

Rose's eyes went wide. "Who is it?"

Crowley stared at the name on the display.

"It's Gertie's number."

CHAPTER 38

It couldn't be Gertie. It had to be Price calling from her phone. Crowley steeled himself for a mind game, then answered.

"Hello?"

"Jake, dear, did I wake you?"

Crowley frowned, stunned to hear Gertie herself on the phone and sounding entirely relaxed.

"Er, no. Rose and I are out for an early walk."

"This early? You're on holiday, you know. You could allow yourself a little luxury."

"I guess so. Are you okay, Auntie?"

Trudy laughed, an almost girlish sound. "I certainly am. I've been indulging in a bit of luxury myself, actually. Matthew, that dear man, bought me a surprise present yesterday and I spent the day at a luxury spa being thoroughly pampered. We spent the night here, I'm calling from their best suite if you can imagine it. There's an enormous spa bath right in the middle of the room, raised up like a giant watery throne."

"Price is there with you?"

"Yes, of course. We've had a lovely time. And don't make any crude jokes. At my age, I'm sound asleep by nine o'clock."

Crowley swallowed, shook his head, trying to straighten up his thoughts. Rose looked at him, one eyebrow raised. He gave her a confused half-smile. "I'm so glad to hear that," he said lamely to his aunt.

"Anyway, Matthew and I were talking over breakfast, and despite the luxury, we're leaving shortly. I felt bad that you're only here for a few days and we're indulging ourselves like this. So we thought we'd love you two to come over to my place for dinner tonight. Make the most of you before you fly off again. Do say you'll come along!"

Crowley's head was spinning. "Yes, of course. We'll see you at your place around 5pm?"

"Sounds perfect," Trudy said. "We're going to spoil ourselves with massages and hot mud baths today before we head off, so expect me to be as relaxed as you've ever known me when you come around. I plan to have a skin treatment too, so you may not even recognize me."

"You'll have to make sure you introduce yourself again when I arrive then," Crowley said, forcing humor past his confusion.

What the hell was Price playing at? At least he knew now that Gertie had been having a wonderful time while Crowley thought she'd been abducted and held in a damp cell somewhere, suffering at Price's mercy. But it only made the whole thing more baffling.

After he hung up, he explained the situation to Rose.

"What the hell is he playing at?" she asked.

"Exactly what I just asked myself. But there's nothing we can do but play along for now."

"So what do we do until tonight?"

"There's nothing we can do. I guess we just be tourists and do some sightseeing."

Rose laughed, without much humor. "I'm not really going to be able to enjoy the city's wonders with this stuff hanging over us."

Crowley shrugged. "Me either. But let's just kill time until tonight. We can start with a good breakfast. If nothing else, at least we'll be rested and well-fed."

"And maybe we can find something constructive to do with the time," Rose said, tapping Poe's journal against her knee.

Crowley admitted to himself that he was nervous as they rode the elevator up to Trudy's apartment. He'd managed to keep himself busy throughout most of the day with a variety of tasks, including confirming that Clyde was all right. But now that the moment was at hand, worry was creeping in. He said as much to Rose, and she agreed with him.

"What if he tries something crazy?" she asked.

Crowley shrugged, shook his head. "I'll stick close to him. We can't really predict his actions, and that's how Price wants it. It's his one advantage."

Rose smiled, gave a soft nod. "Oh well, let's see how it goes."

Trudy answered the door herself. "Hello, darlings! Come in, come in."

Crowley hugged and kissed his aunt, noting that she seemed genuinely unfazed by anything. He had wondered if she might exhibit signs of stress, as maybe Price had her acting in his interests, but she seemed entirely unaware of any tension.

"Gabriela has gone down to Texas for a couple of days, to see her family down there. A bereavement."

"Oh, that's no good," Rose said.

Trudy smiled. "Gabriela's great-grandmother. She was ninety-eight and lived a full life. Gabriela is heartbroken, of course, they were close, but she's also rather pragmatic about it. I find a lot of Mexicans are."

"Some cultures have a much more ready and healthy relationship with death, I think," Rose said.

"Exactly that! The Americans and, good God, especially the British, you'd think death was a dirty word. Anyway, the upshot is that we're fending for ourselves this evening and that's fine with me. I've been exercising the old roast dinner skills once again as we all enjoyed it so much before. I've roasted a lovely leg of lamb, roast potatoes and vegetables, and there's apple crumble and custard for dessert."

"Holy cow, Auntie!" Crowley said. "We'll never leave if you keep up like this." He forced the jollity past nerves pulled taut as parachute ropes, glancing left and right for a sign of Price.

"Your beau not here?" Rose asked, voicing Crowley's concern.

Was the man planning something awful?

"He should be along shortly. He had business at the New York office to attend to, so when we left the spa, I came home to start cooking, and he went there. I can't imagine he'll be much long—"

She was interrupted by a rap-tap-tap at the door, then it clicked from someone using their own key and opened. Price stepped inside and smiled broadly when he saw them all standing in the hallway.

"There you all are!" he said, with friendly ease. "Am I late?"

"Not at all," Trudy said, pecking him on the cheek. "These two have just arrived too, so I'd say you were right on time."

Crowley was wary, his nerves firing. He remembered scouting seemingly abandoned buildings with his squad in Afghanistan, everyone tense as they passed in practiced unison from room to room, checking for insurgents or booby-traps. The tension in his system now echoed those missions, the sensation that things could get awful and violent at any moment. Price gave him a sidelong look, his mouth tweaked up at one side in a half-smile that was partly smug, partly genuine in humor. Was the bastard enjoying this?

Regardless, Crowley remained ready to move in an instant, should Price try to draw a weapon, but he saw no telltale bulge of a concealed handgun. Price's suit was well-fitted, tailor-made, of course. The thing about fine clothing was that it was incredibly hard to conceal a firearm underneath, but Crowley took little comfort from the seemingly unarmed nature of the man. Something was definitely up, some play would be made. He desperately wanted to anticipate what that might be. Well, maybe he wouldn't need it if he could make a play first.

"Shall we take the air?" Price asked Crowley suddenly. The question came with a smile, but his eyes made it clear he didn't want to be denied.

Crowley felt an urge to mess with him. "We've only just arrived, shouldn't we stay together?"

Price's cheeks twitched as his teeth clenched. "It's a fine evening, and I've just been stuck in a rather unpleasant cab for the past half hour. I'm sure you've heard the reputation of New York taxis."

"I have, though I wonder if it isn't a little unfair and prejudiced."

Price inclined his head in acquiescence. "It almost certainly is, but this one, sadly, rather fulfilled the stereotype."

"I need to see to the last of the dinner preparations," Trudy said. "Could you organize drinks first, Matthew?"

"You go and enjoy the balcony," Rose said, giving Crowley a nod. "I'll make our drinks. You like scotch, same as Jake, right?" she asked Price.

"Yes, thank you," Price said with another smile. "Trudy has a fine selection. Why don't you surprise us?"

Crowley enjoyed stretching Price's act of civility, but he went with him to the balcony anyway. As they closed the door behind them, he took a moment to enjoy the movement of the still warm breeze. Sounds of the traffic drifted up, along with the stronger odors of New York, but the air was pleasant up here, he couldn't deny that. The sky was just descending into twilight, peach on one horizon, already darkening to indigo on the other.

"We have played something of a game, you and I," Price said, putting both palms on the stone balustrade and leaning forward, straight-armed, to take in the view. His demeanor seemed relaxed, but there was an edge to his voice Crowley couldn't quite place.

"Is it a game to you?" Crowley asked. "All this death?"

A smile twitched Price's lips, but he kept his eyes forward, not meeting Crowley's gaze. "There are many degrees of game, Jake. But I mean specifically you and I, and the dance we've been reluctantly engaged in."

Crowley clenched his jaw, tempted to up-end Price right over the stone wall of the balcony, send him sailing to a violent end on the street below. It would be satisfying, but he held his action and his tongue for the time being.

After a moment more of silence, Price said, "I think I owe you some explanation. My life has been beset by grief. And, many times, betrayal. I don't mind admitting that there have been periods of genuine madness in between, but is it not often said that genius and madness go hand in hand?"

Crowley barked a laugh. "Are you calling yourself a genius?"

Price finally turned to look at Crowley, his eyes sparkling with mirth. "Can you really deny that I outwit the vast majority of men, Jake? I'm over three-hundred years old." That bald-faced admission took Crowley back for a moment, and Price laughed in almost boyish glee. "You can't pretend you don't know. And much as you might wish to believe it's not true, does it really take me telling you to finally make it real?"

"At what cost, though?" Crowley asked. "Your long life at the expense of so many others."

"Worthless lives. The lowest of the low. Criminals, parasites. If anything, I'm culling the herd." Price waved one hand, brushing away countless murders as irrelevant. " But that's not why I do it. It's all for love, Jake. That's the thing. It's always been for love, and after so many long years of grief and anger, I've finally found love again. Real, heartwarming love."

"With my aunt?"

"Who else? And that's what this is all for, Jake. Her, your aunt. She's central to it all. I was so close to giving everything up. A man gets tired, you know, living for so long. But she makes me feel young again. For the first time in centuries, if you can believe that."

"I'm not sure I can," Crowley said.

"Real love is rare." Price smiled, his face softening. "Do you love Rose? Because treasure her if you do."

"And that's what this is all about? Love?"

Price nodded. "Yes, it really is. And that's all I want now. At long last, I've found real love again, and I want it to be the completion of my work. I need the information you have from Poe for one last batch of the elixir, just enough for Trudy and myself, and that will be the end of it."

"Happily ever after?" Crowley asked, incredulous. "You think Trudy will agree to such a thing? Have you even asked her? Not everyone thinks immortality is a good thing." He was stunned to be talking so casually about such bizarre ideas. Did he himself think immortality was good? There was an appeal to living a long life, but living forever? And living it as an old person? Perhaps immortality at thirty or forty, but a woman her seventies? An endless life of dotage seemed like a kind of hell.

"She's healthy for her age, and the treatment has certain rejuvenating benefits. We've discussed it in theory," Price said. "I've tested the waters, asked what she thinks of such ideas, and I like to think I know her mind."

"Bedroom fancy is very different to real life," Crowley said, immediately regretting the mental image of his aunt and Price in the bedroom.

"I'll even share my half of the formula with you," Price said, changing tack. "You have Poe's journal, so you already have his half. That means you'd have the entire thing to do with as you see fit. Immortality for yourself and those you love. The betterment of humankind. I don't mind. As long as Trudy and I have our chance."

Crowley scoffed, lost momentarily for words.

"I love her, Jake," Price said, his voice threaded with seemingly genuine pain. "If it weren't for her, I'd stop entirely. I'm not lying about that. I'd all but given up before she came along. Can you understand?" His eyes searched Crowley's face, beseeching. "Do you really know love yet, young Jake Crowley? True, deep, soul-burning love?"

Crowley felt scoured by Price's scrutiny and looked away, still plagued with doubts about the man.

Price turned and quickly pulled something from his jacket pocket. Crowley moved on instinct, twisting to one side and seized Price's wrist, looking for the gun or knife. But Price held a sheet of paper, scrawled with tight writing in blue biro.

"The formula," Price said. "To prove my sincerity."

Crowley looked at the small sheet in Price's grip. Slowly, he reached out and took it.

"Can you deny your beloved aunt this?" Price asked. "Trust me, she would cherish the chance. She would hate you for taking it away from her. You don't know age yet, the fear that comes with it." Price stepped back, turned to look out over the city view again. "The other option is to throw me off this balcony right now. I assure you a revenant is not immune to a crushed skull. But I know you won't do that to your dear old Gertie. Will you?"

Crowley looked inside, saw Trudy and Rose smiling and chatting. Rose held a tray with their drinks on it. He imagined the scene going on forever, he and Rose enjoying eternal life even as Price and Trudy did. The concept made his head swim.

He pocketed the slip of paper Price had given him. "Okay," he said, letting out a slow breath. "All right."

Price turned back, a beatific grin splitting his face. "Well done, my boy! Thank you!"

He reached out, and they shook hands.

There was a tapping on the glass of the door behind them. Rose stood there, holding the tray, using her foot to attract their attention. Trudy seemed to have returned to the kitchen. Crowley opened the door, gave Rose a subtle nod.

Rose held out the tray, a scotch on each side. Price stepped forward quickly, reached across, and took the glass on Crowley's side. "Sorry,' he said. "New alliances are always shaky."

They laughed, albeit a little uncomfortably, and Rose went back inside. "I'll help Trudy with the dinner," she said from the doorway. "You okay here?"

"All good," Crowley said.

He held his glass up. "Cheers."

Price nodded, tapped his glass to Crowley's. The chink of glass was high and musical in the evening air.

"To life," Crowley said and tipped his glass up, draining the shot. It was smooth and peaty, a pleasant burn on the way down.

"To life," Price agreed and drank his. "I won't forget this, Jake. And neither will Trudy."

The smile faltered on his face. He looked at the glass in his hand, then at Crowley, his brows creasing together. He grunted and gripped his stomach with his free hand.

"You're an animal," Crowley said, his voice low and steady. "A predator. A true vampire."

"I can't believe you." Price grunted again and doubled over. "How could you take a chance? What if I hadn't taken your glass?"

"It wouldn't have mattered. They were both the same.

You're an evil murderer, Matthew Price, and you may be a genius. But you clearly don't know everything. You see, Poe's journal was filled with all kinds of things beyond his own formula. He was quite appalled at your methods, so he came up with a recipe to counteract the effects of your formula, incomplete though it was. You've managed to extend your life for a long time at the expense of the lives of others. But the effect that's keeping you alive is cumulative, isn't it?"

"Damn you," Price said, his breath now coming more easily. He slowly stood up straight again, wincing and knuckling his back. "What have you done?"

"What have I undone would be a better question." Crowley lifted his empty glass again, smiling. "If Poe is right, undoing the cumulative effect of your centuries of murder means you will succumb to the ravages of age incredibly quickly now. Far more quickly than your methods can counteract."

Red rage burned in Price's eyes, raw hatred. His lips peeled back from his teeth in a snarl. "That hurt like a kidney stone," he said, searching Crowley's eyes with his own. He plainly saw the truths there.

"Poe's hypothesis was right, wasn't it," Crowley said. "Your longevity has been an ongoing process of topping up, always on the brink of collapsing under you. All these years, all the deaths at your hands to maintain the extended life you've hung onto so tenuously. No wonder you so desperately wanted to get the true formula. And no wonder Poe hid it from you. I think he hoped you'd falter on your own, but his counter-elixir was there in case. I wonder why he never used it on you?"

"Even you don't know everything," Price said, his voice tinged with an acid edge.

"No. Especially given how simple the counter-elixir was. In the modern world, the requisite plant-based ingredients are surprisingly easy to acquire. Rose and I spent the day collecting them. Thanks for not making this a lunch date, by the way. We wouldn't have had time." Crowley smiled but kept his distance in case Price pounced in a moment of rage. "And they dissolve in water. Or whiskey."

But the man's face relaxed, some kind of resignation sliding in. He nodded begrudgingly. "How long do I have?"

"Poe reckoned probably a month before everything inside of you collapsed to the entropy you've been holding off for so long."

"And how do you know I won't kill you between now and then?"

Crowley smiled, lifted his palms in a gesture of acceptance. "You could try. But I'm prepared to take that chance because for some reason I actually believe that you do love my aunt. I think that's true and you wouldn't put her through the grief of losing both of us. Would you?"

Price nodded, let out a long sigh. "Damn you. You're right about that. I have many flaws, but when I love, I love deeply. I suggest we go back inside and enjoy a pleasant evening together with your aunt. And then after that, I'll have to break the news to her that I am in the late stages of terminal cancer."

CHAPTER 39

Walking back to their hotel, Crowley and Rose headed through Central Park. Stunned by the evening's events, they paused to stand on the ramparts of Belvedere Castle. The miniature castle, created in 1869, gave commanding views over the Great Lawn to the north and the Ramble to the south. The night was warm, moonlight bathed them as they leaned on the pale gray stone, looking out. A soft breeze carried scents of grass and the sound of leaves rustling in the oasis in the middle of the great city. It was peaceful. Crowley wondered if this was the sort of thing that a person could enjoy forever, but he figured even the most beautiful things would grow old and stale with enough time. A finite life held greater wonder.

"Despite everything, I feel a little bad for him," Crowley said, admitting aloud his thoughts.

"He killed so many people," Rose said. "I have no sympathy for him at all."

"No, I suppose I don't have sympathy either. But he lived for so long in the pursuit of one thing, and came so close until we took it all away."

"Poe took it away really," Rose said. "We just acted on the theories he never saw through."

Still not wholly trusting Price, they'd waited in another room while he broke the news to Trudy. She'd handled it with courage and grace. The Fawcett way, she called it. Even after Price had left, they'd offered to stay, but his aunt had asked for some time alone. Crowley didn't like it, but neither did he believe Price was a threat to his aunt. Not only because of the man's feelings for her but also because he'd lied to Price about the effects of the formula. If Poe was correct, the man had a lot less than a month left. His body would already be feeling the effects.

"I have to admit, Price truly seems to love your aunt. I could tell it broke her heart."

"Seems that way, but when a person has got as much money as Gertie, you never truly know."

"Love or money. Everything seems to come back to those two things every time, huh?" Rose leaned her head against Crowley's shoulder. "I wonder which one it really was for Price."

"I've already told you it was love."

They startled, spun around to see where the voice behind them had come from. Matthew Price stood there, holding a pistol low and close to his stomach. He moved it a little left and right, to cover them both. Crowley was in no doubt that he would fire if given any provocation. Crowley ground his teeth. Stupid! He should have known it had gone too smoothly, that Price had accepted his fate too readily.

"You didn't really expect me to give up just like that, did you?" Price kept a safe distance between them. Close enough that he would certainly not miss if he fired, but far enough away that Crowley couldn't jump him. Crowley felt Rose tense beside him, knew she was making the same mental calculations. He hoped she would be smart enough not to make a move. Not yet, at least.

"I want the journal," Price said. "You're absolutely right that my own formula is one of multiplication. It holds only when constantly renewed and, as the years pass, it has to be renewed ever more frequently. So no doubt Poe is right that now, counteracted, my demise will be swift. I'll never be able to renew my own temporary longevity. But that doesn't matter anymore. You have the journal, which means you have Poe's half of the formula, which means I can finally have the genuine elixir of immortality I've always sought."

Crowley shook his head, frowning. "It doesn't work like that. To make the elixir that Poe took will take at least thirty days. Because it's thirty days for his half, then more time for the combination with yours. You don't have that long. You'll be dead long before it's ready." Crowley couldn't help grinning cruelly. "Isn't that ironic, Matt?"

Rose sucked in a gasp, shocked at his effrontery. What was to stop Price from just shooting them now?

Crowley's heart raced. He hoped he hadn't pushed too hard. But he needed the man angry, rash even if there was to be an opening to save themselves.

Price's face twisted in anger. "You petty, tiny, children! Give me the journal! If I have the recipe for what you tricked me into taking last night, I can reverse-engineer an antidote and buy myself time to make the proper elixir!"

Crowley frowned. "Do you really think that's possible? Because I get the feeling you aren't as smart as your partner, Edgar. You've always fallen just a bit short of him, haven't you?

Been a bit more unstable. I can see it in your eyes. You're not so certain you can do this, are you?"

"It doesn't matter!" Price yelled, spit flying from his lips. "I will try. You think after all these years I'm just going to quit? To lay down and die at your hands? Give me the journal!"

"Why don't you use your witchcraft?" Rose said, understanding what Crowley was up to. Sarcasm dripped from her tone.

A crooked smile spread from one side of Price's mouth. "Witchcraft. Such a misunderstood word. Such a misunderstood craft. I've watched the corruption of that perception over the years, and it's made me laugh and sad by turns." His anger appeared to dissipate slightly as he spoke.

"But you are a witch, aren't you?" Rose pressed.

Price's eyes narrowed a moment, and Crowley thought the man was deciding whether to talk or not. He was angry, all he wanted was the journal, but he was plainly narcissistic too. How could he not be, given his killing hundreds of people to extend his own existence?

"I was once a Witchfinder, in Massachusetts," Price said. Crowley smiled softly, pleased the man had given in to his selfishness. The longer he went without shooting, the less likely he was to fire. "I was the most zealous," Price went on. "Then I saw something that changed my life. I had rooted out and exposed numerous covens, dozens of solo witches practicing their black arts, but most were simple midwives and herbalists. Some were mediums of varying skills, I suppose, but all were harmless. Of course, back then I didn't see it like that. They were women of Satan, and they had to be hanged. We burned fewer than popular culture, or even the history books, would have you believe. Most were drowned or hanged.

"But then one night, in the course of my work, I tracked down a coven to a small house, deep in the woods. Far removed from the public eye, it took me a long time to find. But once I knew its location, I waited until I was sure they were planning a ritual. Catch them red-handed, yes? No possibility that they could get off the hook of my accusations. And I had one of my underlings with me, an apprentice who was shaping up to be a fine witch hunter. When we reached the small cottage, we spied on the coven as they were in the midst of a ceremony, and I knew I would have concrete evidence against them. Some horrific blood sacrifice, I expected. These were the real black deal, not some cunning woman with a knowledge of plants and folklore. But instead, I witnessed something incredible."

Price's eyes had glazed slightly with the recollection. The gun still pointed right at them, but Crowley noticed the man's white-knuckled grip on it had eased somewhat. He didn't want to pounce too soon, and honestly, the story was fascinating. But he only listened with one ear, watching for an opening all the while.

"They healed that boy," Price said, his voice softened with wonder. "That child's withered and useless arm was made whole and functional again. It was true magic, not some dark art. It was the holiest magic, the power of healing, like Christ with the blind man or the lame man. On the one hand, these witches wielding Christ-like power was both terrifying and blasphemous. But it was wondrous too. As I watched this miracle, my wife lay at home, dying from an illness no doctor could cure. I told you before that when I love, I love completely, deeply. I would have given anything to save my wife. The healing properties of the real magic of those witches sang to me."

Price shook his head slightly at the memory, looking past Crowley now, staring into the past. "But I had my apprentice with me, yes? A promising young man. He didn't see everything that had happened, but he understood enough. He was true to the cause and wanted to arrest everyone there. I was forced to make a hasty decision, one that would change the course of my life. I killed him there and then, and hid his body in the woods. It was the first time I killed."

"How many so-called witches had you put to death before that?" Rose said, aghast. "It was far from the first time you'd killed."

Price favored her with a condescending smile. "It was the first time I had taken a life with my own hands, rather than my accusations and evidence. Regardless, I turned then. The witchfinder secretly became a witch."

"I should have realized sooner that you were a witch," Rose said. "Even your company, SaleMed, has Salem right there in the name."

"Yes, a bit of whimsy on my part. I first tried to learn their healing arts, but my skills were not the same as theirs. Something that worked for them would often not work for me. That coven would give me no secrets. No one would trust a Witchfinder of my reputation." Price's face darkened. "My wife died anyway."

His eyes narrowed, his face tightened. The pain of his loss was still evident, hundreds of years later. His love for his wife seemed undiminished by time. "So I devoted my life to fighting a battle against mortality, against death."

Crowley couldn't help the laugh that burst from him. "That's ironic, considering how many lives you've taken in order to save your own."

Price shrugged it off, his attention back on them, the light in his eyes sharp again. Crowley thought maybe they'd missed a chance to jump him, if there had ever been one. "Insignificant, unremarkable people who aren't missed," Price said.

"Jazz wasn't unremarkable!" Rose said fiercely, anger making her cheeks livid.

Price smiled. "I don't care. The knowledge in my head makes me more valuable than all my victims combined. And that includes the two of you. I only need one of you to tell me where the journal is, so let's make sure we know I'm serious, shall we?"

He raised his pistol and fired.

CHAPTER 40

Crowley moved instinctively, shoving Rose to one side and using the momentum to launch himself the other way. Price's pistol boomed, flashing in the night, and Crowley felt and heard the bullet whizz by his ear. Too close! Rose was smart enough to keep moving, tucking and rolling in behind a section of wall. Crowley matched her in the opposite direction, hoping Price would keep tracking him and leave Rose to get away.

To ensure Price did keep his eye away from Rose, Crowley launched himself up and away at an angle. He knew it was futile, there was no way he could cover the space between himself and Price, but if he simply kept moving, and kept Price's attention away from Rose, that would be enough in the immediate moment. From the corner of his eye, he saw Rose running low, moving around the low wall trying to flank Price. Then the witch fired again and Crowley barked in pain as the bullet zinged his shoulder, tearing through his jacket and sending a line of fire across his deltoid muscle. He ignored it, hoping it as only a flesh wound. He'd been shot before and, while he felt the pain and the heat of the shot, he hadn't felt an impact. Dampness soaked his jacket as the blood flowed, but that could wait until later.

Crowley ducked and rolled, and prepared to launch himself at Price in a suicidal last ditch attempt, when a figure flew out of the dark and crashed into their attacker. At first, Crowley thought Rose had impossibly covered ground right around behind Price, but her low run had been short-lived and she now crouched behind the cover of another wall a mere ten feet from where she'd started, hemmed in.

Price and the surprise assailant grappled, fighting for control of the gun. Crowley took the opportunity to run back across the rampart. He hauled Rose to her feet, intending to get them both out of there while they had the distraction, offering a silent thanks to whoever had interrupted Price's attack. Was it a simple good Samaritan or someone else?

As the thought went through Crowley's mind, the pistol went off again. Crowley couldn't leave whoever it was to the fight on their own, and he turned only to see their rescuer slowly release his grip on Price and slide to the ground.

Growling in anger, Crowley was on Price in an instant. He grabbed the man's wrist as he tried to turn and bring his weapon to bear once more. Despite the burn in his own shoulder, Crowley forced Price's gun hand wide, grabbed the man's neck with his other hand, and drove him back against the ramparts.

Price cursed, spitting fury. "I'll kill you, Crowley. And when I get the journal from Rose, I'll kill her too!" They wrestled, Price surprisingly strong for his age and rapidly deteriorating condition. Crowley ignored his ranting, tried to maneuver the man into a position where he could drive in a knee, or even a head-butt. "Then once I've reversed the effects of the poison you dosed me with," Price went on, spittle flying, "I'm going to marry your aunt. She'll need someone to comfort her after the death of her favorite nephew!"

"Will you shut up!" Rose shouted, her fist flying in from the side to crack into Price's jaw. The man grunted in pain, his strength momentarily sagging away. With a roar, Crowley flipped Price up and over the rampart.

Price spun in the air like a rag doll, his high-pitched scream piercing the night. He bounced once off the castle wall, the screaming cutting short with a grunt, then smacked into the rough gray rocks far below and slid to a stop. His limbs were crooked, a dark pool of blood quickly spreading from his shattered skull.

Crowley nodded to Rose. "About bloody time he was finished."

She returned his nod, and they ran to the fallen man and crouched on either side of him. He seemed barely alive, but Crowley was thankful he wasn't dead yet. There was a chance. His face was very familiar. Under a mop of curly black hair, the man's eyes flickered.

"Is he alive?" he asked in a weak voice.

"Price?"

The man nodded.

"No," Crowley said. "He's dead. And good riddance."

The man drew in a shaky breath. "I couldn't agree more."

"Are you Edgar?" Rose asked.

The man nodded subtly. "Edgar Allen Poe. A pleasure to meet you at last, Rose Black. And you, Jake Crowley."

"Done your homework, eh?" Crowley asked.

"I've been watching you, trying to catch up with events. Only just in time, it seems, but perhaps you didn't need me at all."

Crowley let out a laugh. "Are you kidding? He had us like fish in a barrel. We'd be done for now if you hadn't come along when you did."

"I'll call 911," Rose said, scrabbling for her phone.

"There's no need," Poe said.

"What do you mean, no need?"

"I'm so sorry for all the damage I've done. All the people who died."

"Price had been conducting his rituals long before he met you," Crowley said. "And he would have continued to do so even if you two had never met."

"Of course. But so many times I could have stopped him, were I only brave enough. But I always thought, what if I fail? And then he has power over me, and tortures the formula out of me. I didn't know if I could truly resist him. He uses barbaric methods you wouldn't believe."

"Why didn't you destroy the journal right away too?" Rose asked.

Poe smiled ruefully, shook his head. "All those years ago, when I realized what Price really was, the evil he conducted, I suffered a bout of madness. I was appalled, vexed, and I lost my mind. I sank into a blackness that lasted days. When I came to, I couldn't find the journal, I had no idea what I'd done with it. I made a cursory search, but feared that if I didn't flee immediately, Price would find me, capture me, and extract the information. If not by torture, then perhaps witchcraft. I had to hope I'd destroyed the journal already, even in my madness, but I could never be sure. Regardless, I destroyed my lab and supplies and fled. I've periodically returned, to search for the journal, to check for any news of its discovery."

"Which is why people think they see your ghost sometimes," Rose said. "They actually see you."

Poe nodded. "So where is the journal now?"

Crowley and Rose shared a quick glance. "We have it," Crowley said. "It's safe. No one else knows we have it but you and Price. So only you now."

"Promise me you'll destroy it? It's too dangerous. Don't be tempted by it."

Crowley nodded, looked up to Rose and she smiled, gave a single nod back.

"We swear," Crowley said.

"Good. Thank you. Now quickly, get out of here in case anyone else comes along. You don't want to be entangled with Price's death."

"No!" Rose said, digging in her pocket again. "We have to call you an ambulance. We'll deal with the Price thing."

"It's already in hand," Poe said with a smile. He held up a smartphone, then grinned at the expressions on their faces. "I may have been around for 200 years, but that doesn't mean I'm not a modern man. I called for help while you fought Price, my man will be along any time now."

"Are you going to be okay?" Rose asked.

"I think so. I've survived this long, after all. I'll report Price's death, say the man mugged me here, and that he fell over the ramparts as we struggled, but not before he got a shot off into me. My man will act as a witness. Now please, go."

Crowley looked down at Poe, his face ashen, but his smile in place. "Edgar Allan Poe," Crowley said. "I can't believe it."

Poe's smile widened. "Isn't life a funny thing? But no autographs. Go!"

"Thank you again," Crowley said, squeezing the man's shoulder once before he stood. "For everything."

Rose leaned down and kissed Poe on the cheek, then joined Crowley.

"So," Crowley said as they started walking. "How have you enjoyed our vacation in the Big Apple."

"Different to how I expected, if I'm honest. Maybe we should try again."

Crowley kissed her. "Let's start over in the morning."

They hurried away into the night.

Epilogue

On a quiet street in Salem, Massachusetts, not far from Remond Park, a man approached an old three-story house. The home was like others in the neighborhood, rectangular with an A-frame roof, siding painted a pale cream. Flowerbeds surrounded it on three sides. In the driveway stood a battered blue pick-up truck. The back window of the pick-up had a sticker that read, *May Your Actions Be Returned Threefold.* No one else was abroad in the darkness of the night as the man passed under the pool of yellow light from a streetlamp and walked between the pick-up and the house, heading for the door along one side.

He was a big man, well over six feet tall, broad and round-shouldered. His movement belied a kind of contained strength, but there was subtle grace there too. But as he raised his hand to knock, the action was stilted, nervous. The knock seemed strangely loud in the quiet street.

After a few seconds, the door was answered by a woman of indeterminate middle age, her long iron-gray hair tied back in a loose ponytail. "Derek?"

The big man nodded. "Am I late?"

"Not at all. But everyone is here. We're so glad you found us, Derek. Please come in."

Derek went inside, the aroma of sandalwood incense and coffee instantly apparent. The woman offered to take his coat, and he shrugged it off, stood awkwardly.

"I'm Glenda," the woman said. "Come in."

She led Derek into a large lounge room filled with floral-patterned furniture and polished wood cabinets. Six other people sat in the room, a variety of men and women, widely ranging in age. Derek saw one young woman with alabaster skin and long red hair who looked no more than twenty. The oldest-looking was a man with skin like wrinkled teak and a bald head who appeared to be at least eighty years old.

"Tea or coffee?" Glenda asked, gesturing for Derek to take an unoccupied armchair.

"No, thank you." He lowered himself into the chair, looking

nervously around at the group, who returned his perusal with friendly expressions.

Glenda sat as well and smiled. "Now, Derek, first of all, you must understand you're among friends. We're also very serious about what we do, and we've investigated thoroughly, so we know a lot more about you than you know about us. Of course, that will change in time. We have no secrets within our coven. But you said you had something of great value to earn your place as the eighth of us since Marjory passed."

Derek swallowed, nodded. "I'm grateful to you for accepting me, so I offer this as my pass of entry. I feel guilty because it's stolen. This woman I know, she's a friend of the girl I love. Well, loved. Anyway, I've kind of been shadowing her. Not really stalking," he said quickly. "It's not her that I care about. Being around her makes me feel closer to…" He sat up straight, cleared his throat. "Anyway, I knew she was up to something…sketchy. I broke into the place she was staying, and I found this book. I knew right away it was dangerous and would be safer in the hands of a good coven than anywhere else. I'm pretty sure she would have destroyed it, and I couldn't let that happen."

Glenda appeared skeptical but curious. "And what is it, dear?"

Derek took a deep breath. "It's a journal. An ancient and powerful book with many secrets. Have you heard of Edgar Allan Poe?"

"Gone, you say?" Poe lay in silk sheets in his house at Telegraph Hill, South Boston. The bullet wound still hurt like hell, but painkillers were dealing with the worst of it. Thankfully his vital organs had avoided any severe damage, and blood loss was the only real risk. But transfusions had taken care of that.

"Yes," Sarah Mason said. "I checked every inch of that hotel room. The only other options are that they have it on them, they hid it somewhere else, or they did indeed destroy it."

Poe nodded, sipped tea from a china cup as he lay back against a pile of soft pillows. "Let's hope for the latter, eh? If nothing else, at least I think the trail of people who know about it is finally dead. It ends with us, Jake Crowley and Rose Black. I think they're decent enough people that we can trust them. If they don't destroy it, perhaps they won't abuse it either."

Sarah tied back her long blonde hair, revealing more of a face that looked little more than thirty or so, completely belying the fact that she had been born in 1903. The last of the elixir that Poe had saved had been his gift to her when she agreed to marry him. He had refused to ever make any more. The cost was too high, but the one dose that remained in his possession for so many years was too valuable to destroy. And immortality was lonely, watching so many people grow old and die. Never getting too close to anyone, as they'd see him remain the same while they surrendered to the ravages of time. But Sarah understood.

"Let me take a look at that dressing," she said. "We need to change it again today."

"I made a smart move marrying a doctor, did I not?"

Sarah smiled. "The irony of an immortal man needing a doctor is not lost on either of us, I'd wager." She leaned down and kissed him, then drew back the sheet to see to the dressing on the last gift Matthew Price had given his old friend.

Lily Black answered her phone, annoyed to have been disturbed. But this was one phone she always answered. "Tell me you have good news," she said, without preamble.

A gravelly voice on the other end said, "As a matter of fact, I do. I'm in New York City, and I've finally found them. Your sister and her boyfriend seem to be enjoying a vacation."

"Is that so?" Damn! Why hadn't Jazz let her know? She'd maintained the fiction of friendship with that obnoxious snoop for years, solely for the purpose of keeping tabs on Rose. Jazz had it bad for Rose and had maintained their friendship, which made her the occasional source of grade A gossip. But not this time, apparently. "Where are they now?"

"About to board the Ellis Island ferry out to the Statue of Liberty. I've tracked them to their hotel too, so I know where they're staying."

Lily smiled, her lips curling up in slow satisfaction. "Excellent. Don't make any moves, but don't lose them. I can be in New York by the morning."

THE END

ABOUT THE AUTHORS

David Wood is the USA Today bestselling author of the popular action-adventure series, The Dane Maddock Adventures, and many other works. Under his David Debord pen name he is the author of the Absent Gods fantasy series. When not writing, he hosts the Wood on Words podcast and co-hosts the Authorcast podcast. David and his family live in Santa Fe, New Mexico. Visit him online at www.davidwoodweb.com.

Alan Baxter is a British-Australian author who writes supernatural thrillers and urban horror liberally mixed up with crime and noir, rides a motorcycle and loves his dog. He also teaches Kung Fu. He lives among dairy paddocks on the beautiful south coast of NSW, Australia, with his wife, son, dog and cat. Read extracts from his novels, a novella and short stories at his website –www.warriorscribe.com– or find him on Twitter @AlanBaxter and Facebook, and feel free to tell him what you think. About anything.

Made in the USA
Middletown, DE
17 March 2020